d r i v e

"A fun, detail-rich romp with unexpected depth that takes a deep dive into the inner workings of NASCAR racing in the late '80s and early '90s. Inspired by the author's real-life experience as the daughter of a NASCAR team owner and the sister of a racing star, this is as close to the action as you'll get without a pit pass. I cheered and cried in equal measure."

—**Kristin Harmel, international bestselling novelist of**
The Winemaker's Wife* and *The Room on Rue Amélie

"In a tale that mirrors the twists and turns on a racetrack, Susan Strecker weaves a story of love and loss against the backdrop of the NASCAR circuit. You'll fall in love with journalist Piper Pierson, driver Colt Porter, and the charming cast of characters that guide them to the book's stunning conclusion. *Drive* will make you want to get behind the wheel, and its message of fearlessness, of loving the life you're given, will stay with you long after you cross the finish line."

—**Cheryl Della Pietra, author of *Gonzo Girl***

"*Drive* perfectly captures life in the NASCAR Winston Cup racing scene of yesteryear and is a captivating tale. It kept me up all night reading. I could feel the passion as this story took me back to the path I endured to get into the highest level of motorsports. Loved the heart and soul of this story, and the paths we take with family and the thrilling journeys they lead to. I could not put it down. While reading *Drive,* I felt like I was back in the '80s driving on the NASCAR circuit and enjoying everything that is wonderful about the sport."

—**Shawna Robinson, former NASCAR driver**

"Strong themes of family loyalty and self-blame flow through this well-paced story of tragedy, forgiveness, fast cars, and the very human people who own them and drive them."

—**Susan Cushman, author of the novel *Cherry Bomb* and the short story collection *Friends of the Library***

"*Drive* by Susan Strecker is a book that will change your mind about life, grief and loss. As tired as I was one night, I could not put it down. You will come to love all these very personable characters. They are so real and relatable. I know nothing of NASCAR, but you don't need to. You are driven into the world of a tight-knit family trying to do the right thing for their daughter and their company. Colt, the new driver for the family's NASCAR race team, gallops into Piper's heart and shows her that life is worth living. Do what you love and experience it because life takes you for a ride. Powerful page turner you will want to share with a friend."

—**Suzanne Lucey, owner of Page 158 Books**

Drive

by Susan Strecker

ISBN 978-1-63393-928-8

Published by

 köehlerbooks™

210 60th Street
Virginia Beach, VA 23451
800–435–4811
www.koehlerbooks.com

"Susan Strecker's third novel serves up a combination of high-stakes racing and romance, a peek into the business of NASCAR teams, and the emotional highs and lows of success. Piper and Colt will steal hearts and inspire readers to live life fully without regret."

—Jeanne E. Fredriksen, book reviewer

"Fast-paced and emotionally driven. With unexpected plot twists, *Drive* takes the reader through the characters' stories, through their transformation and commitments, narrating about their life-altering revelations and rediscovering freedom. A must-read discovery journey for all fans of fantastic storytelling!"

—Elena Granoth, Library Director, Morris Public Library

"A propulsive novel that is guaranteed to get heads and hearts racing. So buckle up and hold on tight because Susan Strecker is about to take you on an exhilarating ride. *Drive* is a victory lap from one of fiction's freshest voices."

—John Valerie, Book reviewer

"*Drive* is the kind of story one easily gets lost in, and is sorry to leave though you've raced to the end."

—Su Epstein, Ph.D. Library Director, Saxton B. Little Free Library

d r i v e

A NOVEL

Susan Strecker (signature)

SUSAN STRECKER

VIRGINIA BEACH
CAPE CHARLES

For my brothers—Rick and Rob
Because I love you

1

There was a time—before my father's accident—when all I wanted to be was a race car driver. I could change a tire before I turned twelve and learned to drive a stick on my fourteenth birthday. I had no need for college. Short tracks and super speedways were my classrooms, and famous drivers were my professors. My dad and I had it all figured out. I'd drive for his team and take over Pierson Racing when he retired.

Then he almost died testing at a crap little track in Tennessee. And after he recovered, I couldn't get near a race without hyperventilating. I traded my dreams of becoming the first successful female driver for a degree in journalism and understood what it was to miss something I never had.

Two weeks after graduating college, I was having dinner with my best friend, Liza, at Sandwich Construction, the most famous race car bar in the South.

"I'm so glad you're here," Liza said, squirting ketchup on her fries. "It seems like applying for journalism jobs *is* your job."

A TV above the bar had the evening news on and was loudly replaying a clip of Vice President Dan Quayle telling the nation that "a mind is a terrible thing to lose." I asked the bartender to turn down the volume and then spoke to Liza.

"It might as well be," I said. I'd been sending my resume and writing samples to newspapers and magazines for months. I'd had a handful of interviews that led nowhere and had received several letters and messages on my answering machine politely telling me *thanks, but no thanks*. Regardless, I refused to listen to the voice in my head telling me I was never leaving Charlotte. "You're so lucky you got your dream job." Liza had been recruited by the biggest advertising agency in Charlotte. I'd secretly hoped she'd turn down the offer and we'd move to New York or LA together. But she loved the firm and they loved her.

A guy with bright-blue eyes and hair the color of black coffee entered the bar. I put down my burger and watched as he sat next to Liza. Wearing a monogrammed button-down, he probably wasn't a local. And he definitely wasn't a driver.

Liza reached for a saltshaker, strategically brushing her arm against our neighbor. "Howdy," she said in a manufactured Southern drawl. She was from Boston. We were randomly paired as roommates our freshman year at UNC and had been best friends ever since. "I'm Liza and this is Piper." She pointed a blue fingernail at him. "And you are?"

He extended his hand, eyeing Liza's cleavage while he spoke. "Tack Richards."

"Are you waiting on someone?" she asked. Nothing subtle about Liza.

"Can't say that I am. I moved south for a job and haven't met many people yet. But my neighbor said this place has the best onion rings around." Tack's teeth were so white I couldn't stop staring at them.

Liza shimmied closer. "People only come to this area for two reasons. Quarter horses and car racing." She sized him up. "What do you think, Piper? Is Tack a cowboy or a driver?"

I hated talking to strangers. "Nice to meet you, Tack. I'm Piper Pierson." I didn't quite meet his eye.

"So, what's your guess?" he asked. "Your friend thinks I'm here to buy a horse or drive a race car."

Liza kicked my foot, probably pissed that he'd forgotten her name.

I hopped off my barstool. "You're not tan enough to be a cowboy." His shirt was starched. "And you're much too smooth to be a driver. I vote PR for a race team."

"Ooh, so close," he said. "I'm the new editor in chief at *NASCAR Weekly*."

"Well, isn't it a small world," Liza said. "My girl Piper wants to be a writer." I looked away, embarrassed. She poked me in the ribs. "Tack works for *NASCAR Weekly*. Isn't that a great coincidence, Piper?"

It really wasn't. The last thing I wanted to do was work in that industry. My hope was that a cubicle at *Cosmopolitan* or even *Good Housekeeping* awaited.

"My dad reads your paper religiously," I said. "Congratulations on your new job."

"Thanks," he said. "So, you're interested in journalism?"

"Yes, but I was thinking of something a little more mainstream like *Rolling Stone, People* or *Entertainment Weekly*."

"Those are awfully ambitious goals," Tack said, not unkindly. "Have you had any offers?"

"I've had a few interviews," I said, irritated that Liza had brought it up. "But nothing yet. I better get a job soon or my father is going to make me work for him for the summer." I held up my foot. "Do I look like I could jump pit wall in sandals?"

"Wait a minute. You're Planter Pierson's daughter?" he asked.

How many times have I been asked that in my life?

"In living color," I replied.

"Like Pierson Racing? As in the owners of the Whitley Chewing Gum team?"

"The one and only."

"Is your resume in the pile of mail I haven't opened yet?"

"Nope."

He reached in his wallet and handed me a business card. "Why don't you drop it in the mail to me? The newspaper is hiring right now."

"Thanks, but stock car racing has been my world my whole life. I think it's time I try something new."

Tack slid his business card toward me. "Just take it. You might change your mind," he said.

Liza had finished her burger and paid our tab. I could tell by the way she was tapping her fingers on the bar that she was bored and mad that I was monopolizing Tack's time.

"I think it's time for us to go," I told him. "It was nice to meet you. Good luck at the paper."

•   •   •

I wasn't surprised when my father called the next day asking if I'd sent my resume to the new editor of *Weekly*. With driver point standings, feature articles, race schedules and a bit of gossip mixed in, that newspaper was our bible.

"Do I even want to know how you found out in less than ten hours that I met Tack Richards last night?" I asked him. I was flipping through a stack of fashion and home-improvement magazines on my bed hoping to find some interesting *help wanted* ads.

"I think the better question is why haven't you applied to *Weekly*. You'd be a natural."

"Maybe I didn't know they were hiring," I said, circling an ad that seemed promising.

"I've seen your spreadsheets. You have a list of every newspaper, magazine and journal this side of the Mississippi in need of writers. Don't tell me you didn't know, Noodle."

I sighed, thinking about how mad he'd be if I told him I hadn't confined my search to the East Coast. Plenty of papers in Denver, Sacramento and Chicago had my resume.

"I knew they're hiring. I just don't want to work there."

I could tell by the lack of sound coming through the phone that my father was holding his breath, which meant he was annoyed. "You want to tell me what's going on here?"

"You know, Daddy. I used to love racing. Now I don't. Maybe it's time for me to get on a plane and make a go of it somewhere else."

"If you're so over it, why do you go to almost every race with your mother and me?"

I glanced at the framed photographs covering one entire bedroom wall. My life, from infancy to college graduation, was photographically chronicled. My parents and our race cars were in almost every picture.

"I go to the races for the same reason horses run back into burning barns. It's all I know."

The sound of metal colliding and then collapsing, of my mother screaming for her husband, and of sirens blaring as rescuers tried to extract my father's limp body from the cockpit played on a loop in my head like a soundtrack.

My dad was as stubborn a man as I'd ever met, refusing to abandon the only life he knew. That accident left him in constant pain. Even still, he was determined, as he said, to keep on keeping on. He would carry on as a team owner, and my mother and I would do whatever we had to, to support him—including going to races that made me want to vomit.

"It's not too late for you to be the first girl driver to tear up stock car racing. You don't need to defect to Yankeeville or the

Wild West and pretend you don't love this sport."

I was so tired of this discussion.

"Me being a driver is off the table. You know that."

"But you were so good."

"I was good. And then December happened. Remember, Daddy?"

"You do recall that I was the one who got hurt, right?"

"Yeah. And you almost died. So, forgive me for not wanting a job that only reminds me of how I nearly lost you."

"Oh, Piper. The important bit here, the thing that you're missing, is that I didn't bite it. I'm fine. So, you can stop worrying about me now."

Fine was not a word I'd use to describe my dad.

"Whatever. Can we talk about something else, please?"

He chuckled. "You drove a go-kart like a hellcat. Youngest driver and first girl to ever win the NC Enduro Championship. And you moved up to Dash cars like they were overgrown karts. You weren't afraid of anything."

Daytona Dash cars *were* glorified go-karts. Practically anybody could drive one.

"Exactly. And look where that got me."

"I know you know how many Winston Cup champions began their careers racing karts."

"Just about all of them," I submitted. Yes, it was a logical path, like the way many Major League Baseball players started in Little League as children. I hated remembering how good I was. It made me ache to get behind the wheel again. "And do you want to tell Mama that I'm going to drive again or should I?"

"You got me there. Your mother would disown you and put a bounty on my head if I let you get in a race car these days."

My mom was the loveliest creature I'd ever seen—tall, willowy, never used a curse word or was in a bad mood. But my father was right. She'd hunt us both down if we resurrected our decade-old plan of turning me into the best female race car driver in history.

"So why are we even talking about it? I don't want to race anymore. And she would freak the f—"

"Don't you finish that sentence." Twenty-two years old and I wasn't allowed to curse in front of my parents. "Let's not get in a tangle about this again. All I'm saying is that you *have* real talent. Just because you haven't sat in a race car in five years doesn't mean you forgot how to drive. If you want to change gears from writing to racing, we'll figure out a way to medicate your mother without her knowing."

I rolled my eyes. "Let's not get ahead of ourselves. Have you forgotten I don't even drive a street car anymore?"

He guffawed. "That's temporary. One day you'll get tired of begging rides everywhere. I'm not worried."

"Keep telling yourself that, Daddy."

I loved my dad, but he had no clue what was going on in my head. The first and only time I tried to drive after his accident, I threw up all over the steering wheel. There was no way I was driving any kind of car again. Ever.

I needed to get off the phone before he started asking questions I didn't want to answer.

"Please, Daddy, don't harass Tack. All I did was have a casual conversation with a guy in a bar. No one said anything about me applying for a job or them hiring me. And even if I do go for an interview, there's a whole big, blue ocean between me writing about racing and actually doing it."

"You don't have to write for that—or any—newspaper, you know. You have options."

Options meant driving. I envisioned my father trying to climb the old set of stairs leading to the attic, complete with his bum hip, and unearthing the fire suit and helmet I'd long ago packed away.

"Thanks, Daddy. I appreciate the support. But I *want* something new. Sometimes I think it'd be great to move north or west or diagonally and get a job at *Spin* and write articles about the B-52s." Before he could ruin my happy fantasy with a pesky dose of pragmatics, I added, "And by *write articles* I mean fetch coffee for others if I have to."

"Nonsense. In a couple of years, people will fall all over themselves to bring *you* coffee."

My parents were my biggest supporters, and sometimes I thought they believed in me too much. If they honestly thought I could do anything, then they would only be disappointed when I didn't.

"I know you know this, but you have a standing offer to work for me."

"Dad!" I said sharply. "You know I'll never drive again. So, quit asking."

"There are lots of other jobs you could do here besides the big one. You name it; it's yours—marketing, PR, manager, whatever you want."

What I wanted was to hang up and call a travel agent.

"Father, please give it a rest. Must you stick your nose in everything I do?"

"You're a great writer. And with your background and depth of knowledge, *NASCAR Weekly* would be foolish not to hire you. So, let's compromise there. If you're not ready to race again just yet, meet with Tack and stay in the sport you love. Please?"

"Correction," I protested. "The sport I used to love."

We were quiet for a moment, and I knew we were thinking the same thing—that my writing about NASCAR was inevitable.

"Maybe I should move to New York and get a job filing at *Vanity Fair*. At least then I'd get away from the ghosts," I said.

"I hate to break this to you, little girl, but ghosts can fly. They'd follow you right on to anywhere you went. You need to let this go.

They're my ghosts—not yours."

I heard a noise in the background, and I knew he was tapping his wedding band on his desk. It's what he did when he was remembering.

An ad for a copyeditor in a gardening magazine caught my eye. I knew nothing about gardening and didn't want to copyedit, but I was desperate.

"I'll talk to you later," I said. "Love you, Big D."

• • •

My nylons were too tight, and I'd sweated through the silk blouse I picked out the night before.

"Good morning," I said, knocking on Tack's open door. "Thanks again for the opportunity to chat."

Sitting behind his shiny, chestnut desk, Tack seemed more banker than editor. He came to the doorway where we shook hands.

"Glad you changed your mind," he said. "Have a seat. Can I get you something to drink?"

My mouth was so dry my tongue stuck to its roof. "No thanks, I'm all set."

Just as I knew I would, I'd ended up mailing Tack my resume and a few articles I wrote in college. I was surprised by his almost immediate response and invitation to meet with him. I wondered if my dad or one of his people had done some lobbying.

Tack had my articles in hand as he motioned to a small, cloth couch and took a seat in a matching chair adjacent to it.

"I read the articles you wrote for your school paper. They were something else."

I cracked a smile. "That's a nice way of putting it. The last one about campus security got me invited to seek course credits elsewhere."

"They fired you?"

"You accuse one retired detective of slacking on the job and suddenly you're a pariah."

"Pariah or no, you're very talented," he said.

"Thank you. I worked hard in college and even published a few freelance pieces in small magazines."

He held up my resume. "Yes, I see that. You're impressive on paper and your articles are excellent."

I licked my lips. I needed something to drink. "I hear a *but* coming."

"But why are you here? I have to say, I was surprised when I got your resume. You seemed pretty reluctant the other night."

"Because I wasn't kidding when I said my dad was going to make me work for him if I didn't get a real job. I would love to go to New York and write for one of the famous glossies up there, but *Weekly* is a great paper. I grew up reading it. And you seem like a good guy. So here I am." I held up my hands as if resting my defense. "I don't really want to spend my time changing tires with the boys in fire suits, but I'd be happy to write about them."

"You're an odd duck, Piper Pierson. Most kids in your position would be begging to have a career in the industry."

"What can I say? I guess I want to make it on my own."

That wasn't a complete untruth. My father worked for everything he had, and I wanted to, also. Neither of my parents had gone to college, so as far as they were concerned, footing the bill for eighty thousand dollars' worth of school was the same as giving me that money. They also believed in Paul Getty's mantra that children of the wealthy needed jobs or they'd feel worthless. *Maybe it was Rockefeller or Vanderbilt who said that. No matter.*

"That's a respectable goal." Tack took two bottles of water from a mini fridge in the corner. "I wish more people had your work ethic."

I chugged half the bottle Tack had handed me.

"I have great parents," I said. "But may I ask you a question? I'm sure you've gotten tons of resumes from people with more experience. Why even give me an interview?"

He laced his fingers behind his head and stretched.

"I already told you that you've got talent. And I believe in taking chances on people who deserve it. I'd probably be a traveling shoe salesman if my first boss hadn't given me a shot."

"I didn't know that was a real job." Usually, I could tell when someone was bullshitting me, but this time I wasn't so sure. I wanted to make sure I wasn't sitting here because of my dad. I met Tack's eyes. They were open wide, unblinking, waiting for me to respond. He seemed genuine.

He sighed loudly. "I was expecting a little more enthusiasm. Are you sure this job is something you want?"

I never wore pantyhose, and I felt like my lower body was being strangled. It was hard not to squirm. "Of course," I said, "Why else would I be here?"

Tack smiled. "That's exactly what I am trying to figure out."

He opened a cabinet behind his desk and fiddled with a radio. A country song I didn't recognize played through speakers in the ceiling. He sat, sang along to the music for a moment, then made eye contact with me.

"With your background, I think you'd be a great fit here, but I don't want to make you do anything you're uncomfortable with. Do you need time to think about it?"

I loved and hated the sport. I grew up playing soccer in the infields at racetracks and watching pit crews with the same fascination as others watched football cheerleaders. I started racing karts as soon as I was old enough and began testing the smaller Daytona Dash cars well before I got my license. I had a future in the male-dominated industry, and I had loved it.

I hated what racing took from my family, but I loved the familiarity of the tracks and the smell of spinning tires being warmed up. I knew where I had to stand in the pits to avoid the sun, and I enjoyed the celebrity of being Planter Pierson's kid. I'd never met anyone who didn't love him and, by extension, adore me.

I answered Tack without thinking.

"Racing is my home." I'd been telling myself for months that if *Time* or *Popular Mechanic* or even *Housewives R Us* offered me a job, I'd be on the next flight out of Charlotte. But this felt right.

Tack stood and shook my hand. "Welcome aboard, kid.'

•   •   •

The first person I told about my working at the newspaper was my best friend.

"Are you sure this is what you want?" Liza asked. She filled a plastic cup with Lucky Charms and started eating it with no milk.

"The job?" I asked. "Sure."

She put down her cereal. "Last week you were begging me to move to Philly or Seattle or Oshkosh with you. Now you're happy to stay put and write about cars going around in circles?"

Liza loved my parents like they were her own, but she'd never understood what they did for a living.

I opened the refrigerator, stared at a coffee yogurt, then closed it. I was starving and craved a sausage, egg and cheese sandwich from McDonald's.

"Beggars can't be choosers," I told her. "I've had like four phone interviews and none of them have gone anywhere. At least this is a job."

"Do you want to know what I think?"

"No. But I have a feeling you're going to tell me anyway."

"You *say* you hate racing. You make noise about wanting to get out of the South. But you jumped at the first opportunity to stay here. You were never going to leave. You'd last two days without your parents."

This was precisely the reason I loved Liza; she spit the truth no matter if I wanted to hear it or not.

"You'd miss me too much if I left town without you." That's what I'd deluded myself into believing since accepting Tack's offer—that other people needed me to stay. I gave Liza a quick peck on the cheek. "Let me know if you might get home before midnight. We can grab some dinner. But now I've got to get to my parents and tell them I took the job."

"See?" she yelled from the kitchen as I left. "You could have just called them." She was laughing, but she had a point.

• • •

All the way to the race shop in the back of the cab, I couldn't stop thinking about what Liza said. Maybe I was afraid to be by myself. I yapped about wanting to make it on my own, but there was never a doubt in my mind that I'd take the *Weekly* job if given the chance.

I stood in the parking lot after I paid the driver, telling myself it'd be okay if I went home and called Tack. I could tell him something had come up, that I appreciated the opportunity, but it wasn't the right fit. And then I could wait for my parents to kick my ass for backing out of a commitment. I dug a mint out of my pocket, put it in my mouth and told myself to be grateful.

I found my father in his office at the race shop. I stood in the entryway and knocked on the wall. He had a stack of eight-by-ten headshots on his desk and was splitting them into two piles. "Daddy," I said from the hall.

"Noodle," he replied without looking up. I waited for him to invite me in, but he kept sorting and taking notes. My dad had all kinds of ridiculous sayings. One of them was that he was "as patient as a hungry cheetah waiting on a zebra." I tried to wait out the cheetah, but he kept on with what he was doing. When he started to whistle, I knew he wasn't going to budge.

"I took the job," I finally said.

"I know." He stopped shuffling through the headshots and held up one of a good-looking Busch driver whose name I couldn't remember.

"So, you did talk to him."

He shrugged. "I have a good relationship with the media. You know that."

He did. It was some weird version of keeping his friends close and his enemies closer. Except the press loved him.

"Tack said he's never had to persuade someone to take a job before."

"*Persuade* is a strong word."

I started to sit in the chair across from his desk, but he pushed himself up and came around it. He scooped up a couple of photos and handed them to me. "I need to stretch for a second."

I watched him try to touch his toes, then we both sat on a cream-colored suede couch. I gave him the pictures and a kiss on the cheek.

"I had some questions and felt I owed it to Tack to be honest. I told him racing is not my first love and if I'd gotten an offer from someone else, I would have taken it."

My father gave me a look. "Rubbish. Racing *is* your first love and we all know it. I'm glad you got your foolish head on straight and signed on the dotted line."

"As much as I thought I wanted to get away from here, I think it'll be fun. He seems really nice."

He handed me the picture of the Busch driver that I'd seen on his desk.

"What do you think of this guy?"

These men must have been prospective replacement drivers

for Mack. I took the photo and stared at a blue-eyed boy who couldn't have been more than eighteen. He looked a lot like the kid who jumped over pit wall and ran to my dad's car after his accident.

"I think he looks like he's not old enough to have a learner's permit."

I handed the photo back to him.

"Don't worry. Little Donny isn't coming to our stable. He's just one of the masses I have to send a regret note to."

Only my dad would send *I'm sorry I didn't hire you* letters to the hundred or so drivers he'd turned away.

"So, it's really happening?" My heart hurt with the thought of having a new driver. Mack Marlin had been driving for our team almost as long as I'd been alive. I couldn't imagine there was anyone out there who could take his place.

"It has to, P. Mack's doctor gave him clearance to finish out the year, but his meds aren't working as well as they used to. The folks at the Mayo Clinic said once that happens, his symptoms will only get worse." He picked up a picture of a talented young driver who was better known for his attitude than his ability. "It's time."

"I'm sorry, Daddy. I can't imagine how hard this must be for you."

He sighed. "It's not so much that Mack's retiring, because he's really not. Come February, he won't be driving anymore, but he'll still be in the shop running strategy and tactics. I just can't imagine we'll ever find anyone as good as him."

My dad and Mack had won five Winston Cup championships together. There was no one as good as Mack Marlin.

"Do you even want to try?" I asked.

He put down the picture and leveled his gaze. "As opposed to what? Give up and sell the team?"

I reached across the couch and patted his hand.

"That's not what I meant. Are you going to go after an established driver or start with someone young? Someone who you can shape into a driver like Mack? Choose a kid with a lot of heart and you can make up for any lack of talent. You know you can build another champion."

He grinned, slyly.

"You've already found somebody, haven't you?"

"I love you, Piper." He stood, indicating it was time for me to go.

"But?"

"But you have a big mouth." He winked.

"You're not going to tell me who our new driver is, are you?"

He walked me to the door and kissed the top of my head. "Of course I am. You'll find out at the press conference with everyone else."

"Press conference?" I whined. "When will it be?"

"A month. Month and a half. There are still some details to be worked out on both sides."

He was right to not tell me. There was no way I'd be able to keep that secret for so long.

2

I spent a month at *NASCAR Weekly* writing short articles about smaller tracks building new concession stands, crew chiefs getting married, and a petition asking NASCAR to allow women to wear sandals to races. It wasn't the most stimulating work I'd ever done, but I genuinely loved writing and liked the people I worked with. The job also kept me occupied. Liza and I had lived together all four years of college and decided to stay in the apartment we had off campus until the lease expired in September. But she was so busy at her new job, working sixty hours a week, that I almost never saw her, and the apartment felt too quiet.

I was at my cubicle, chewing on a pencil, cataloguing the notes I'd taken about a small track in Virginia that was considering selling shares to the public to raise enough funds to buy new grandstands. It sounded like a crazy idea to me, but the year before, a fan at a different track had fallen through rotted bleachers and had broken his back. So, I understood the urgency. What I didn't get was how seating that held no more than 3,000 people could cost a half-million dollars.

"Piper P." Tack knocked on my partition. "Come with me."

I picked a tiny bit of eraser out of my teeth.

"Am I in trouble already?"

He led me into his office and closed the door.

"Hardly. Jim Matts stopped by to see me this morning."

"Mr. Matts, the owner of the paper?" This reeked of my father's interference. *Again.* Like he did when I started racing enduro karts but was technically too young until a *mistake* on my paperwork got me in a year before I should have been allowed to compete.

"What did he want?"

"He thinks it's time for you to move on from the puff pieces we've been throwing at you. Sink or swim."

To my surprise, I got excited at the thought of getting out of my cubicle and writing a piece that required human contact, not just a phone call here and there and a day at the library in the microfiche room.

"I'm ready. What am I writing about? Why those new tires are so good for testing but terrible for races? Why in a man's world it pays to be a girl if you want free beer from the creepy vendor at that old track in Kentucky?"

"You're not writing about a *what.* You'll be writing about a *who.* Two *whos*, actually."

"Awesome. Which *whos*?"

I had a terrible thought that I was about to be instructed to write about wives. Not that there was anything wrong with the wives of drivers and team owners. On the contrary, I thought they deserved a lot of credit for giving up careers and committing to following their husbands from one loud racetrack to another. Reason number forty-seven I had no intention of ever marrying into this sport.

My first big assignment was to interview two drivers vying for the Busch Grand National Championship. If Winston Cup was Major League Baseball, Busch was its younger cousin—the minors. Tenured staff covered Winston Cup, which left Busch to me and a few other newbies. The Busch series attracted two types of drivers: young Winston Cup hopefuls and the more experienced drivers who knew their niche.

Brent Austin was thirty-five and had finished in the top ten in the year-end point standings six of the last seven years. He'd found his forte and didn't have enough of an ego to chase the kings of Winston Cup. That he'd never tried to run in the more difficult series made me respect the hell out of him. He was happy and successful right where he was. The other front-runner was Colt Porter, a kid about my age in his third year of running Busch. We used to run Daytona Dash cars together as teenagers.

Brent and Colt were racing in Braselton, Georgia, which was a three-and-a-half-hour drive. It was too far to take a cab and lacked nearby train stations. I hadn't volunteered to Tack that I didn't drive, so when he suggested I carpool with one of the reporters who covered Winston Cup, I wondered if Papa Pierson had tipped him off.

Ken Dilaurentis, the most senior staff writer and the nicest co-worker I had, left Moorestown on Thursday, planning to catch our drivers after practice. We listened to MRN, Motor Racing Network, all the way there and knew a nasty rainstorm had put practice on hold.

Braselton Motor Speedway was 210 miles from my apartment, and when I told my dad I'd gotten my first out-of-state assignment, he acted as if I'd be going to the moon. Thanks to my father and the emergency kit he put together for me, I had a big umbrella in Ken's car, which I grabbed before heading to will call to get my credentials. I also had a thin, silver blanket, a flare gun, a gallon of water and a two-in-one device that would break glass and cut through a seatbelt. Unfortunately, the goodies were in the trunk, so it probably wouldn't do us much good if Ken drove off a bridge or plowed into a roadside ditch.

I got my credentials, snapped them into a Pierson Racing lanyard and set out toward a sea of motorhomes. I didn't know which was Colt's, so I headed to one the same color as his race car. When I got close enough, I saw the initials *CP* with a circle around them painted on a wheel cover on the back of the vehicle.

I was nervous walking over. I'd read every back issue of *NASCAR Weekly* that mentioned Colt Porter, and I knew he was a superstar in the making. He was handsome enough to be on TV and talented enough to be a contender in any faction of the sport. I read all the articles I'd found on him twice, hoping to get a feel for his persona. Would he welcome a rookie reporter, or would he think he was too important to waste his time with me? The pieces I found about him mentioned only his stats—from all his wins, top-five finishes and qualifying first for races, to how he got his start in racing the same way I had—in go-karts.

I'd stood on many a podium with Colt, trading top honors with him when we both drove in the Daytona Dash series. Yet, I knew very little about him as a person. I didn't know if he had siblings, if he was close to his parents, or if he'd always wanted to race. I wondered how personal to get for the story.

Two pit crew guys were standing in front of Colt's rig smoking cigarettes. *Stay casual, Pierson,* I told myself as I got closer. With black linen pants, a white button-down blouse, a Coach backpack and my mess of blond locks tied up in a French twist, I hoped they wouldn't mistake me for a race fan trying to get an autograph.

"Hey," I greeted the tire changers or gas can catchers or windshield washers or whoever they were. "Is Colt around?"

They stared at each other for a few seconds, apparently deciding if they should grant me access to this year's potential Busch champion.

"Up there." One of them motioned with his chin. "Just knock first."

I stepped toward the front of the rig and took a deep breath. I knocked, heard someone telling me to come in, and I climbed the steps leading to the sport's hottest young star.

Sitting on a gray suede couch were Colt, a pretty, dark-haired girl, and a man dressed in an ElectroAde uniform.

"Hey." I turned to Colt and he stood. "I'm Piper Pierson with *NASCAR Weekly*." We shook hands, and I felt silly introducing myself to him as if we'd never met. But I didn't want him to remember me as the girl who quit racing. I wanted him to know me now as the kick-ass journalist. "Two of your guys out front told me I could come in." A toilet flushed and a door opened. Then my father came out of the bathroom. "Dad? What the heck?"

"Shit," he said, looking as guilty as if I'd caught him without a flashlight during a hurricane. "Piper. What are you doing here?"

"I'm on assignment. I told you last week I was coming to interview Colt Porter and Brent Austin. Remember you wanted me to ask Ken when the last time his tires were rotated?"

Most of the time I loved being an only child, but every once and again I thought a sibling would have taken up some of my father's nervous energy.

"Did Ken fill up his tank before y'all left?" he asked. "There's nothing worse than running low on fuel when you're in the middle of nowhere."

"Yes, Father," I answered. "Now are you going to tell me what you're doing here?"

Colt Porter watched, amused. My dad and Colt stood shoulder to shoulder.

"Meet our new driver," my dad said.

I'd grown up with Mack Marlin. He was like an uncle to me. He was burly and mustached, hands thick with callouses. He was built like a wrestler and had been keeping the pretty, bad-boy drivers away from me since I was twelve. Now, one of them was taking his job.

Colt reached out to shake my hand again and kissed it instead. "Miss Pierson," he said. "I am honored to be a part of your legendary team. I will make your father proud."

I was too stunned to speak or sit down, so I stood there stupidly in Colt Porter's motorhome with my mouth open and my leather backpack hanging off my shoulder.

"Surprise," my dad said. "With everything that's going on, I forgot you were going to be here."

I looked between my dad and Colt. My father had been searching for a new driver since Mack got his diagnosis a year ago. I long suspected that he would sell the team before he'd have anyone else drive for us.

"So, you knew last month when I stopped by the shop to see you? You'd already hired Colt? He's the driver you'd selected but wouldn't tell me about?" *Is this assignment another set-up by my dad? His way of keeping tabs on me at work?*

My father came to me and put his arm around my shoulders. "Take a walk outside with me." Then he turned to Colt, shook his hand and said, "Thank you for your time. Great things await us."

"Will you excuse me for a minute?" I said to Colt and his friends, following my dad into the misty rain. The two men who'd seemingly been standing guard were gone.

"What the heck, Daddy? Why didn't you tell me Colt is Mack's replacement?"

My father gave me a sharp look, and I immediately realized my mistake. "There is no replacement for Mack. Never will be. I found someone who will drive for us next year."

My dad cried for two weeks after Mack's career-ending diagnosis of Parkinson's disease. That he had finally hired another driver told me he accepted Mack wouldn't be running for us come February.

"I'm sorry I didn't say anything when you came to see me. But it's not official yet. I wanted to wait until the contracts were signed." He took a toothpick from a tin in his back pocket and chewed it. "And we all know you like to talk more than a bird on a wire."

"I tell one reporter one time that you were planning on firing your head tire changer and I'm forever the town crier."

He grinned. "That opened a great big can of trouble."

I smiled sheepishly at the memory. "Probably wouldn't have been so bad if it hadn't been Mom's brother."

"Don't remind me. Your mother was as mad as a mama bear whose cub had been taken from her."

It started to rain harder, and I was reminded that we were out here talking because my father had hired the man-child I was supposed to interview.

"What does Mack think? About Colt Porter?"

My dad spit out a splinter. "He handpicked the boy. I would never hire someone without his blessing."

"I can't believe this is really happening. Is he good enough?" I motioned toward the motorhome.

"I've done my homework, little one. And I do believe he might be the best young driver that ever was."

"That's high praise coming from you."

"We'll talk more about it when you get home. But I've got to get back to the shop."

"Okay, Daddy." He kissed me on the forehead and started to walk away. "Wait a minute," I called. "Why'd you come all the way to Georgia to talk to Colt?"

He gave me a hangdog grin. "Would you believe me if I told you another team was courting him, so I had to make my move?"

I crossed my arms. "Why no. No, I wouldn't."

"It could happen."

"If Colt Porter were considering any other team besides yours, you wouldn't want him. Everyone knows you're the best. So, you want to tell me what's really going on here?"

"I never could hoodwink you. Truth be told, I didn't forget that you were coming to interview Colt."

"I figured." Lightning illuminated the sky, and I wanted to get back inside.

"You're a pretty girl, and Colt's going to be spending an awful lot of time with us."

His concern was misplaced. I hadn't dated anyone in almost two years. "I suppose I should be thankful that you're always looking out for me. But seriously, Dad. Don't you think it's an inch from psychotic to come all the way here to do something that could have waited four days?"

He held his hands up in surrender. "I really did have a few *other* things to wrap up with him. And there's an engine builder here who I understand is unhappy with his current place of employment. You know how much I hate the telephone, and I figured if I could kill two birds with one stone, then it wasn't a wasted trip."

"And embarrassing your only child was just an added bonus?"

"Listen, Noodle, I have to get back to the mother ship. Call me when you get home so I know you're safe, okay?"

I hugged him goodbye. "Yes sir."

"And remember what I taught you. Anything can be used—"

"As a weapon," I finished for him. "I know. My keys can poke out someone's eyes, a swift kick to a boy's tender area can put him on the ground, and most berries are nonpoisonous."

My father was a self-professed survivalist.

"That's my girl."

He kissed me again, and I watched him go, his gait unsteady and one hand in his pocket. He gave me one last wave before he turned and disappeared behind a transporter.

Back in the motorhome, Colt was sitting on the couch and started to stand up to greet me, but I waved him off.

"So, that just happened," he said.

"I did not see this coming," I said more to myself than him.

"Roll with it, Pierson. We're going to be a great pair."

I tucked a loose strand of hair behind my ear. "How could you possibly know? We just met."

"Uh, I was talking about your dad and me."

My cheeks flushed scarlet.

"Okay then." I looked away. "As you know, my name is Piper Pierson and I work for *NASCAR Weekly*. I called your shop a few days ago and made an appointment with your office manager to interview you. Is now a good time?"

Thunder rumbled outside, and the sky darkened.

"I'm all yours, Piper Pierson, daughter of my new boss, Planter Pierson, the winningest team owner in NASCAR history." Colt leaned back, knees open, arms on the back of the cushion, assuming the carefree pose of the young and arrogant.

"Please don't do that. When I'm on the clock, I am not Planter's daughter. I'm just a journalist for a newspaper. And I'm supposed to write a piece about you and Brent Austin and your competition and camaraderie both off and on the track. Not listen to you kiss up because of who my father is." I meant to be funny, but I could tell by Colt's expression he was stricken by my words.

"My mistake, Ms. Pierson, writer of the newspaper articles, no relation to that team owner guy." I cracked a smile. "Now, let's get down to business. What can I do you for?"

"Can I ask you something, off the record?" I reached in my bag and fished out a pad and pen. I inherited a neurosis from my father that allowed me to only write in black ink. "How does your current owner feel about you switching teams?"

If he said he didn't give a crap because he was headed for the big leagues, that was a red flag that I'd have to tell my father about.

"Darlin', I don't know what your daddy told you out there in the rain, but when he interviewed me, I said I couldn't accept offers until I talked to Mr. Thompson." He was referring to his team's owner. "Cal Thompson has been like a father to me and I would never leave without his blessing."

I'd rarely heard a driver besides Mack speak so graciously.

"I take it he gave it to you?"

Colt's eyes got glassy, and he blinked hard a few times.

"He said whether we win the Busch championship or not, we'd had a great run together and that it was time for me to move on to a bigger team. Said it'd be the perfect way to kick off the nineties." No wonder my dad hired him. There was nothing not to like. "Anything else? Off the record?"

"Nope." I opened my notebook. All the questions I'd written down when I got the assignment now seemed superficial.

"Then sit your pretty self down and I'll tell you how I'm going to win this thing."

I didn't know where to sit. There were still two people in the transporter I hadn't been introduced to, and I felt stupid plopping down next to a stranger.

"Before we begin," he said, "I have to ask you if you're going to be here a while."

"That's up to you and Mother Nature. I'd be happy to talk with you until it stops raining or until I overstay my welcome."

"In that case, I need to do two things. First, let me introduce you." *Thank God.* "And then I need to make us lunch. I hate to talk about myself on an empty stomach."

He winked at me, and I was distracted by his charm and dark-brown eyes. Colt motioned to the man sitting in a swivel chair. "This fine young gent is Scott Stephenson. He's the best pit crew member you will ever have the privilege to meet. They say races are won and lost in the pits, and this guy, along with the rest of my team, hasn't let me down yet. I don't reckon any of them will."

I shook Scott's hand. I'd read about him while I was researching this assignment. Colt mentioned him so often I suspected they were friends long before he started racing. When I turned my attention back to Colt, the girl who hadn't said a word had scooted closer to him on the sofa, and he now had his arm around her.

"And this dark-haired beauty is my sister, Sasha."

"Nice to meet you, Piper," she said.

"You're his sister?" I said, shaking her hand. I looked between the two of them. "I can see it now. You have the same eyes."

"Maybe," Colt said. "But Sasha got the looks in the family. She takes after our mama."

"Then she must be beautiful, too," I said, turning to face Colt. "Pardon me for asking, but what's for lunch?"

Colt touched my cheek on his way to the fridge. "I love a girl who's all about the food." I noticed a jagged scar close to his left eye, and I wanted to reach out and touch it.

After fixing four plates of grilled salmon over mixed greens and warming fresh bread, Colt settled down and told me to fire away.

"Before we officially begin, I have one more question that has nothing to do with racing."

"Oh no," he groaned. "Does everyone in the world know about that night?"

Sasha interjected. "Come on, Colt. It's not as if y'all are local town folk. What made you think nobody was going to recognize you?" Everyone laughed, and I had no idea what they were talking about. She caught my confused expression.

"You never heard about the night my big brother and another driver who shall remain nameless but may or may or may not drive the number 39 car almost got arrested for disturbing the peace? Girlfriend, where have you been?"

"It really wasn't a big deal," Colt quipped. "My friend has a not-so-nice neighbor, and one night after a few games of poker, we thought we'd teach old Farmer Larson a lesson. We weren't going to steal his car, really. We just wanted to move it around the corner so he would think that it got stolen."

"But dumb and dumber made a little too much noise trying to hot-wire the thing and woke up Mrs. Farmer Larson," Sasha interjected, laughing. "It's a good thing yours truly can flirt because the sheriff was dying to arrest those two idiots and sell the story to some rag magazine."

"Yowza, Colt," I teased. "Sounds like you better think of something really nice to do for your sister."

"He already did." She giggled. "He set me up with a very eligible Winston Cup driver."

Colt turned his attention back to me.

"So, what did you want to ask? Now that Sasha has made me unnecessarily fess up." He pointed at his sister and shook his finger.

"Oh," I muttered absently. "I was curious how you got the scar by your eye."

He rubbed the left side of his face. "I smashed my face on a rock while I was walking my dog."

"Were you drunk?"

Sasha laughed. "No. He was about nine years old and was trying to walk Julie and ride his bike at the same time."

"But she was a beagle and her little legs couldn't go very fast," Colt added, "so I had to peddle really slowly and my bike tipped over."

"However," Sasha continued, "Julie the wonder dog ran home and barked in the front yard until our mom followed her back to the crash site. Four hours and seventeen stitches later, Colt and Julie came home from the emergency room—each wearing an eye patch."

It was cute how Colt and Sasha seemed so in tune with each other, and it made me wish I had a sibling.

"That's a good dog," I said, peeking out the window. "The sun is trying to come out, so we better get moving."

I flipped through my notebook until I found my list of

questions. "Right now, you're only two points ahead of Brent Austin. How do you plan on winning the points chase?"

He leaned in and stage-whispered, "I have a top-secret, foolproof plan."

I was surprised he'd tell me, a novice reporter, his strategy. I held my pen, waiting.

"I'm gonna win more races." Then he winked at me.

I scribbled down his words and waited. Finally, I said, "Is there more to that?"

"No," he said simply. "If we want to win the championship, we have to win more races and finish better than Brent."

"Don't feel bad," Sasha called from the kitchen where she was putting more bread in a basket. "One thing you need to remember about my brother. If you ask a simple question, you'll get a simple answer."

"All right," I said, taking inventory of the remaining *simple* questions I'd prepared before the interview. "How important is it to win the championship? You're only twenty-three. You have lots of years of racing left."

I thought I'd get a one-word answer like *really* or *very*. But instead he said, "I do and I don't. I'm young. I love racing. I plan on doing this forever. But forever could last thirty more years or it could end tomorrow. Racing is a dangerous sport."

I winced. No one knew that better than my family.

"You never know what's going to happen, so we better enjoy this beautiful life while we've got it." He reached behind him and took a bottle of water from the windowsill. "But, in terms of importance, it's more crucial to me that I drive well and take a lesson from the big dogs than it is to win a championship this year. I just try to run each race the best I can and learn from my mistakes."

Interviewing Colt Porter was like talking to a ninety-year-old war veteran trapped in a young man's body. As I flipped through my notes for a question that didn't sound like a four-year-old had thought of it, one of the smoking guys from outside came in.

"Sorry to interrupt, Colt. Practice has been rained out."

"Thanks, Jake," Colt said and then got up. "Good job today, everyone. Tomorrow we'll show 'em what we can do."

He changed the radio station from MRN, which had been rebroadcasting endless interviews to fill dead air, to a rock station. On his way back to the couches, he stopped at a cabinet and returned with a bottle of Cuervo 1800 and several shot glasses. He filled them and put one in front of me.

"Welcome to the family, Pierson. We don't dick around in here with lemons and salt. Bottoms up." We touched our glasses and he slammed his shot. My empty glass hit the table before his. "Hot damn, girlfriend. I think I'm in love." He slid in the dinette and put his arm around me.

"Thanks for the drink," I said. "But I need to get going and find your rival and ask him a few *simple* questions for my article."

By the time I found Brent's trailer, it was pouring. His crew chief told me Brent had left for the day because of the rain, so I headed to will call where Ken and I were planning to touch base at five o'clock. I bought a coffee and reviewed my notes while I waited for him.

"Hey, Piper," Ken greeted, dashing under the awning where I'd been waiting. "How'd your interviews go?"

"One down, one to go," I said. "The rain foiled my plans to meet with Brent. How was your day?"

"All good. Lots of notes. Now I just need to get typing." The rain stopped and he closed the umbrella he'd been carrying. "Ready to go to the hotel?"

"If you don't mind, I'm going to stick around for a while. I'll grab a cab a bit later."

"Sure thing. I'll leave your bag with the front desk in case I'm out when you get there."

"You're the best, Ken. Thanks so much." I waited until he'd walked out of sight before I turned toward Colt's motorhome.

• • •

That night ended at seven the next morning in Colt's motorhome with me hungover and fully dressed in his bed. I thought about trying to sneak out while he slept, I was mortified that I'd passed out in his room. But I went to the couch where he was sleeping and poked him until he opened his eyes.

"So, I'll see you later," I said as I tucked in my shirt.

"Come on, stay a little while longer," he whined.

"I'd love to, but I need to interview Brent Austin, get home and write this article." I tried to maintain eye contact as I talked, but I kept looking at what was under his blanket.

"Oh yeah, my buddy Brent. It's a good thing it rained yesterday."

"Why's that a good thing?" I feigned unconcern, but I'd been so happy the day before when Brent Austin's crew chief told me he left the track as soon as the rainout was called.

"Because Brent left, and you came back to be with me instead of leaving to interview him."

I glanced around the room for my backpack. "Anyhoo, I should get a move on and find Mr. Austin. Then I'm heading back to Moorestown."

"Can't you stick around and watch me win tomorrow?"

I had grave disdain for cocky men, but Colt was so charming, he came across confident, not arrogant.

"No can do." I wanted to stay, but I wasn't about to tell him that. "After I interview your competition, I have to find a rock and crawl under it."

Colt slid off the couch and wrapped a towel around his waist even though he was wearing boxers. His chest was smooth and muscled. "Nothing happened. Remember?"

"Speaking of." I dropped my eyes. "Sorry I put the moves on you last night." It'd been years since I cared about anyone enough to flirt. "I don't normally drink. And now I remember why."

He patted the couch next to him, but I didn't sit. "Don't be. I'm flattered. But we both know why your dad came to see me here when he easily could have waited until I was back in North Carolina."

"He's always been a little overprotective of me. But don't worry about my father. I know how to handle him."

In truth, I had no idea what to do about my dad. I studied Colt as I spoke. He was as close to perfection as I'd ever seen—young, great looking, talented, charming and successful. I found my bag and checked to make sure my notebook was in it.

"I like you, Piper."

I couldn't stop from smiling. "I need to get going. I've got work to do." As if Brent Austin would be up for an interview at seven in the morning.

"Can I call you?"

"If you can find my number." I gathered my bag, walked to the couch and rested my hand on his shoulder for a moment. "But I'm unlisted."

I quietly closed the motorhome door behind me and checked my watch. When I called Ken the night before to let him know I wasn't coming back to the hotel, we made plans to meet at will call at 9 a.m. to head back to Moorestown.

•   •   •

I hadn't exactly planned on staying overnight at the track. But my survivalist father taught me to be prepared, so I kept a brush, a toothbrush and toothpaste in my purse. I bought a cute top from a vendor and cleaned myself up in the bathroom. Then I bought a twenty-ounce Mountain Dew and a bagel with extra cream cheese and ate at an empty picnic table killing time. I spent almost an hour going through my notes. I finished my bagel, tossed my soda in a trashcan and headed to Brent Austin's transporter.

"Morning," I said to the same stocky man who I'd talked to the previous afternoon. He was sitting at a small table by the ramp with a paper and pen. "Is Brent around? I'd love to talk to him before practice starts."

"You and me both. He spent the better part of the night at the ER and is currently at the infield care center." He held up the paper, which I could see now was a list of drivers' names. Some had been crossed out. "I'm not so sure he's going to recover in time for the race. So, I'm looking for someone to drive for him, just in case." There was a time when I thought I could be anyone's relief driver.

"Do you mind if I ask what happened?"

He motioned to a chair on the other side of the table. Coffee was brewing, and it smelled so good I wanted to ask for a cup. "The doc thinks it's food poisoning. When practice got rained out yesterday, he took off for an early dinner. He's getting IV fluids right now and with any luck he'll be able to race tomorrow." He glanced at the paper. "But I like to have a backup plan."

"Oh no. What restaurant?" I asked, thinking of the delicious lunch Colt had prepared the day before. And then the not-so-delicious takeout pizza we had for dinner.

"Have you heard about the snazzy new restaurant that just opened in Atlanta? The one whose bar is a fish tank?" I told him I knew of it but had never been. "Consider yourself warned. Stay away from the squab."

As if I'd ever eat a pigeon. My stomach turned with the thought of Brent throwing up baby bird all night. I felt the tequila roiling. I thanked the man for his time and left him with a scribbled note asking Brent to call me when he felt up to it. I got a large cup of coffee that didn't smell nearly as good as what was in Brent's trailer, found a payphone and left a message for Tack telling him I was unable to interview Brent. I stopped near Colt's motorhome and got close enough to hear voices coming from it. I wanted to knock, but it seemed entirely too needy. So, I waited at will call for Ken. When he got there a minute before nine o'clock, I thanked him for picking me up, and we headed north on I-85. We listened to MRN all the way home, hoping to get an update on Happy Hour, the last practice before a race. But I never heard anything about Colt.

·   ·   ·

When I got to my apartment, I fumbled with my key, still feeling like the world was a little lopsided. I heard my answering machine beeping. When I opened the door, the space around me smelled still and stale. The air-conditioning wasn't on, and it was hot in the living room. It didn't look as though Liza had been home since I left. I opened a few windows, turned on the overhead fan by the sectional and threw away a carton of noodles that had been on the counter when I left. Then I checked the answering machine. One message was from Tack, and the other three were from Colt wanting to know if he could see me when he got back to Charlotte. I should have known he'd figure out how to get my number before I even got home. The phone rang and I prayed it was Brent Austin.

"This is Piper," I said.

"What's happening, hot stuff?"

I couldn't stop myself from smiling, and I was glad Colt couldn't see me.

"Hey, I was just thinking about you. What's going on?"

"Were you wishing you didn't have to leave me today?"

That's exactly what I was thinking, but he didn't need to know that.

"Did you hear that your competition is sick?"

"Yeah. I just came back from the infield care center. Turns out there's a nasty bird flu going around. Poor guy's been puking for twelve hours." I was about to correct him and say that it was food poisoning, but then I got the joke. *Poor Brent? Poor me.* I needed to interview him before Monday, and it seemed like that wasn't going to happen.

"I guess that's good news for you if he can't run tomorrow. But it means I'm totally screwed."

"First off, that is not how I want to win the championship. Second, what does Brent being sick have to do with you?"

I could tell by his tone that I'd offended him. My father said insulting a man's integrity was as bad as insulting his family.

"I'm sorry," I said. "I didn't mean it like that. It's just that this is my first feature piece and it's due on Monday. If Mr. Austin is too sick to talk to me, I don't know what I'm going to do."

"How good are you?"

"Good enough," I said, annoyed. "Why?" Maybe I was wrong about him. Maybe he wasn't as mature as he'd come across when I interviewed him.

He laughed, irritating me even more. "I meant how good are you at your job? Can you put together the article in a few hours?"

My school had a great journalism department, one of the reasons I'd chosen it. I'd started at its newspaper as a freshman and was used to deadlines. I liked the pressure of knowing I had only a certain amount of time to get something done. It kept me from procrastinating. And I'd already put together a solid outline.

"Sure. Why?"

"It must be your lucky day, Pierson. Brent happens to be a friend. I'll make a deal with you. If you'll have dinner with us Sunday night, we'll finish the interviews. Provided he's feeling better, of course. Sound like a plan?"

Relief rushed at me like a blast of cold air on a hot day.

"Will you both be back by then?" Even though Busch races were on Saturdays or occasionally Friday nights, many drivers stayed at the tracks all weekend.

"Most definitely. I'm a homebody. I'd rather watch Cup races from my couch than be stuck at a hot and crowded track."

Colt was not at all like what I thought he'd be. Many young drivers hung out at races just to meet girls.

"Can I put that in the article?" I asked.

"I'd be disappointed if you didn't. People need to know that I'm just like everyone else."

"Oh yeah, because most twenty-three-year-olds have half-a-million-dollar motorhomes and a personal chef."

"I bought my rig used and I'll be paying it off forever, and there is no chef." His voice got low, and I knew I'd upset him again. *Shit! What's wrong with me?* I was trying too hard, something I never did. I felt like a jerk.

"But that salmon was so good."

"I cook well," he said. "Now grab a pen and a paper so I can give you directions to my place."

It wasn't lost on me that he let me off the hook for making assumptions about him, and I was reminded what my supervisor at school had told me on my first day. *There's no room for guessing in good journalism.*

I dug through a junk drawer, tried two pens that were both dry and settled for a Sharpie. "Okay," I finally said. "I'm ready."

3

I'd told Liza all about Colt, so on Sunday while I showered and got ready for dinner at his house, she lay on my bed and kept me company. Since she started with the advertising agency, we hadn't seen much of each other, and I was grateful to have a few minutes with her.

"Which ad campaign are you working on now?" I asked.

"None. But I have mastered the art of operating the cappuccino machine," she said brightly. "Apparently, my rise to stardom is not as meteoric as I thought it would be."

"Even after you landed that big coffee company as a client?" I took off my shirt, and Liza grabbed another from my closet and tossed it to me. I put it on and twirled.

"How do I look?"

"You look like you like this guy," she said.

I sat again and put on smoky blue eye shadow, thinking about how being with Colt felt different.

"Let's not go there."

She rolled over on her back. "Why not? You're twenty-two. Not ninety-two. What do you have against fun?"

"I'm fun," I murmured.

She sat up. "Really? When was the last time you kissed a boy?"

"Point taken."

"Getting back to the subject. You look like you like this guy. Are you going to go for it?"

"Did you miss what he does for a living?"

She stood and put her hands on my cheeks. "Your dad is fine. It wasn't your fault. You need to let yourself live a little."

Aside from my parents, Liza was the only person I'd ever talked to about my father's accident. "It was my fault," I said quietly. "You know that."

"It was an accident." She let go of my face and put her hands on her hips. "By definition that means it wasn't anyone's fault."

That wasn't even a little accurate. "*I* caused the wreck that almost killed my father."

She took me by the hand, and we sat on the end of my bed. It'd taken me two years to tell Liza what really happened. I hadn't planned on it, but when she kept pressuring me to get a driver's license I finally broke down and told her I had one, but I'd never use it again.

"Stop it," she scolded. "It was an accident and you know it. Could have happened to anyone."

"That's what my parents told the press. To protect me. The rest of the world thinks my dad was being kind and let some no-driving kid test with him at that Tennessee track. No one but you knows that I was the rookie in the car who begged my dad to let me run a few laps with him."

"It doesn't matter who was driving that other car. You didn't mean to hurt your dad." She squeezed my hand and then let go. "And look at him. He's as good as new. He'd get back in a race car in a heartbeat if your mom would let him."

After my dad was released from the hospital five years ago, I was the one who begged him not to race in the off-season anymore. Like with everything else in my life, my father held a press conference and gave a well-rehearsed speech about hanging up his driving shoes to concentrate on the race team. I'd spent my life in front of cameras and learned early on that I never spoke to the press unless someone told me what to say.

I spun my watch on my wrist. "I've got to get going. Wish me luck."

"Luck," she said, then stood. "For what?"

"That I don't screw up my first big article."

She picked up a lip liner from my bureau and stained her mouth a dark wine color. "You don't need luck for that. But I will wish that you get your head on straight and realize that you like this boy."

There was never any fooling Liza. "I don't like him," I lied. "Besides, even if I did, there's the small problem that come February he's going to be working for my father."

Liza put down the lip pencil and sat on the bed next to me.

"Do you really think your dad would have a problem if you two dated?"

"Well, you know how much he likes to quote that old racing buddy of his."

"Never stick your dick in the cash register," we said at the same time.

Liza scrunched her eyebrows together. "That seems strange to me. Your parents are usually so cool."

Good point. They had never pretended that I was a saint or that I didn't live in a reckless, privileged world. Instead of telling my friends and me not to drink, my father told us never to drink and drive. As long as I called him for a safe ride, he wouldn't ask questions or punish me. I exercised that option four times when I was in high school asking him to pick me up from parties where I'd been drinking. And true to his word, he'd driven me home, handed me two aspirin and a bottle of water and kissed me goodnight.

"Yeah, well. What can I say? Even Planter and Poppi Pierson have their moments of parentaldom."

"That's too bad." Liza leaned back on a mound of pillows. "I've seen that Colt boy on TV. He's pretty cute."

"Tell me about it." I put on a little mascara, blended the eye shadow a bit more and presented myself to Liza for inspection.

• • •

Liza dropped me off at Colt's on her way to meet some friends from work for dinner. When he opened his front door, he was singing, "Hey, good lookin', whatcha got cookin'?" His voice was uneven and off key—and I loved it.

"How's your day?" he asked, leading me into his house.

"Better now," I replied. "By the way, how was the race? Did Mother Nature cooperate?"

It stopped raining before sunrise on Saturday, the maintenance crew had spent three hours on the jet dryers, and the race started on time. I watched Cup races on TV when I wasn't at them, but I hadn't paid attention to Busch in years. All that changed the second I let myself into Colt's motorhome.

"Yeah—we got it in. It was okay."

"Just okay? Did you blow a tire or something?" I wanted to give him a congratulatory hug. But I was afraid if I told him I didn't pee for three hours for fear of missing the camera panning in on him, he'd get spooked.

"No, nothing like that. My guys did a great job getting me in and out of the pits, but I couldn't get Billie Jean into the stall fast enough each time. It felt like it took ten minutes to get to where the guys could do their stuff."

"Billie Jean?"

His cheeks reddened. "I name all my cars after girls in songs."

I'd had a friend in college who did that with her horses.

"You and my dad will get along just fine." I stepped farther into the foyer, trying to get a look inside. "Or maybe not. He gives his cars girl names that start with P. There could be a standoff between you two."

Without missing a beat Colt said, "We could start with Peggy Sue and Proud Mary. That would work, right?"

"I'm sure you will figure something out. Now, other than Billie Jean not wanting to stay in her stall, how was the race?" Knowing he'd won, I wondered why he was giving me such a dismal recount of a great finish. "Where'd you end up?"

"Oh, my guys won the race for me, but I drove like shit."

That was Colt—wise and humble.

Colt led me into the kitchen and introduced me to Brent Austin. I reached out to shake his hand, but he stepped away.

"I'm sorry, Piper. I'm still not feeling a hundred percent. And even though the doctor is convinced it was the squab, I don't want to risk getting anyone sick."

I put my hand down. "Oh, no problem. But can I ask you something?"

"Sure, I guess. Are we starting the interview already?"

Colt went to the refrigerator and opened three cans of Busch. Brent told him no thank you and got a bottled water instead.

I took a sip of beer, hoping to settle my nerves. I hadn't realized until I got there how much I wanted the night to go well.

"What made you think it was a good idea to eat a pigeon?" I asked.

Colt wiped his mouth. "Oh, Pierson, I asked him that very same thing yesterday morning."

Brent covered his mouth with his hand. "Please don't say that word."

"You mean pigeon?" Colt asked. "What about cow brains or fish eyes? Are those okay?"

"So, Piper," Brent said, ignoring Colt and smiling. "Your dad has been one of my longtime heroes. I'm probably not so far from retiring and I've often thought about owning a team when I'm done driving. I hope I could be half as successful as your father."

"That's very kind of you to say, Mr. Austin."

"Brent, please. I mean it. I'm not sure I would have had the guts to keep going in any capacity if I'd had an accident like your dad's. Did they ever even figure out exactly what happened?"

My father had confidentiality clauses in any contract he signed, so if something catastrophic happened, no money-grubbing hack could sell the story to a tabloid without being sued. Other than a handful of people who had witnessed the accident but were legally bound to secrecy, no one knew that I was the driver who caused his wreck.

I hated thinking about it, never mind talking about it.

"Your house is beautiful, Colt," I said. He was washing broccoli at the sink. "Brent, would you mind giving me a tour while Colt cooks?"

The two men exchanged worried glances. "Sure thing," Brent said. "Wait until you see the view. You'll never want to leave, especially at sunset."

While Brent gave me a tour of the house overlooking Lake Norman, Colt made beef stroganoff. He offered me a bite as he was stirring the reduction. It was so good that when he had his back turned, I glanced in the trash to see if there were takeout boxes from Del Frisco's.

Colt's kitchen was huge and had the telltale signs of a great chef. The top of the island was a chopping block. His knives cost more than my best cashmere sweater. The dishwasher made no noise. The refrigerator was stocked with lettuce, cucumbers and tomatoes from his garden. I'd been in plenty of houses with beautiful kitchens that'd never been used. One of my dad's best friends and a fellow team owner had a faucet over his gas stove so pots could be filled while on the burners. But he claimed he didn't know how to boil water.

Colt went into the front yard to cut flowers as Brent continued my tour. A deck ran the length of the house facing the lake. Two jet skis and a boat were tied to a dock out the back door.

Our last stop was Colt's bathroom because Brent insisted that I see the shower.

"No offense," I said. "But we can skip this part. I have little desire to see a single man's bathroom." Pee stains on the toilet seat and hair in the shower drain were not how I wanted to remember Colt's house.

"You're going to want to see this one," Brent said.

He took me to a wooden room about the size of my own bedroom with benches against three walls. Showerheads came from every direction. Colt's shower was also a sauna. There was not a stray hair in sight. Creased white towels hung from racks.

By the time the tour of a house that could be showcased in *Architectural Digest* ended, Colt had set the table, opened a bottle of Stag's Leap cabernet, and put wildflowers in a trophy from one of his many Busch victories.

"My lady." He pulled out a chair at the island for me, and I fleetingly thought he was too good to be true. "Dinner will be ready in a few minutes. Let's sit and have a glass of wine."

I sat next to Brent, sipping wine and eating a cheese I couldn't identify. It had a bite to it but wasn't really spicy. "What kind is this?" I put another piece on a stone-ground cracker and ate it. "It's so good."

Colt stood so close to me I could smell his deodorant. "It's called Dragon Cheese. I get it at a specialty shop in Davidson." I took another piece and he eyed me. I handed it to him, then made one for Brent, as if I'd meant to dole out appetizers. I wanted more, but now I felt self-conscious.

"You look hungry," Colt said to me. "Let's eat."

Colt served the three of us. The beef smelled so good I didn't want to wait the minute it took for Colt and Brent to get their food. I took a bite before Colt put down the serving tray. Being a good Southern wife, my mother was an excellent cook and had passed that gift on to me. While my mom was all about exactly following recipes created by famous chefs, I liked to experiment. Cilantro instead of basil, braised lamb rather than roasted, red pepper sauce in lieu of tomato. I was already thinking of meals I could make for Colt but wasn't sure anything I cooked would be as good as this.

I'd finished half the food on my plate when I realized Colt and Brent were staring at me, smiling.

"What?" I asked. "Haven't you ever seen a girl pig out before?" I wiped my mouth with a cloth napkin that Colt had folded into the shape of a sailboat. "It's so good, I can't help myself."

"My wife eats before we go out to dinner so no one will see her chewing," Brent said. "Says it's unladylike."

"Then she'd hate me," I told him. "Because I love to eat."

"Clearly," Colt said.

I made a face at him. "I blame you. It's just so good."

"It's true," he said to Brent. "You should have seen her inhale my salmon salad on Thursday when she interviewed me. I didn't know if I should be impressed or horrified."

"Impressed," Brent and I said at the same time. "Okay, boys," I said to keep myself from finishing my meal before they were even halfway done with theirs. "Tell me everything I need to know to write a fabulous article."

"Brent's terrified of spiders," Colt said.

"Really?" I asked. "You drive a race car on a track with thirty other cars going almost two hundred miles an hour and you're afraid of a tiny creature that makes your life better by eating mosquitos?"

"Easy for you to say. You never had a big brother whose pet tarantula escaped and reappeared on your face in the middle of the night."

"A tarantula?" I asked. "But they're so fuzzy and cute. My great-grandmother in Brownsville, Texas, had pet tarantulas. They're harmless."

Brent reached for a piece of rosemary focaccia. "I see I'm not going to get any sympathy from you."

"Definitely not. *Charlotte's Web* was my favorite book when I was a kid. I named all of Grammie's spiders Charlotte."

"That must have been confusing for them." Colt smirked.

"Oh sure, go ahead and mock. But my parents call me to trap spiders and set them free. I like the little eight-legged guys."

Brent shivered in his seat. "I'm getting a little freaked out over here. Any chance we can change the subject and talk about something else? Like how I'm going to kick this youngster's ass and win the Busch championship?"

I stabbed a piece of beef off his plate with my fork. "I don't know, old man. I'm liking finding things out about you two that have nothing to do with cars. I mean, I get it. Dowlet Tires put you on the pole, but they inevitably blow before the end of a race. You gotta go with Goodyear all the way, even if you're slower in practice and qualifying. And drivers and crew chiefs will say they like to start from the pole, but hardly anyone wins when they start in first, so the outside pole or second row is much preferred."

Colt and Brent were staring at me. I couldn't tell if they were amused or annoyed by my mini rant.

"Boys," I said dramatically, with the back of my hand on my forehead. "Please tell me something about you. Not race car drivers Brent and Colt. But something about you as people. I'm begging you."

They exchanged glances. "I love to talk about myself," Colt finally said. "But you told me in my motorhome that you were supposed to write an article about our strategies to win the title. My fear of wearing hats because I think it's going to make my hair thin has nothing to do with me as a driver."

He was being sincere, so I tried hard not to smile. I could totally see Colt checking the top of his head in the mirror every morning, searching for the beginning of a bald spot.

"That's exactly my point," I said. "When it comes down to it, consistency is going to win the championship. And maybe a little bit of luck. Everyone knows that." Brent sat up in his seat, and I worried that I'd offended them.

"I'm not taking anything away from you two. Because you're both super talented." Colt's eyebrows scrunched, and Brent gripped his fork. "Listen. I like to be prepared, so I read everything I could find about you as soon as I got this assignment. My father has every Busch and Cup race, as well as a bazillion driver interviews, on VHS. He watches old races the way football players watch film. Believe me when I tell you that I've done my homework. I can tell you that you, Brent, have won at every track you've ever raced."

He nodded in appreciation.

"And you, Colt, have never had a DNF. But I don't know why you wanted to race or how your families feel about it or if you even have families." Colt started to speak, but I stopped him. "Don't worry about what I was *supposed* to write. My father's favorite saying is that he'd rather beg forgiveness than ask permission. I'm hoping I'll get so much good info from you two, my boss won't have any choice but to be awed by my talent and initiative."

"You're a little cocky," Colt said.

"Funny," I shot back. "I told my roommate the same thing about you." But he was right. I hadn't felt this good about myself since before my dad's accident.

Colt cleared our plates. "So you've been talking about me." He turned to Brent. "Did you hear that?"

"Sure did," he said. "I think she likes you."

My face went hot. "I like you both and I'd like you both a little more if you'd stop teasing me and start talking."

•   •   •

My time with Colt and Brent passed too quickly. I took notes until we cleared our dessert plates and drank our coffee, not so much for the article, but so I wouldn't forget anything Colt said. We covered all the important stuff—how great crew chiefs produced great drivers, why super speedways were more fun than short tracks and how they kept their friendship going despite being fierce rivals. Eventually I convinced them that it wouldn't be their fault if I got fired for writing off topic, and we started talking about silly things like how Colt hated V8 but loved tomato juice.

"But it's the same thing," I said. "What do you think V8 is made of?"

"I'm telling you." He looked to Brent for encouragement. "The taste is completely different. Tomato juice is nature's perfect drink. V8, on the other hand, tastes like feet."

Stories about Colt's favorite track or worst wreck made me feel like I'd known him for years. I pictured myself in his pit at Sonoma when he didn't think he had to slow down for the road course's hairpin turns and literally flew off the track into the catch fence. I could see his brown eyes getting wide the first time he stepped onto Daytona's race surface.

I could tell from the reverence in his voice when he talked about his current team owner and the love with which he spoke of his parents that he would make both my father and Mack proud. There were plenty of drivers out there who could put a car in the winner's circle, but not all of them would become an integral part of the team.

Brent and I cleaned the kitchen while Colt gathered pictures for me to use for the article. He came back with a stack of photos, and Brent excused himself to go to the bathroom.

"Please stay a while longer," Colt whispered in my ear after the bathroom door closed. "We can pick up where we left off."

We'd left off with me passed out drunk in his bed. "Sorry." I shut off the sink and dried my hands. "I have a curfew. My roommate is coming to get me. She gets very lonely without me."

"Did your car die?" he asked, looking out the window.

"I don't drive," I said.

"*You*?" He leaned in close to me. "Don't think that just because I haven't said anything I don't remember you. You were the only driver who kicked my ass in the Dash cars." I started to talk, but he must have seen the way my mouth pulled down in a frown. "Clearly not the time to bring that up." He folded a damp dishtowel into squares. "Well, why don't I run you home?"

"It's okay. I asked Liza to meet me here"—I looked at the microwave clock—"about now."

Brent returned and wiped down the slate counters one more time. "My work here is done," he said. "Piper, it was a pleasure to finally meet you in person. Please let me know if you need anything else for your article."

"The pleasure was mine," I said, hugging him. "My only problem is now I have too much great stuff to write about." Headlights shone in the window above the sink. "Let me grab my notebook and I'll walk out with you."

I gave Colt a quick kiss on the cheek, said goodnight to Brent in the driveway, then returned to my apartment to start my 2,000-word assignment.

• • •

The next day, I submitted my first big article for *NASCAR Weekly*. Twenty minutes after I put it on Tack's desk, he called me into his office.

"Piper," he started in a tone that made me want to go back to my cubicle. "Close the door."

I couldn't imagine what I'd done wrong. "Is everything okay?"

"This piece," he said, his voice way too loud. He held up the typed pages I'd submitted. "It's not what we talked about. This is more dating profile than race strategy."

Shit! Apparently begging forgiveness wasn't going to be so easy. In truth, I hadn't given my defiance much thought. I'd written a good article, and I foolishly assumed that Tack would love it and magically forget that I hadn't done what he asked of me.

"I'm sorry, Tack. It's just that these two guys have so much personality and I thought readers would be more interested in them as people than as competitors. I mean, one of them is going to blow a tire or run out of fuel or get caught up in a wreck and the other is going to win the championship. That's how good they are. It's going to come down to circumstances." I sounded just like my dad.

Tack pushed back in his chair. "I agree with all of that, but that wasn't the assignment."

"But it's a good piece, right?" I groveled.

"That's beside the point. I can't have the new hire going rogue."

I deserved this but thought he'd pardon my insubordination because it all worked out in the end. I could see why he'd have to make an example of me.

"I know I already said this, but I truly am sorry. I'll go clean out my stuff." I stood, thinking about how much I hated to disappoint my parents. They were going to be so pissed.

"Settle down, Piper. You're not fired."

I turned back toward him. "I'm not?"

"No. But that was your first and last warning to do what you're assigned."

"Yes sir," I said contritely. "I understand."

"Now sit down and tell me how you got this material. It sounds like you're writing about two of your best friends."

"You told me to interview the top two contenders for the Busch championship and I did."

He flipped to the second page. "How on earth did you get Colt to tell you that he sleeps with the hall light on or—" He ran his finger to the last paragraph. "—that Brent was a tenor in his church choir as a kid?"

I fluttered my eyelashes at my pretty-boy boss. "You'd be surprised how far asking nicely can get you."

He unbuttoned his monogrammed cuffs and rolled up his sleeves. "If you promise to stay on task, I've got good or bad news, depending on how you look at it."

I squirmed in the squishy leather chair. "Uh oh," I said. "Are you making me the copyeditor because you're so impressed there weren't any mistakes in my article?" When proofing my work, I used a trick my eighth-grade English teacher, Mr. Hershnik, taught me. First, I read it out loud, and then I read it from end to beginning.

"Kid, you're going to a lot more races."

"I can do that," I said. "I'll make you proud, Tack. I promise."

4

In addition to UNC, I'd also gotten into Drew University, Boston College and the University of Arizona. But there was never any doubt that I'd stay in North Carolina. I only applied to the other schools to make it seem like I was considering being on my own. My parents told me I should go wherever I wanted and that they'd visit as much as I would allow.

They were my whole life. I missed my senior prom because we were racing at Dover. I was eighteen, and they trusted me in the house alone for the weekend. But, like on so many other occasions, I chose family over friends and went on the road with my parents. I was always afraid that if I wasn't with them at a race, something bad would happen.

After the Tennessee wreck, my parents made me go to my high school's counselor for a semester. She said what I felt was a phenomenon called *magical thinking*. For me, the magic was that as long as I went to races, no one would get hurt. Thinking I could control fate was stupid enough, but my philosophy made no sense since I was the one who slammed my car into my father's and almost killed him. It didn't matter what my parents said, or what schools I got into; there was no way I was going to college someplace far from home.

I was afraid when I got to Chapel Hill that my roommate would think I was a baby for wanting to go home as much as I did. But it was the first time Liza had really been away from Boston, and visiting my parents and eating my mother's comfort food made Liza feel a little less homesick. So, at least once a month we'd pack our bags and head to Moorestown for the weekend.

●   ●   ●

On my way to my parents' house on Saturday, I ran into Sandwich Construction, the site of my chance meeting with Tack, to pick up lunch for my mom and me. Colt was eating in the bar area with his parents. I recognized them from the articles I'd read. He looked just like his father. I hadn't seen Colt since the night he cooked dinner for Brent Austin and me, and although I thought about him all the time, I didn't call him. I'd never been the girl who chased boys. In high school I didn't have to. And in college I didn't want to.

I couldn't hear what Colt's father was saying, but his expression was serious, so I didn't interrupt their meal. I wasn't even sure if Colt had seen me until he yelled my name so loudly the entire bar fell silent. Crimson-cheeked, I headed to his table.

"Hello, very loud person," I greeted. He was wearing pressed pants and a button-down shirt, as if he'd dressed up for his mom and dad.

He stood, took my hand and kissed my cheek. "Sorry about that, but I didn't want you to get away without meeting my parents." I was wearing baggy jeans, a plain white T-shirt and tennis shoes. I wished I was wearing something nicer, but Liza teased me that this was my uniform.

"Mom, Dad, this is Piper Pierson. Piper—these are my parents, Meri and Doug Porter."

I extended my hand to each of them. "Mr. and Mrs. Porter, it's a pleasure to meet you. My parents and I are thrilled Colt will be a part of our team next year."

Doug Porter stood, and his mannerisms were strikingly similar to Colt's. He brushed his fingers through his hair and shifted his weight from one foot to the other. "Piper Pierson. Daughter of Planter Pierson, I presume?"

"The one and only," I said. He shook my hand vigorously as if I were one of the boys. "Your father is one hell of an owner. He's genius, I tell you, genius. How he built his stable from one dirt-track car to his current team is legendary. We are so honored that Colt is going to be a part of that legacy next year."

Mr. Porter didn't let go of my hand, and we stood there, awkwardly connected.

"He's a smart cookie, all right." My hand was getting sweaty, and I wanted it back.

"*Smart?* Smart is knowing how to do calculus. Your dad is *brilliant*. Penske and Childress got nothing on him," Colt's dad said, referencing two of the sport's most famous team owners. He finally released me, and I fought the urge to wipe my palm on my jeans. I tried to make eye contact with Colt, but he was staring at the floor.

Meri Porter rose and took my hand in both of hers, then air-kissed me. "Piper," she said. "You are the spitting image of your mother. I'd recognize you anywhere."

"Thank you, Mrs. Porter. That's quite a compliment."

She threw back her head. "Oh please, call me Meri. I'm so looking forward to the new season. I think we're all going to get along famously."

"Absolutely," I said. There was a beat of silence, and I felt like I was keeping them from something. "I need to get going." Liza was waiting for me in the parking lot. She was going to drop me off in Moorestown on her way to a client meeting. "But it was really nice to meet you. I look forward to seeing you all more often."

A few years earlier, my dad told me he got tired of making the commute from Moorestown into Charlotte where Pierson Racing was housed. So, he built a 25,000-square-foot garage on the hundred acres we had at home. When it was under construction I overheard my parents discussing the cost. My dad said it was money well spent if it made it easier for me to spend time with them. Then he asked my mother if she thought I'd ever drive a car again. Now, I suspected I would find my way over there more often.

The bartender brought me my food. I shook Colt's parents' hands again and gave him a wave. "I look forward to seeing you again soon."

"Hey, Pierson," Colt called to my back.

My lunch was burning my hands through the bag. "Yes?" I turned to him.

"Don't be a stranger," he said, then winked at me.

● ● ●

My timing was bad, and my mom was out by the time I got home with lunch. She left a note saying she was at the grocery store and would be back soon, so I put her lunch in the fridge and sat out on the back deck eating mine, listening to the radio. The phone rang, and I ran into the kitchen to answer it, then remembered I didn't live there anymore.

"Hello?" I asked, then quickly added, "Pierson residence."

"What's happenin', hot stuff?" Colt greeted, quoting his favorite movie, *Sixteen Candles*.

"How did you know I was here?" I asked, pouring myself a Mountain Dew and heading back onto the deck.

"It wasn't a huge leap. I didn't think you ventured forty minutes from your apartment to get a hamburger." I could hear him tapping a pen, something he'd told me was a nervous habit when I interviewed him. "I'm sorry about my parents," he said.

I put the phone on speaker on my lap and continued eating my chicken wings. "What are you apologizing for? They were nice."

"My dad can be a little . . . intense. I was hoping to hide him from you for a while longer."

"How quickly you forget." I looked around for a napkin, and when I couldn't find one, I wiped my orange fingers on my jeans. "At least your father didn't show up at my place of work telling me to stay away from you."

"Braselton wasn't that bad. He's just looking out for you. It was sweet."

There was silence, and I couldn't help but feel that something was on Colt's mind.

"You okay?" I asked. "You're never this quiet." I said it like I'd spent more than a couple evenings with him. That was the thing about Colt. I felt like I'd known him forever.

"I'd been thinking about introducing you to my mom and dad."

He had? We'd only hung out twice, hadn't even kissed. "Meeting the parents is usually a good thing. Why do you sound like someone ran over your cat?"

His breathing was rhythmic. If I didn't know any better, I'd say he was scratching his head, trying to think of what to say next.

"I like you, Piper." I cringed because his tone told me this was not necessarily good news. "Remember when my sister told you in Braselton that I wasn't dating anyone?" After I'd come back from Brent Austin's transporter, Sasha had casually mentioned her brother was single.

"Oh." His words stung. "You're with someone. As long as we're confessing our sins, I have a strict no-dating-drivers rule. So, it's all good."

"What?" His voice was flat. "I . . . I didn't know that."

"Yeah, it's just easier."

"Well, okay then. Forget I said anything."

"It's okay. What were you going to say?"

"Nothing. It doesn't matter now."

"Come on, just tell me. I'm sorry I interrupted you."

He sighed. "Not that you care, but I did have a girlfriend . . . once. And even though we broke up a while ago, she's still close to my family. I just didn't want you to be bothered by it."

"You are a good man, Colt Porter."

His voice brightened. "Why don't I zip over to your parents' house and I'll tell you everything you need to know about me?"

With hot sauce smeared on my jeans and the evening I had planned with my mom, it wasn't the right time to see him. "You're sweet. But my dad's away this weekend, so I'm hanging out with my mom."

"Of course." He sounded apologetic.

I heard the garage door open and my mom's car pull in. "My mother's home. I'll talk to you later."

I was reaching for the end-call button when I heard him say, "Piper?"

"What?"

"I'm gonna make you change your mind."

I laughed. "I wish it were that easy."

"Just remember one thing."

I heard music coming from the kitchen and my mother singing along. It was a country version of a Stones song. *You can't always get what you want, but if you try sometimes, you get what you need.* "What's that?"

"You can't help who you love."

I'd been telling myself otherwise for five years. I came in the kitchen, held up the phone so my mom would know I was talking to someone, and threw the empty box of wings in a little trashcan by an old, white desk I'd had since middle school. The Stones cover ended and went into a Emmylou Harris song.

"I gotta go. My mom just got home and we have plans—"

"Hang on a second," Colt said. "Someone's at the door."

After a few moments, Colt came back on the line. "Did you send me something?" he asked.

"No, why? Did someone send you their panties?"

"I don't know." He sounded worried. "There's a box on my doorstep. A long one, like the kind roses come in, but bigger."

Even my old, married father still occasionally got phone numbers and bras in the mail. A year ago his random gifts had gone from lingerie to loony when someone sent him a poem that would have made Poe proud. It was all dark times and *can't live without you.* I could only imagine the things girls sent Colt.

"Let me see what it is." I heard him open a drawer, and then there was the sound of scissors or a knife cutting through cardboard. "Fuck!" he yelled. "What the fuck?"

Most drivers I knew were rugged, macho even. But the scream that came from Colt reminded me of when I was little and my friends and I would shriek for no reason.

"What's wrong? Did one of your crew guys send you a gag gift?"

"It's a fox," he said.

"What do you mean a fox? A stuffed animal?"

"No. A fox. A reddish-grey, dead fox."

My skin went cold. "Jesus, Colt. Hang up and call the police. That's so creepy."

I put on my shoes and wiped buffalo sauce off my hands.

"Wait a minute." His voice was shaky. "It's not addressed to me."

Relief rushed through me. "Thank God. But who sends someone a dead fox?"

"Well, it's not my name, but it is my address. I'm so used to getting packages, mostly promotional stuff, that I didn't even look at the name. It's addressed to 'The Right Stuff.' How weird is this?"

"Did you say 'The Right Stuff'?" I asked.

"Yeah. Why?"

"That's the taxidermy shop in Davidson my dad takes the elk he hunts to. I picked one up for him once. I think it was on Rock Ledge Drive. Isn't that your street, too?"

"Yes, but in Moorestown." He sounded relieved. "Must have been a mix-up."

I felt my heart beating. When the girl who sent my dad the poems followed my mother home one day, my dad took a restraining order out on her. She never came near us again, but I'd heard of other drivers waking up to crazy, obsessed fans standing in their bedrooms.

"Do you want me to come over?"

"It's okay, Pipes. I'll look up the company in the phonebook and call them. Go have fun with your mom."

"Are you sure? What are you going to do with it?"

"I have a big freezer in the garage. I'll put it in there until I can figure out what's going on."

"Will you call me later, please?" I asked. "Let me know you're okay."

I hung up, and my mother came out of the den. "What was that about?" she asked.

"What was what?"

"Was that Colt on the phone? It sounded like something was wrong."

My heart raced. "Colt? Why would you think that?"

She led me to the living room, and we sat on the loveseat.

"Just because I never went to college doesn't mean I'm a dummy. So why don't you tell me what's going on."

Being the only child of a man who spent more than 200 days a year traveling meant I had always been extraordinarily close to my mother. We talked about everything—how to properly use a tampon, why smoking pot was less dangerous than drinking, and why, at the age of sixteen, she took me to her gynecologist and put me on the pill. She said if I was going to have sex (whenever that might be), I couldn't count on the boy not to get me pregnant.

But I hadn't been able to talk to anyone about this. Not even her.

"I think Colt and I like each other."

"Is that bad news?"

I picked up a magazine and thumbed through it. "Um, yeah. I don't like race car drivers."

"Apparently you do."

I closed the magazine. "Come on, Mama. You know what I'm talking about."

"Oh, honey. You've got to let that go. You're so young. One of these days you've got to start living your life."

"I am," I snapped. "I went to college. I have a job. I am fine."

She touched my chin, making me look at her.

"No, you're not. But I love you."

5

My father turned to me, clean shaven, new haircut, handsome in his ruggedness.

"Is my tie straight?"

"Come here." I stood on my toes, loosened the tie covered in tiny wrenches and fixed it. "Better."

"Thanks, Noodle."

"I hate being on TV," I groaned. "The camera is not kind. Do I have to be there?"

"There's nothing anyone or anything could do to make you not look good. You are all your mother's daughter. And she's the prettiest girl I've ever seen."

I'd learned in the one and only psychology course I took in college that marriages rarely survived the death of a child or a life-threatening accident or illness. It had something to do with how everyone grieved and coped differently. Not my parents. After Tennessee, they gushed to *Sports Illustrated, NASCAR Weekly* and *The New York Times* that life was full of challenges and the wreck was meant to bring them closer together and make them stronger. They never stopped complimenting each other—on camera or off.

I went along with their story because I knew they spouted it so often and emphatically for my protection. But I didn't think any of us would ever get past what really happened that night in December of 1984 until we publicly told the truth.

"Thanks, Daddy, but this is about announcing Colt as our new driver. It has nothing to do with me."

I'd talked to Colt almost every day since he spent some quality time with a dead fox.

"Oh, but you said the magic word. *Our.* It's our team. He's our driver. So it's *our* press conference. I know you keep saying otherwise, but one day Pierson Racing will be yours. You'd better get used to this." He shooed me away. "Now go dress yourself. And remember, the press is always watching the heir apparent."

My father's life was controlled by what others might think. He said being any kind of public figure brought great scrutiny, and that was one of the reasons why he lived such a clean life. I didn't envy him or any of the other high-profile team owners and drivers who constantly had to worry about being seen ordering more than one beer at dinner or being photographed picking a parking ticket off their windshield.

"More like the *where apparent.* You know I'm never gonna do what you do, right? I'm a journalist, Daddy, not a race team owner. I chose a different life."

He put on his sport coat. "That's what you say now, Noodle, but you already have one foot on the path." I started to protest, but he placed his hand firmly on my shoulder. "And don't you tell me otherwise."

"I'll go get changed," I said. That I'd brought a totally appropriate dress to my parents' house told me I knew I was going to the press conference no matter how much I complained.

"What time do we have to leave?"

"We don't. It's taking place here, at the shop."

I paused in the doorway. "But you hate having the media

anywhere near your personal life." My father was an intensely private man, which was a hard thing to be when you were the king of circle track racing and lived in North Carolina.

"The race shop is fair game. And I asked the press to come in the shop entrance. They won't get anywhere near the house." He slipped a pocket watch in the front of his dress pants. "Now scoot. The team will be here in ten."

While I changed in my old bedroom, I saw Colt's car coming up the driveway. I went outside and waited for him.

"What's up, Pierson?" he asked when he got out.

"I hear we're introducing you to the world today." I'd brought a simple, pale-yellow dress with long sleeves. Seeing Colt in a suit and tie, I wished I had something fancier.

"Darlin', no introductions needed. The world knows me." He kissed my cheek and slipped by me toward the front door.

"Arrogance is not charming," I called after him, but my voice was light.

• • •

I stood smooshed between my parents while my dad and Colt shook hands for an uncomfortably long time amid myriad photographers taking pictures. Then my father, Colt and Cal Thompson, Colt's current team owner, all made statements and took turns answering questions. I was bored and hot and had to pee. After fifteen minutes of telling reporters that Colt would make the transition from Busch to Winston Cup with Cal's support, and how Colt felt he was ready to handle the heavier and faster cars on tracks with the best drivers in the country, my father announced that lunch would be served in the race shop for anyone interested. He was always doing things like that.

My father believed there were certain people you never wanted to make mad—reporters and restaurant servers being on the top of the list. He also loved any chance he got to show off the race shop. It housed a lifetime of trophies, photographs and memories. By inviting the NASCAR press corps to eat with us, my dad got to boast a little and made them feel like we were all on the same side. It was brilliant, really. He was kind by nature and well versed in making everyone feel important, so the media rarely wrote a hostile word about him.

"Mr. Pierson," shouted a young guy I didn't recognize. "Just one more question."

My dad never said no to autograph requests or questions. He would quip privately, "If I'm that interesting, then it's my job to sign my name till my hand cramps." I could recite all his corny sayings.

"Go for it," he said to the young reporter. "I always have time for you."

"Thank you, sir," the kid said, weaving his way to the front of the crowd. "But this one is for your daughter."

"Piper?" my dad asked, stepping back and instinctively putting his arm around my shoulders. "Any questions you have for my family, you can ask me."

That was another thing about my father. It was an understood agreement he had with the press. Nothing about him was ever off limits, but they left my mother and me alone.

I snapped my head up with the sound of my name. I'd been thinking about the puff pastries my mom and I made that morning, and how I was going to work it into conversation with Colt that I was an excellent baker.

"Me?" I asked.

"That's right." The reporter held up his tape recorder.

"Daddy?" I never officially spoke to a member of the press without his permission.

"You may ask," my dad told the kid. "But tread lightly."

"Miss Pierson, Mack Marlin has been with your family

practically since you were born. What will be the dynamics of the team now?"

The question annoyed me. I had nothing to do with the race team and wasn't qualified to answer.

"I cannot speak for the team. But what I can say is that Mack has been like a second daddy to me." Mack stepped forward to stand beside me. "Just because he won't be driving come February doesn't mean he won't still be a part of our team and our family."

The reporter smirked. "That's not exactly what I meant. One day this team will be yours. What will that be like?"

"My father has no plans to retire. Ever. He's certainly not going anywhere this century. As for me, I'm a journalist, just like all of you. I'm not the story here. This is about my father's race team and their new driver. I'm here to support my dad as his daughter—not as his heir apparent. I have no professional or financial connection to the race team. I think we're finished here. The lemonade is getting warm and the steak is getting cold." I waved for people to follow me indoors to the race shop. "The line forms behind me."

The brash kid wouldn't relent. "But when he *is* ready to retire, that will make you Colt's boss."

Just as I was about to snap at him, Colt caught up to me and pulled my arm. "If that ever comes to pass, there's no one I'd rather take orders from," he said to the reporter as we broke left and hurried away from the crowd behind us.

We were almost to the race shop when my dad appeared by Colt's side. "You two look good together," he said.

"Yeah, yeah. I know," I told him. "You and Mack look good in front of the cameras because you could pass for brothers. And Colt and I are young." I gave our new driver a sideways glance. "And pretty. It's all about appearances."

"So young to be such a cynic." He mussed my hair.

Once inside the building, I left Colt with Cal Thompson and Mack, and I found my mother.

"Mom?" I said. "Can I ask you something real quick?"

She excused herself from a couple of model-pretty women reporters and followed me to a hallway leading to the restrooms. "What's up, sugar?"

"Daddy just said the weirdest thing to me." She smiled like she knew what was coming. "He said Colt and I look good together. What was he talking about?"

"Come on, P. Let's get some lunch. The ribs are going fast."

"Mom." I stopped and grabbed her hand. She put her arm around me and guided me to the buffet.

"Let's just say your father wants you to be happy and Colt is a good boy."

I stood, opened-mouthed, waiting for her to say more, but she saw someone she knew and left me alone by the dessert table. I picked up a cream puff, took a bite and set out to find Colt when I saw his parents enter through the side door. My fingers were sticky, and I'd spattered powdered sugar on my dress, so I went to the bathroom to clean myself up before they saw me. I stood in front of the sink, mindlessly washing my hands. Finally, I rejoined the crowd, saw that Colt had been swallowed by a sea of reporters, and ate lunch with the woman who ran the team's hospitality department.

•   •   •

The following Monday, I was sitting in Tack's office, trying to decide if he came from money or just cared a lot about his appearance. His shirts were pressed, his pants creased and his nails perfect.

"Good work rewriting that article about the Busch points leaders," Tack said, leaning against his desk.

"Does that mean you're not mad at me anymore? I really am sorry I went off script."

He patted down a stray hair on top of his head, and I wondered how he knew it was out of place. "All is forgiven if you keep writing like this. And if you tell me how you got those guys to open up to you like that." The piece that eventually went to print wasn't nearly as interesting as the first one I wrote. But I'd learned my lesson to keep my head down and my questions banal.

My mind slipped for a moment back to dinner with Colt and Brent. "Busch has a nice bunch of drivers." I shrugged. "Everyone's so friendly, they were happy to talk." I was afraid if I told Tack that I knew Colt from my racing days, he'd start asking questions I didn't want to answer.

"Did you know when I gave you the assignment that Colt was your team's new driver?" A senior writer with dark nose hair passed by Tack's office and gave me a dirty look.

"It's my dad's team," I said loud enough for her to hear. "It'll never be mine. And no, I did not know. My father had already signed him and wasn't planning on telling me until the press conference we had last week, but I kind of found out by accident. So, I knew when I wrote the article, but not when I went to Braselton."

"I guess that explains why Colt and Brent were so willing to talk to you."

"Due respect, sir," I said, getting up to close the door. The girl with the nose hair was still lurking, so I turned my attention to her. "Do you need Tack?" I asked her.

"Uh, no," she said quickly. "I just heard you talking about Colt Porter. I met him last year covering a Busch race. He's a great guy."

Tack got up and stood by me at the door. "Excuse us for a few minutes, Amy," he said to her. "We just need to finish up in here."

"Anyway," I said after he sat. "I believe they gave me a great interview because I am good at what I do. I asked them thoughtful, open-ended questions that required extensive answers, researched them before the meeting and took my cues from them. If they went off on a tangent about high school, I stayed with it."

I told people this was why I didn't want to take over Pierson Racing after my dad retired. I never wanted anybody to think things were handed to me. That was part of it, for sure, but I couldn't be responsible for putting people I cared about in harm's way every weekend.

Tack held up his palms and dropped his eyes for a moment. "My apologies, Piper. You're a talented journalist and I didn't mean to imply otherwise."

He opened a manila folder that had been on his desk and removed a photograph, then handed it to me. "Mr. Matts came to me last night with a brilliant but difficult idea for an article. After a lengthy discussion, we decided you might be the person to tackle this."

My heart thumped as I stared at a picture of Tim Richmond, one of the most prolific Winston Cup drivers ever. "You want me to interview Mr. Richmond? Why? I'm the greenest employee you have."

"For the same reason that I unintentionally offended you. He'll talk to you."

Suddenly my skirt felt too tight, and I wanted out of there. "What makes you think that?"

"I know your dad is friends with him."

My parents had always treated me like an adult. They never used baby talk or colored difficult conversations with euphemisms and unwarranted hope. When my dad's best friend from high school killed himself, they told me he was too sad to want to live anymore. When the cat I got for my sixth birthday got flattened by the garbage truck, they didn't tell me that Snootis Frootis ran away. They simply told me the truth; then we buried her together. And from the time I was old enough to understand, my dad had warned me that some people might treat me differently because I had a famous family. Classmates might be nice to me because they thought I could get them tickets to a race. Or boys might ask me out because they might meet Mack or another driver. Maybe I'd get promotions in my job that I didn't deserve because no one wanted to make Planter Pierson mad.

And my parents wondered why I wanted to have a career far, far away from NASCAR.

"My dad is friends with everyone," I said sourly. "I've only met Tim in passing, and it was a long time ago. Way before he quit racing."

Tack sat up in his chair and straightened his tie. "Take this as a compliment, Piper. It means the head honchos have faith in you."

I shifted in my seat, trying to adjust the waistband of my skirt. "I appreciate that, Tack. I really do. But please don't give me special consideration because I'm a Pierson. It's insulting to me and unfair to my colleagues."

I wished I'd left the door open so nose-hair Amy could hear that.

"How about this? You got the assignment because you can handle a challenge. And believe me, this will be nothing like the puff pieces we gave you the first month you were here."

"Can you at least tell me why you want this piece written?"

"Because Tim was a great driver and he's all but disappeared."

"He's more than great. He's a legend." At one point in his career, my father talked about Tim coming to drive for us, expanding our team to two drivers. But then everything changed. "Someone with more experience should get this gig."

Tim was sick. That was fact. But no one knew for certain what was wrong with him, and he didn't need some rookie reporter—family acquaintance or not—snooping around in his personal business. Above all else, my family respected other people's privacy. There was no way I was going to write about whatever was going on with Tim Richmond.

"I'm sorry, Tack. But I have to respectfully decline."

"That's the problem with coming out of the gate with a bang. You set the bar very high for yourself."

"Thank you for your confidence in me. But I'm not the right person for this. Would you please give it to someone else?"

"Listen, Piper. This is a direct order from Jim Matts. Neither one of us can afford to defy him."

"I'm glad he liked my bit on Brent and Colt, but this story is way above my pay grade."

Tim had a reputation of being a very nice man, and the few interactions I'd had with him over the years didn't indicate otherwise. He was so lovely that once he heard my name, he'd probably feel obligated to talk to me.

Tack tilted back in his chair, as if studying me.

"You sound like you know what's going on with him. That alone is a good reason for you to take the lead on this. I can assign someone to help you, if that's what you need."

Sweat dampened the back of my shirt. "I know he's sick, but I don't know what's wrong with him. I really don't. He and my dad were close before he moved away. Although no one has ever said anything, I get the feeling he left because of his health."

"Moved away?" he asked. *Shit.* I'd already said too much. "See, you know more about him than the rest of us. I thought he was still around these parts, but not racing anymore. Someone said he has lupus or MS."

I pulled my blouse away from my chest and fanned myself for a second. "Can I please talk to my father about this before I say yes?"

Tack leaned forward and touched his nameplate. "What does this say?"

"Tack Richards, editor in chief."

"And what does your nameplate say?"

I looked behind me, as if I could see my cubicle in the bullpen through the closed door. "Um, I don't have one."

"Exactly. That's because I'm your boss. So no, you may not ask your father's permission. I understand your father is used to having the world fall at his feet. But *NASCAR Weekly* is *my* playground." I was taken aback by his condescending tone. "Mr. Matts and I want you to write this article. So write it you shall."

"But I still don't understand why you want me to do it. What about Ken?" I turned toward the closed door again. "He's been here forever."

"Ken *has* been here forever. And you could learn a thing or two from him. But a man like Tim Richmond, who is one of the best in the sport, but who has basically gone into hiding, isn't going to talk to some random reporter. Even someone as respected as Ken Dilaurentis."

I stood and took a step back. "Papa Pierson strikes again. You knew my dad and Tim were friends and your boss told you to give me the story figuring I'd use my name and my contacts to get to him." I spoke slowly, trying to keep the accusation out of my voice.

He held his hands up in a *well, what did you expect* gesture. "Welcome to the business, kid. I'll give you two weeks to get it done."

• • •

I was so pissed when I left Tack's office that I couldn't concentrate on the article I was finishing. Races occasionally got rained out, and it was a huge inconvenience to tracks and fans to reschedule them. Weather permitting, they were always run the first available day, usually a Monday. But some people had to work, so it was hard for them to stay an extra day or two. And many fans flew to races, making it expensive to change plane tickets or spend another night in a hotel. A rescheduled event also meant having to organize food services, vendors, maintenance, track officials and safety crews on short notice.

To avoid the hassles of postponing, tracks had the option to deem a race finished if more than half the laps had been completed. The problem with that was some sources thought officials might be swayed to call a race if certain drivers were in the lead. I was writing an op-ed piece about it, but now I was too angry to even proof it. I thought about going back into Tack's office to protest, but I knew I was being a baby. Racing was a small world, and I'd be foolish to think that my name didn't provide access unavailable to others. Even worse, I knew my dad would tell me to do the job I was hired to do.

• • •

With eleven days left to complete an assignment I hadn't even begun to research, I ran into Colt at the race shop and he asked me to go waterskiing. Now we were at his house but hadn't gotten in the lake yet.

"Piper, what's your twenty?" I was lying on a chaise next to Colt on his back deck. "What has you a million miles away from this?" Colt stood and ran his hands up and down his body. He was wearing bathing trunks and no shirt. For a guy who spent most of his time driving, or in the shop or watching video of past races, he was tanned bronze.

It occurred to me that there was a picture of Colt and Tim Richmond on his dresser. Between them were two Hooters girls. All four of them were model beautiful. "You're friends with Tim Richmond, right?" I asked.

He sat behind me, pressing himself into my back.

"Sure am. He was a hell of a driver."

I got dizzy with the feel of Colt's warm skin against mine and lost my train of thought for a minute, then realized what he had said. "Tim *was* a great driver?"

He leaned away from me and grabbed a beer from a small wooden table next to him. "You know he's sick, right?"

"That's what my dad has told me. Is it serious?"

"You could say that."

"Do you know what's wrong with him?"

Colt stood and sat at the end of the lounge chair so we were facing each other.

"What's with all the questions? Are you writing his biography?"

I felt my face go hot. "Kind of. My editor wants me to write an article about him."

"What the fuck, Piper?" His anger was sudden and fierce. "And you agreed? What the fuck?"

His anger startled me. I reached forward and took his hand. "I hear ya. That was exactly my reaction. I told Tack I couldn't write this piece. But he more or less threatened to fire me if I didn't do it."

"I knew he was a pretty-boy cocksucker."

"Pretty boy?" I asked. "You're not jealous, are you?" He cast his eyes down and didn't answer. "Have you even met him?"

"Yes, I've met him." His voice had softened some. "It's a small world."

"You mean like how when we went to the movies a few weeks ago we ran into four other drivers and their wives?"

"Uh, I hate to break it to you, but that redheaded woman isn't that guy's wife."

"I don't even want to know." I finished my beer and looked for a place to put my empty bottle. When I didn't see one, I tucked it into the cushion of my lounge chair. "Is there a reason I shouldn't write about Tim?"

"I guess that depends on what you're going to say."

I thought about it for a minute. "He's a great driver and seems like a good guy. Can I write that?"

Colt tucked my hair behind my ear. "Do me a favor. Research

him a little and try to figure out why the powers that be at your paper want you to feature him."

Colt made a good point. I'd been so caught off guard by Tack's request that I didn't even think about why he wanted an article about Tim. It'd been more than a year since he raced. Although no one would ever forget him, Tim Richmond was no longer front-page news—or any-page news, for that matter.

"If you still feel like they asked you for the right reasons, then I'll talk to you. Hell, I may even be able to get you a sit-down with him."

My eyes got big. "You know where he is?"

"He's a close friend."

"I should have known. The good guys always stick together."

He reached in the cooler between our chairs. I thought he was going to give me another beer, but he flicked me with ice water. "Us being friends is an advantage for you. So why do you look so sad?"

A seabird landed on the dock below us. It paced from one side to the other, flapping its wings and squawking. It reminded me a little of Mick Jagger in concert.

"I love writing and being a journalist. But I'm not sure I'm meant to be an investigative reporter."

"I know I'm just a simple country boy who turns left for a living. But aren't *journalist* and *reporter* one and the same?"

"Technically, they probably are. But in my mind they're different. A journalist writes about stuff. Anything that people want to read about—movie reviews, folks who accomplish amazing things, advances in medicine. But a reporter—especially an investigative one—digs up dirt about people, uncovers scandals, writes about messy divorces, sudden deaths. The stuff no one wants to talk about."

Colt opened his eyes and squinted while he talked. "I'm not defending the media. Lord knows I get a bit tired of being followed into restaurants and drugstores, but reporters, as you call them, are just doing their jobs."

"I know, but it makes me uncomfortable. I don't want to let Tack down or lose my job. But I also don't want to invade Tim's privacy or put any of his friends"—I reached for Colt's hand—"like you, in a bad position by asking questions I shouldn't."

He squeezed my fingers. "It's sweet that you want to write the feel-good pieces. But, for now, you have to do what your boss tells you to."

"I guess."

I remembered reporters calling us and camping on our front lawn for weeks after my dad was finally able to travel home from Tennessee after his accident. Normally, he would have invited them in for coffee and brought in extra chairs so everyone would be comfortable while he answered endless and identical questions. But he knew the danger of being too cozy with media types, and he always placed protecting his family first. My father wasn't going to let anyone know that I was involved in that accident.

After he was home for a few days, I heard him tell my mother that I needed privacy to heal. Half of Charlotte was convinced that whatever happened hadn't been at a track. I heard rumors that he'd gotten in a bar fight, stepped out on my mother and had the shit beat out of him by an angry husband, and even that he'd been in a small plane crash. I told my parents they should talk to the press. I hated that anyone might think my mom and dad treated each other badly. But they refused. My father told me again that the media understood his family was off limits.

"How about this?" I said to Colt. "Give me a few days to do some research and I'll convince you why you should help me with this assignment."

"If I do help you, what's my reward?"

My stomach felt funny, but in a good way. "Wouldn't you like to know," I teased.

• • •

Knowing Colt wouldn't give me anything unless I did my homework, I went to the Hickory Grove Library and set out to learn all I could about Tim Richmond. With Tack's permission, I spent the next morning in the archives and found several old articles from our very own *NASCAR Weekly,* a few from the *Charlotte Observer* and one from *Sports Illustrated.* They didn't tell me much more than I already knew. But one theme was evident in everything I read, and I thought that might be my hook. I wanted to share with Colt what I'd learned and the direction I thought the article should take, so I called him from a payphone in the library. I was supposed to be back in the office by lunchtime, but I called Tack after I spoke to Colt and told him I had a lead to pursue.

An hour later I was at Colt's office at his race shop in Moorestown, with the door closed. "Don't get any funny ideas," he said, leaning back in a leather chair. "There are cameras everywhere."

I stared at his mouth. "Jeez. You make it sound like I have impure thoughts."

"Don't you?" *Good grief*—he was cute when he grinned at me like that.

I pulled a small notebook out of my bag. "I can't write this story," I said.

He swiveled his chair away from me. "Really, Piper? You too? That's pretty shitty."

My stomach knotted. "What are you talking about? You were mad at me yesterday when I said I had to write the piece and now you're pissed when I tell you I can't?"

When he faced me again, his eyes were hard, and his mouth was a straight line.

"What's wrong? You can't make this a puff piece and it's too hard to dig deep and write about the tough stuff?"

"Fuck you," I spat. "I can't write this article because I'd be repeating what everyone already knows. Tim is a superstar talent who got a raw deal. He doesn't deserve what's happening to him. But what's the point of reciting stats about how successful he was? *That* article's been written a million times. And I won't pry into his personal life and write about his illness, whatever that may be. If that's what Tack wants, he might as well fire me now because I won't do it."

Colt stood and came toward me, but I stepped away. I had to finish my thought.

"If Tack will let me write an article honoring him, I'd love that. I can't contribute anything new about him other than reporting on his health, and I won't do that. So, what else is there to write about, if not making it a tribute piece?"

Colt went back to his desk. "You're something else, Piper Pierson. You're like a sweet little Jack Russel who grabs onto something and won't let go."

I cocked my head at him. "Did you just compare me to a dog?"

"It was a compliment. A weird one, but still a compliment."

He got two cans of Coke out of a small, brown fridge in the corner of his office, gave one to me and sat next to me on the couch. I opened the can and downed half of it. I loved soda, but it made me belch like a man. I couldn't hold it in and accidentally burped right in Colt's face.

"You're a charmer, Pierson. I'll give you that."

"I have many talents," I said. "Now, do you want to hear my thoughts on Tim Richmond?"

He waved at the air between us. "Please."

"I'm not so sure he'd be quite this famous if not for two things."

"He's a kick-ass driver and he's fearless?" Colt quipped.

"Yes, he is both those things." I flipped through a couple pages of the notes I'd made earlier that morning. "He's also very attractive, and he's not your typical good ol' boy."

"Is he better looking than me?" Colt pouted.

"No one's better looking than you." I meant that. My breath got screwy every time I saw him.

"What do you mean, he's not your typical driver?"

"First off, he was born in Ohio and is from a wealthy family."

With multi-million-dollar sponsors and huge payouts, there was a lot of money to be had in our sport. But almost no one I knew in NASCAR came from money.

"So far, so good. But what else?"

I tried to think how to phrase what I wanted to say without it coming across as a put-down.

"It's no secret that most drivers, including you, of course"—I winked at him—"could take apart their cars and put them back together blindfolded. But word on the street is that Tim can't even change a tire."

Colt frowned and I continued.

"But what he can do is coax a car out of hitting the wall, navigate one safely to pit road after it's blown a tire, and fly down the straights at super speedways going more than two hundred miles an hour. He's an amazing driver, but he doesn't know that much about cars."

A friend from Chapel Hill had expensive show horses she kept at a barn that did all the work for her. She'd roll up to the stables in her breeches and boots and get on the horse, but she had no idea how to put its saddle on or take care of the animals. I supposed the two sports weren't that different.

"I guess you did do your homework."

"Does that mean I get a gold star?"

"Why don't I make you dinner tonight? You'll get more than that." Colt cooked as well as any restaurant chef. "But I digress. What else did you come up with?"

I didn't need my notes for this part. I was sure I'd figured out what was making Tim Richmond so sick, but I'd never print it. "I know that by the end of the 1985 season, Rick Hendrick created a new team so he could hire Tim to be its driver. Together they went on to win seven races in 1986."

Even with winning a quarter of the races on that year's schedule, Tim only managed a third-place finish in the point standings. Conundrums like that led to revampings of the points system.

Colt leaned back in his chair and closed his eyes. "Go on. So far you're nailing it."

"This is where the rumors come in. Near the end of the '86 season, people started talking about Tim's health. He supposedly said he had a nasty flu that wouldn't go away."

Colt scoffed and reached for the soda he'd put on the floor by his feet. "That was one hell of a flu."

I rolled my eyes. "You know what? I don't blame Tim for lying," I said, then caught myself. "*If he was.* His health is no one's business." Colt looked like he was going to say something but didn't, so I continued. "He got better a few times and the vultures backed off. But as soon as he got sick again and started losing weight, they were all over him."

"Damn media," Colt grumbled.

My father had taught me to respect the media and accept them as part of our lives.

"Easy now. Just like you told me yesterday, they were just doing their jobs. Some people think chasing a football down a field is a silly career path. But we all choose what we want to do for a living."

That said, I still wasn't sure this was what I wanted to do with my life. I felt a little slimy looking into Tim Richmond's non-racing life.

"Playing football doesn't invade anyone's privacy."

"You need to come for dinner one night at my parents' house. We have this discussion all the time. I know I was bellyaching yesterday about the media never having any discretion, and here I am defending the industry. We need to look at it from both sides of the fence. Yes, journalists and reporters dig up dirt and take pictures of celebrities when they're kissing other people's wives, but this is the life you signed up for. If you didn't want the paparazzi to follow you around, you should have been a physics teacher."

"I aced science in high school. I could totally do that."

I imagined Colt wearing wire-rimmed glasses explaining the theory of relativity to a couple of teenaged girls in low-cut shirts.

"I got us off track. What happened after the media noticed Tim was sick again?"

This next part I did not learn at the library. I'd remembered my dad talking to Tim on the phone right after he returned from getting treatment for one of his illnesses. I hadn't given it much thought then, but now I was piecing it together.

"By the end of the year, Tim checked himself into the Cleveland Clinic under a false name. I can't say this for certain, but I am pretty sure he was diagnosed with full-blown AIDS." Colt winced, and I quickly added, "I promise that even if I were able to confirm that, I'd never print it."

"You can stop there," he said.

"No. I can't. Tim was advised to keep his condition quiet, so he simply said he was having some health issues and would be taking most of the next year off from racing."

"Jesus, Piper. You could be writing his biography." His tone was soft, and I knew he meant it as a compliment.

"I'm just trying to honor one of our own." Not everyone in the industry wanted to hear about an insider who might bring negative press coverage. I consulted my notes again. "So, I'm willing to bet that Tim was secretly getting treated for AIDS. Whatever it was, he responded to the meds. A couple of months into the '87 season, he felt well enough to drive in back-to-back races at Pocono and Riverside. In his usual *do it right or don't do it at all* fashion, he won both races."

Colt fist-pumped the air, a salute to his friend.

"But," I continued, my voice sour, "even with two great showings, Tim was sidelined."

"I remember that," Colt said. "It was bullshit then and it's bullshit now. Off the record, what do you think that was about?"

"I've thought a lot about that very question." I held Colt's hand and squeezed it "Can we just go on the assumption that Tim has HIV or AIDS?" He nodded but kept his eyes down, which made me think he'd known all along. "We still don't know much about AIDS. I mean, six or seven years ago, no one had ever heard of it. Then there was all this talk that it came from monkeys and only gay people can get it. It's ridiculous. It's sexually transmitted. Anyone who has sex can get it, but I think because it primarily affects gay men, certain powers that be don't want to be associated with it. Homophobia at its worst. Regardless of how Tim got the disease, it doesn't negate the fact that he was treated unfairly."

"It's such bullshit," Colt said again. His eyes turned glassy.

"Pretty much. But Tim wasn't going to go away quietly. He sat out the rest of the season, but when it came time for the Daytona 500 qualifier, he was determined to run."

"Damn straight he was determined," Colt huffed. "The Busch Clash starts off the season, and it's an invitational. The only way you get to the Daytona 500. It's an honor for any of us to qualify for that race."

He wasn't telling me anything I hadn't known since I was three, but I let him talk.

"The 500 is our Super Bowl."

"This is where Tim showed the world what he was made of. Knowing the strict anti-drug-use rules, he stopped taking his meds right after New Year's. He then had his doctor give him a blood test that revealed no drugs of any kind in his system. As he predicted, when Tim put out a press release saying he would come back to run the Busch Clash, a new rule went into effect allowing drivers to be tested at will."

Colt chugged the rest of his Coke and tossed the can in the trash. "Fuckers!"

I reached out and squeezed his hand.

"Here's the bitch of it all. The only driver subjected to this outrageous new rule was Tim."

"Goddamn, I hate bureaucrats." Colt got up and paced the room. I waited for him to sit before I spoke again.

"You and me, both. But Tim had them beat. He knew the test would be negative and they'd have no proof he was sick."

"As if it's a crime to be dying." Colt sounded so sad talking about his friend that I hugged him. "Piper," he said into my shoulder. "How do you know all this? I mean, we all know he's sick. Most of us have guessed he has AIDS, but how do you know about the drug test? He got slapped with a gag order. And I only know that because I was with him when he got served. He swore me to secrecy."

Colt shifted in his seat, nervous.

"I'm good at my job. Don't worry. Your secrets are safe with me. And I won't publish anything about Tim that you don't want me to. My intent is to honor him, not degrade him."

"You're a doll." He pursed his lips like he was kissing me.

I found my place in my notes and continued. "So, imagine Tim's surprise when he learned he was suspended indefinitely for having banned substances in his system."

"Did I mention there are fuckers everywhere?"

"Oh, it gets worse. When Tim demanded to know what the drugs were, he was refused the results. When he insisted on another tox screen, they conceded and retested him. Not surprisingly, those results were negative. The only substances found in his blood were Sudafed and Advil. Regardless of the benign results, his suspension wasn't reversed."

"Shit. I knew something had gone down. But Tim wouldn't talk about it. What happened next?"

"You know what happened next, Colt. Everyone who watched the Daytona 500 two years ago knows."

"Jesus. I forgot about that. That was the coolest thing I've ever seen."

"Did you know that he was in that plane when it flew over the 500 with a banner that said, *Fans—I miss you. Tim Richmond*?"

"As sick as he was?"

"Yep, it was his final act of defiance. He was told he couldn't race again until he surrendered his medical records."

"So, the banner was his last *fuck you* to the Man?"

I nodded. "Remember the standing ovation he got as that plane flew over the track?"

"That was Tim's last public appearance."

"Do you know where he's been the last two years? There haven't been any reported sightings." That was the one thing I couldn't figure out.

"He lives with his mother in West Palm Beach," Colt said.

I pushed my chair back, kicked off my high-heeled sandals, and put my feet on Colt's lap. "So that's my story. Or, more specifically, Tim's story."

"Piper. You are pretty all right. That's an amazing tale."

I loved it that Colt thought I was good at my job. It gave me confidence that perhaps this was the right career choice.

"Thank you. Can you answer one question for me, please?"

"Speak."

"How come you didn't know any of this? Do you keep in touch with him?"

"Yeah, we talk once a week or so. I know he's sick and living in Florida. But he's never said anything about his legal battles."

"Do you think someone's paying him to keep his mouth shut? Or is it all legal at this point? The gag order and everything?"

"I honestly don't know. I believe you when you say you didn't know where he was or how to get in touch with him. So, they can't go after him for talking when he wasn't supposed to. And your sources are covered by the First Amendment. So, I guess no matter what's going on, the world is going to know about it when your article comes out."

I had a flash of getting sued for libel, and for being a girl in a man's world.

I shrugged and held up my palms. "Oh well. I'm just doing my job."

"I don't mean this the way it sounds, but I don't think anyone expected you to dig up this much info."

"Is that a nice way of saying no one expected me to be this good?"

He grinned. "You said it, not me. I'd love to know what else you're good at."

6

I took a commuter train from the station near Colt's shop to the one a few blocks from my apartment, then walked home. My feet hurt, and my shoes dug into my baby toes. As I sat in the kitchen listening to a message from Tack telling me I was Kentucky bound for the Louisville race, I thought about how much easier my life would be if I just started driving again. But when I closed my eyes, I saw myself climbing out the window of my car at that track in Tennessee and running to my dad.

Tack's voice brought me back to the present. There was a hotshot new crew chief who'd been hired in the middle of the season after his predecessor had a heart attack. Since coming on board, his rookie driver hadn't finished out of the top ten. Apparently, I had to find out what made him so good. Or what made him make his eighteen-year-old driver so good. Tack left my flight information and told me to come home with another killer story. I had hoped to have the weekend to finish my piece on Tim Richmond, but now I'd have to wrap it up before I left so I could see Colt before the weekend.

When I got to the track Friday morning, I headed to the rookie's transporter to find his crew chief. But I was told both men were in a team meeting and to come back in an hour. So, I went to the ElectroAde rig, but a crew member I hadn't met yet told me Colt was in his motorhome. I thanked him and wandered in and out of rows of houses on wheels till I found Colt's. A tall blond man with a slightly crooked front tooth greeted me outside the door. The imperfection made him seem honest and genuine.

"Hello," he said, extending his hand. "I'm Scott Stephenson. We met—"

"At the Braselton race," I interrupted. "How could I forget the best tire changer in all the land?"

He held onto my hand after we shook. "You flatter me so, Piper. It's nice to see you again."

"You too," I said, shifting my weight. He was blocking the entrance to the transporter, and I wanted to get in and say hi to Colt before I had to go back for my interview. "Colt's lucky to have you around. Honestly, I'm surprised a Winston Cup team hasn't stolen you away yet."

"That's nice of you to say. But Colt and I have been best friends since we were little. I'll stay with him until one of us dies," he said, then laughed.

For as much driver and crew chief swapping as went on in our sport, loyalty ran fierce and deep.

I held up my notebook as if my visit wasn't social. "I need a few minutes of Colt's time." I waited for him to move so I could climb the two steps to Colt's mobile treehouse. "Duty calls." The way Scott stood with his arms crossed and feet shoulder-width apart made me think he was sent outside to make sure no one got in. He didn't budge.

"Do I need a secret password?" Through the light-blue curtains, I saw the silhouettes of two people sitting at the same table I'd eaten at the first time I met Colt.

Scott put his arm around my shoulders and turned me around so I was facing the garage area.

"Let me buy you breakfast," he said as I realized I was being led away from the motorhome, which could only mean Colt was in there with a girl. "Colt should be out of his meeting in about an hour."

After fifty minutes, two surprisingly good cups of coffee and an overcooked bagel, I thanked Scott for breakfast and told him I needed to touch base with Colt about our plans for that night, then run back over to the rookie's rig and catch up with his crew chief.

"Here's the thing, Piper. Colt's pretty busy today. I'm not sure if he'll have time to see you."

I scoffed but reminded myself that I couldn't get mad at Colt if he was here hooking up with another girl. I had been resolute in my refusal to date him. Of course he wasn't going to wait around for me.

"No big deal," I said, waving my hand. "Thanks for the coffee. And the bagel." I wiped crumbs off my pants.

It still bothered me that I couldn't wear anything fashionable at the track. Bare shoulders, opened-toe shoes and dresses or pants that ended above the ankle weren't allowed in the restricted areas of the garages, hot pits and transporters.

"It's not what you think. There's no girl in there."

I didn't believe him. "Sure. I'll see you later."

"It was Mr. Thompson," he called to my back. "And Colt didn't want to see you because he was in there crying."

I laughed without thinking about it. "Seriously? Why?"

"Because Colt loves Cal Thompson like a father and it's just hitting him that he's leaving next season."

"Oh, that's so sweet." I still thought this kid was too good to be true. "Well, I need to get back to the rookie. Tell Colt I was looking for him."

Practice had started, and it was hard to hear Scott over the twenty or so cars on the track. He leaned in close to me and spoke. "Colt has no idea how lucky he's gotten with you."

"You're so lovely. But we're not together." As I walked away, I couldn't shake the feeling that there was something no one was telling me.

• • •

I spent the next two days sitting with the new crew chief as often as I could. I found that the more time I spent with subjects, the more relaxed they felt around me. And the more willing they were to talk. I ran into Colt a few times, but I was so busy interviewing the crew chief, his staff and his young driver that I didn't have much time to spend with him. It was almost better that way. All drivers, even the nice ones, got cocky at races. It bothered me, and I liked feeling as if my job was just as important as Colt's.

I wrote a good piece on Ray Sharon, the genius crew chief of the rookie kid. I didn't dare stray from exactly what Tuck instructed me to write about—Mr. Sharon's uncanny ability to teach new drivers the ability to feel, a skill it usually took many years to develop. It was a tricky piece because the driver had never placed in the top ten with his old crew chief. So, I had to highlight everything that Ray Sharon was doing right without making it sound like the old crew chief was doing something wrong.

In my five sessions with Ray, he told me he drowned as a child, and before he was resuscitated, he experienced what he believed to be Heaven. And that he was an identical twin, and when his brother, Roy, fell down a flight of stairs and broke his arm, he felt a crushing pain in his same arm. But I didn't write any of that. I stuck to the facts and wrote an informative, albeit a little dry, piece.

My flight left after the race started, but thanks to a rain delay, I was in my apartment on the couch watching the end of it when that little rookie beat Colt. I couldn't help but smile. It was mean,

I knew, but Colt hadn't tried to spend any time with me, even though he'd told me how psyched he was that I'd be in Kentucky all weekend.

The next day, I proofed the article, then took a cab to work to leave it for Tack. Normally, I rode my bike or took the commuter train and walked from the station, but I was too tired. I rounded the corner to Tack's office and heard music playing.

"Tack?" I called, glad I'd brought the miniature can of mace on my keychain, just in case it was an intruder who liked to boogie while he broke and entered. My father would be so proud.

Tack came out of his office, messy hair, shirt untucked, as if he'd just woken up. "Piper," he said, covering a yawn, "what are you doing here?"

I held up a manila envelope. "Turning in my piece about Ray Sharon. Were you asleep?"

He grinned. "Maybe. Amy's been out sick since you've been gone. I was just trying to get caught up." He yawned again. "Are you in a hurry? I made some coffee . . . " He checked his watch. "A while ago. Have a cup while I read your piece."

The truth was, I was determined not to call Colt, and Liza was out, probably hogtied to her desk doing grunt work. I was bored and lonely. "Sounds good," I told him. "You go start reading and I'll bring you a cup. Sugar, no cream, right?"

"Thanks, Piper." I watched him walk into his office.

This wasn't the first weekend I'd seen Tack at the paper. He seemed to be one of those freaky, dedicated people like my father, who equated himself to a shark—always having to be in motion. I put two packets of sugar in his coffee, stuffed two more in my pocket just in case and found a big mug for myself and filled it. My father had taught me to appreciate black coffee when I was a teenager. Said it got the job done and no time was wasted with frothy milk and sugar substitutes. I brought our drinks into his office and sat on the couch while he read.

After a few minutes, he placed the papers on his desk and started to speak, then stopped himself.

"This is exactly what I asked for," he said.

"Is that a bad thing?" I asked.

"Well." He rubbed his temples as if he had a headache. "No. It's informative. I got a solid sense of Ray's racing background and what makes him so good with his driver. But it's missing something."

I'd written two articles for this assignment. The one Tack had asked for and the one I wanted to write. I pulled the draft of the second copy out of my back pocket and handed it to him.

"You can't get mad at me because I did exactly what you asked and delivered it a day early. But I spent a lot of time with Ray." I didn't disclose that one of the reasons I was in his transporter so often and for so long was because I was hiding from Colt.

"Ray told me everything there was to know about his job and why he was so good at it. But then we started talking more about him as a person. He's a single father of two girls and they live with him full time in the off-season. How many men do you know who'd take on that kind of responsibility?"

I liked to think my own dad would have done it for me, but I wasn't sure.

"I might have told Ray that readers feel more connected to subjects when they know something special about them. And the more the readers of our newspaper identify with him and his team, the more likely they are to buy the sponsor's products. After that, he told me all kinds of things about himself. Like how he had an imaginary friend named Raisin when he was a kid and how he almost drowned as a teenager when his drunk father capsized their RIB. And that he learned to cook so his girls wouldn't miss their mom so much when they were with him."

Tack had picked up the folded draft and was reading—and smiling.

I sipped my coffee while I waited for him to finish. He lay the articles side by side on his desk and broke out his green Sharpie and scribbled words in the margins of both copies.

"Can you guess what I'm going to say next?" he asked.

"I wrote a kick-ass human interest story and you're going to use my second piece?"

"You clearly have a talent for making people talk to you. I mean, really tell you things about their lives that wouldn't normally go in a piece about how they manage to stay in the top ten in almost every race. You are gifted, Piper."

"Thank you." I wanted to ask if he'd had time to read my tribute piece about Tim Richmond, but I was afraid to ask. I'd worked hard on it and was proud of the result, but I still didn't have a clear understanding of why he wanted me to write it or what I was supposed to write about.

"I think you know which piece I'm going to use." I cracked a smile but didn't say anything. "Why don't you get on home? I'm sure you have better things to do than hang out with your boss on a Sunday."

I really didn't, but I left anyway.

•   •   •

Since turning in my piece on Ray Sharon, I'd had a phone conversation with an official at a short track in the South. My source's name was Roger Waters. I did the math; he was too old for his parents to have gotten stoned to Pink Floyd's *Dark Side of the Moon* and conceive him on a waterbed. But the thought made me smile.

Roger gave me a simple answer to a complex problem that had Busch and Winston Cup drivers threatening to boycott the September night race. When the track was repaved two years before, the facility's owners gave the job to the lowest bidder, who then gave them exactly what they paid for—a shitty job.

According to Mr. Waters, the only thing that would stop the track from sticking to cars' tires was repaving it correctly.

I called my dad to ask him if Roger's facts checked out and to tell him I had a present for him. "This is kismet," he said. "I was fixin' to call and tell you to report to base camp." I could tell from the tone of his voice that it was important.

The front door of my parents' house was unlocked, so I let myself in. "Mama? Daddy?" I called, but neither of them answered. I found my mother hunched over a book at a small desk in the den with the door open.

"Are you okay?" I asked from the entryway. She half raised her head and gave me the just-a-moment finger. But after a minute, she was still reading, so I let her be. I took a seat on the couch in the living room and picked up a magazine when my dad came out of the bathroom, closing the door behind him. He came to me and we hugged. I reached in my purse to make sure I'd remembered his present.

I took the tissue-wrapped book out of my bag and held it up. "I got you something."

He sighed loudly and sat. "Well, I'll be damned. I ask you over for a scolding and you bring me a gift." He took it from me and sniffed it. "Is it a box of chocolates?"

"That'd be the flattest bunch of chocolates ever."

He started to unwrap his gift, but I snatched it from him. "Not so fast. What'd I do now to get myself in a pot of hot water?"

He playfully took the present back from me. "Depending on what this is, you might be off the hook." He ripped off the white tissue paper and red yarn, a Pierson-family wrapping paper tradition, and held up a book called *Survival, Evasion and Escape*. It'd been out of print for years, but I found a copy through a college friend whose mother owned a rare books shop.

His grin told me whatever I'd done to get myself summoned probably didn't seem quite so bad anymore. "I love it." My father was a self-professed hobby survivalist. If he ever got stranded in the desert with no food or water, he'd subsist on cactus thorns and sand.

"I'm glad, Daddy. I was so happy when I found it." I picked it up and flipped through the chapters. "But you might as well say whatever's on your mind." I hated feeling like my parents were mad at me, especially when I hadn't done anything wrong.

"First things first. Did you need some info for an article you're writing?"

I'd almost forgotten about the track-surface piece I was working on. "Oh, yes please. Let me get my notes." I found my notebook in my purse and flipped through pages until I found the outline of my conversation with the security guard. I handed him the notebook.

"Can you read this real quick and tell me if what my"—I made air quotes—"'unnamed source' says is accurate?"

He shook his head slowly while he read. "I had no idea my daughter was so defiant."

His words stung. "I just do as I'm instructed. Tack told me to investigate this lead. And I do believe everything that employee told me is true."

He was quiet for a moment, made a few notes with a pen I'd given him, then finally closed the book and gave it back to me. "Your information is spot on."

I smiled with relief. "Thanks, Daddy."

He held up his hand. "Don't thank me yet, because this brings me to why I wanted to talk to you."

"Uh-oh," I said. My stomach felt like lead.

"I read your article about Tim Richmond." I could tell by the heaviness in his voice that he didn't like it.

"How? It hasn't been published and Tack hasn't gone over it with me. I'm not even sure he's read it yet."

"Don't get your pretty little head in a tizzy, but your boss man sent me an advanced copy."

"What? Why?"

"He wanted my opinion on if I thought it was too—"

"Honest?" I asked, my voice full of hurt.

"*Provocative* might be a better word."

"It was accurate," I snapped. "Colt gave me Tim's number and I talked to him several times to check the accuracy of the article."

Tim had confided that he did, in fact, have full-blown AIDS, but I promised him, just like I had Colt, that I wouldn't put that in print. My story was about what made him an incredible driver and how he was abandoned by the people who claimed to be his family. The reason for the betrayal wasn't nearly as important as the treacherous act itself.

My dad patted my knee. "My Colt gave you Tim's number? I didn't realize you two had gotten that friendly."

"Don't do that, Daddy." He started to protest, but I kept talking. "First you drive all the way to Braselton to give him *the talk*. Then, like a sixteen-year-old prom date, he asks you if he can take me to the movies and you *followed* us there. You most certainly know that we're hanging out."

He dropped his head in defeat. "You're right. I'm sorry. I guess I still think of you as my little girl who needs her daddy. Colt's a good kid. I wouldn't have hired him otherwise. But this isn't about him."

"Then what's it about? Tim? My writing style? The content?"

"You do realize writing about Tim is a hornet's nest, right?"

"Everything I wrote is fact," I said.

"You always did have an iron will. I just want you to be prepared for the backlash. The big dogs in the skyscrapers aren't going to like this article one bit."

My father ran his fingers through his hair, surely trying to think of the best way to tell me my bosses had underestimated me and they'd called him to get me to back off.

"Then they shouldn't have asked me to write it."

My mother still hadn't come out of the office. I thought maybe she didn't want to be stuck in the middle of us and be forced to choose sides.

"Tack approved it," I added, pissed that he didn't have the balls to talk to me himself. His *approval* had been a sticky note on my desk saying he'd gotten the piece and would review it as soon as possible. That he hadn't sent it back to me equaled a thumbs-up in my mind. "And let us not forget he gave me the assignment. If the big dogs don't like it, they need to talk to him."

A cuckoo clock chimed seven times, and if I didn't get out of there, Liza was going to be sitting in the driveway waiting for me.

"Listen, Daddy, don't worry about me. I'm a big girl and I can take whatever heat's coming my way. Go back to your shed and build another sink-proof raft for when the great floods come." I kissed him on the cheek. "I've got to get going. Thanks for the input on the other thing. I'll see you soon."

"Piper, wait," he called to me. "Don't go away mad. I'm trying to help you out here."

"Whatever, Daddy. I never thought you'd be one of them."

"Now hold on, young lady." I stopped and turned toward him. "Tim's been in hiding—"

"You make him sound like a fugitive. He's not hiding."

I couldn't believe I was having this conversation with my super liberal father who was also Tim's friend.

"Look. I'm sorry if the racing world doesn't want to know what the last three years have been like for him, but he had a ton of fans. And I'm guessing they'll want to know what happened to him. Goodnight, Daddy."

When I passed by the den, I saw my mother still hunched over the desk. It was unlike her to not come sit with me when I came over. She was in a chair with wheels on it, shoes off, her feet stroking the bear-skin rug on the floor. My dad had shot that bear, named him Goldilocks, bought a book on taxidermy and tried to turn him into a rug himself. Then he gave up and had it done professionally at that place in Davidson. I hated guns and killing animals, but my father had been so proud of himself for shooting that poor bear in the head, claiming to have killed it without pain or fear, that I never told him I felt nauseous every time I looked at it.

"Mama?" I said from behind her. "Hi."

She swiveled toward me. "Shoofly." Couldn't anyone call me Piper? "I'm sorry I didn't come out to see you. I'm in the middle of something."

"I called Daddy to fact-check an article I'm writing, and he summoned me. If I'd known he was going to yell at me, I would have found someone else to help me out. But here I am."

"Oh, Piper. Your father has never yelled at anyone a day in his life. That's not his style."

She was right. He much preferred the low grumble of the disappointed. But I didn't want to get into it with her, too. She never disagreed with him. It was part of some united-front parenting philosophy that I secretly thought made her weak and him bullheaded.

I peered over her chair and saw a college course catalogue open on the desk behind her.

"Whatcha got there?"

She took both my hands in hers. "I'm going to college." She ducked her head with embarrassment. "One course at a time."

I hugged her hard. "Mama, that's wonderful. What made you decide to do this?"

She closed the den door and we sat.

"I feel silly whispering because I've already told your father all of this. He's the love of my life, the best thing I've ever done. Well, the second best." She patted my hand. "But it's just that"— she was talking quickly—"don't get me wrong, I love my life, I just want—"

"To get a college degree?" I finished for her and hugged her again. "Mama! I think that's wonderful. I'm so proud of you. What does Daddy think?" If me writing about the hard truths of a sick friend made him uncomfortable, I wondered what he'd think of his little missus going to school and—gasp—possibly getting a job one day.

"He thinks it's—" Her laugh was a little too high pitched. "Wonderful."

"Do you know what you want to major in? Where are you going? Have you started yet? Are you going to get a job after you graduate?"

"Jeez, P, slow down. I just got the catalogue in the mail today. I was thinking about signing up for a literature course at the community college in the fall. Just to get my feet wet. See if writing papers and studying for exams is really for me."

I gave her a one-armed hug in her chair. "You'll do great. I can't tell you how proud I am of you." Then I told her I was officially late to meet Liza, and I let myself out the front door without saying goodbye again to my father.

7

When I got to work the next day, I went through my notes and double-checked Roger Waters's facts against what my dad had added, and I was giddy with relief to know the security-guard-turned-snitch knew what he was talking about. While chewing on a pencil and banging out my 2,000-word piece, my phone rang, and the receptionist's extension lit up.

"What's up, Taryn?" I asked when I picked up.

"There's a very cute guy here to see you," she said.

"Me?" I asked, with the pencil still in my mouth. "Where?"

"In the lobby."

I walked through the maze of desks in the bullpen. When I got to the front of the building, Amy was standing too close to Colt. She had one hand on his arm and was twisting her hair with her fingers. "Colt, you—" she started to say, but I interrupted.

"What a nice surprise," I said, stepping between them.

"What's happening, hot stuff?" He leaned in and kissed my cheek, then turned back to Amy. "Thank you for talking with me while I was waiting on Piper. Good to see you again."

"I'm just so flattered you remembered me," Amy said, then looked at me. "Colt and I met last year at a race."

"So you've said." I waited for Amy to leave, and when she didn't, I put my hand on Colt's arm. "Come with me."

When we got back to my desk, I pulled up a chair. "How are you?" We hadn't talked since the Louisville race two weeks earlier.

"You will never believe who called me," he said.

"Who?"

"Paramount Pictures. They want to interview me for a movie."

"Did you get a second job?"

"Ha. Apparently, they're making a film about Winston Cup racing and they want it to be as accurate as possible. So, they're interviewing a bunch of drivers. Isn't that cool?"

"A movie about racing? Forty cars turning left, drunk girls flashing their boobs and guys with no teeth. Awesome."

The irritation in my tone was uncalled for as Colt and I were not committed to each other. We'd only hung out a few times and hadn't even kissed yet. But he had driven out here to see me when he could have just called.

"That's not fair," he said. "Road courses have right-hand turns."

I laughed. "Does it have a name?"

"Yeah, it's called *Days of Thunder* and it's about a really good driver who gets flak from everyone because he knows nothing about cars. He can drive, but he couldn't change a tire if he had to, never mind set up his car."

"Sounds like Tim Richmond."

I wondered if the experimental drug trials Tim told me about were making a difference. All the times I had spoken to Tim on the phone, he said I could ask him anything. But I couldn't make myself go there, and he didn't volunteer the information.

"It does sound like Tim, doesn't it?" Colt said.

"That's exciting." I felt like Amy was watching us. "I should get back to work. Let me know how it goes."

"Hey, my TV interview is in two days. I thought we could have dinner after, and I could tell you all about it."

"I don't know," I said, imagining what I'd wear to dinner. "I write one good article and suddenly they're throwing assignments at me. I might be busy that night."

He leaned back in the chair. "I'm sorry about Louisville. I should have tried harder to make time for you." He was quiet for a moment, then said, "Please go out with me."

I envisioned the evening—nice restaurant, great food, lots of drinks. "I . . . " *would love to* . . . "don't know. Can I call you tomorrow?"

"Sure. No problem." He sounded disappointed. I walked him to the door and watched him leave.

When I got back to my desk, my phone was ringing. "Piper Pierson," I said sourly.

"Good grief, girl, who peed in your Cheerios?"

"Oh shit, Liza, sorry. Colt just left my office."

"Why doesn't that sound like happy news?"

When I was finished filling her in, she said, "Paramount wants to interview him? That's so cool. Will he be in the movie?"

"Liza!" My sweet friend was easily derailed.

"Oh, right—this is about you. I can't believe a nice guy asked you out for dinner. Where does he get off trying to make you understand that not everybody in the race car world is going to bite it?"

Liza had diagnosed me with PTSD and said my dad almost dying was the reason why I hardly ever let myself have any fun. She got it half right. It wasn't that my dad almost died. It was that I almost killed him.

"Are you saying I should have accepted his offer?"

"Cha, Barbie," she said in her best Valley-girl tone. "He's cute. He's famous. And he likes you. What's the problem?"

"Yeah, you're right. Maybe I should call him back and have

one more go at it."

"Shit, Piper, you're falling for him, aren't you? I can hear it in your voice."

"Is that a bad thing?" I asked defensively. "You just this second told me to have dinner with him."

"So you'd get a free meal. Not because it's going to turn into a relationship."

"I have to go. I'm on deadline." I hung up with Liza and then called Colt.

•   •   •

Two days later when I arrived at the five-star restaurant half an hour late, there were no cars in the parking lot. I walked the perimeter of the building but couldn't see through the tinted glass. It'd rained earlier in the day and the air was chilly. I wished I'd brought my soft, cream-colored pashmina wrap. I pulled on the front door and it swung open. A balding man in a tuxedo ushered me in.

"Good evening, Ms. Pierson. We've been anticipating your arrival."

We weaved past twenty or so tables with creaseless cloths and shining silverware to a back room. Colt sat at a table for two with peonies in a crystal vase. He stood when I approached, and I saw that he was wearing a dark-blue tailored suit.

"I was beginning to think you'd stood me up." He pulled out my chair for me and kissed the corner of my mouth.

I was still confused by the empty restaurant and the coincidence of my favorite flower on the table.

"I thought about it," I said.

"Why did you come, then?"

"I got hungry." We both grinned, and I leaned across the table and kissed him on the cheek.

"Speaking of hungry, here come our salads." A waiter in an expensive suit placed two pear-and-gorgonzola salads on the table.

"You caught me," Colt said, reading my expression. "The flowers, the salad, everything tonight will be your favorite. From the crab-stuffed lobster to the bread pudding. This night is all about Piper."

"How, how did you know?" I stuttered. "This is all so . . . incredible."

"I got some help from a little birdie named Liza. After you called me back, I knew I had to do something to win you over. Am I wooing you with my thoughtfulness?"

"Oh, I'm wooed all right." We clinked our wineglasses. "So, tell me about your interview. Did you wow them with your good looks and charm?"

He took a long sip. "Actually, I think I did. The woman who interviewed me said I was nicer, taller and better looking than Tom Cruise."

"No way! Is that who's playing the lead role?"

"I think so, yeah." He tore off a piece of fresh bread and put it on my plate. "Careful," he said. "It's still hot."

"So, what kind of questions did she ask?"

"The usual stuff. What happens if I have to pee in the middle of a race? Does it ever get too hot in the cars? Do I have to be physically fit to drive three hundred miles going a hundred and fifty miles an hour?"

"You must have talked that poor woman's ear off. I can just see you drawing diagrams and explaining in exact detail the physics of how much fluid you have to take in to keep from getting dehydrated and how it's almost more important to know who's behind you in a race rather than who's in front."

His eyes got big. "Were you there?"

"I do listen when you talk, you know."

"I guess you do. I'm so flattered."

Our server brought our entrees, and we talked while we ate. Our conversation was easy. The food was excellent, and we were clearly attracted to each other. But by the time the dessert was served, I didn't think I could go home with him if I didn't tell him about my past. I hated feeling like I was keeping secrets from people I cared about.

"Colt," I finally said.

"Oh no." His smile disappeared and he finished his wine.

"There are a few things I need to tell you." An instrumental version of an old Bob Dylan song came through the speakers. He was my dad's favorite singer, and it reminded me of listening to his greatest hits on the way to races.

"Tell me who he is," he said. "And I'll punch him in the nose."

"I don't think you will—not if you want to keep your job."

He dropped his fork. "You . . . and Mr. Thompson?"

I couldn't stop myself from laughing. "Oh, good lord, no. My parents would beat me senseless if I ever did something as foolish as that."

"Oh, thank God. So, who wrecked you?"

I gave him a lopsided grin. "That's an unfortunate choice of words." I stared at the ceiling, hoping for inspiration or a natural disaster. Then, I just started talking.

"My dad was a pretty successful driver before he founded Pierson Racing more than twenty years ago. He only ever competed in the lower ranks, but he was fearless and talented. Even after he became a full-time owner and won his first championship with Mack, he raced a little in the off-season."

"Um, Piper, I don't know if you know this, but your dad is kinda famous. So I'm aware of his history," Colt said with a wink.

"So, you know about the accident in Tennessee?"

"Of course. Everyone does. Some rookie hit him and almost killed him." He tilted back in his chair. "Man, I'd hate to be that kid. Can you imagine being responsible for almost taking out the most famous car owner in NASCAR history?"

"Colt!" My stomach felt liquid. "Please let me say this."

He leaned forward and his face got serious. "I'm sorry. Go ahead."

"I was the other driver."

"*Ha ha,* Pierson."

"No, really."

Colt's expression turned flat. "For real?"

I saw our waiter coming toward us. I caught his eye and shook my head no, and he veered away.

"Holy hell, Piper. You're serious. Is that why you quit racing? I always thought you'd move up to Busch sooner or later. But once I left the Dash series, I lost track of you." He wiped his mouth with his napkin. "Jesus, Piper. I'm sorry."

I took a sip of my water just to give me something to do.

"I'm going to tell you the whole story now because if I don't, I will probably chicken out forever. So please just let me talk."

He reached across the table and took my hand. It was shaking. "I'm here. I've got you."

"The year I turned seventeen, my birthday landed on the same day that my dad had rented a small track he wanted to test out in East Nowhere, Tennessee. Actually, the track was booked by an assistant who was new and didn't bother to check with anyone about the date. My father was going to cancel since it was my birthday, but I told him we should all go together. I loved racing and cars and hanging out with my parents. It kind of sounded like the perfect birthday to me."

"Oh man, Pierson. You are truly one of a kind."

"Yeah, well. That's one way of looking at it. My dad was supposed to test by himself, but I asked if I could drive with him. For all the driving I did in the Dash series, I'd never been on the track at the same time as him. He said yes, so the crew got one of the backup cars off the transporter and I got dressed.

"I didn't have much experience with those kinds of cars, and it was harder to handle than I thought it'd be. We were out there, flying around, weaving around each other, going high, going low, having a good ol' time. Then, all of a sudden, I slammed on the brakes and veered off onto the apron."

"Did you go all deer in the headlights on your pops?"

"That's a good way of putting it."

"Why? Did you feel a vibration? Or was a tire going down?"

"Nope. Just a case of nerves, I guess. I realized I wasn't in my little go-kart of a Dash car. I was driving a Winston Cup car. The real deal. I saw what my future could be . . . and I freaked."

"We've all been there."

"That's what my dad said. He slowed down and drove tandem next to me and he just talked. About baseball and his favorite football team, the Dallas Cowboys, anything but the fact that we were supposed to be racing each other."

"Sounds very Zen," Colt said. "Your dad is a cool cat. So, what went wrong?"

"I wish I could tell you. I started to feel better, so we got back out on the track and we were almost up to speed. And . . . I don't know . . . I must have freaked out again, because I swerved directly into the driver's side door of my father's car, causing him to spin on the track and slam into the retaining wall."

I sat quiet, remembering how I had screamed my dad's name, expecting to hear his voice come through my headphones, calling me Noodle and telling me everything was okay. But he didn't answer, and an official who was in the pits called for Fire Rescue to get on the track's surface immediately. My mother ripped off her headset and, with impossible grace, started to climb over the wall and run out onto the racetrack. But our rear tire changer grabbed her from behind and held her back.

"Our crew chief was off his perch and across the track before the ambulance got there. It seemed like forever, but it was probably only a minute before Birdie called back to the track to have one of the crew guys drive my mother to the nearest hospital where they were flying my dad, via Trauma Hawk. I wasn't hurt, but they brought me there in an ambulance."

Colt reached for my hand and I let him take it. All these years later, I could still hear the helicopter approaching the track, could see the paramedics putting my father's limp body on the backboard and could remember the antiseptic smell of the hospital.

"He's okay now, Piper. That's all that matters."

"He crushed his pelvic bone and had massive internal bleeding, which caused him to go into cardiac arrest. They'd revived him by the time they got to the hospital, but he was in a coma for six days. They operated on him during that time and the orthopedic surgeon patched him back together the best he could, but he'll have chronic pain forever."

"Is that why he's always up and moving?"

"Yes. Even after the surgery my dad was too unstable to move, so they kept him at Nashville Medical. For three weeks, my mother lived in that hospital room. To this day, I don't recall her showering or eating or ever stepping foot outside the hospital. It was like I'd lost both my parents."

"I understand why your dad quit racing, but why did you?"

I yanked my hand away. "Isn't it obvious?" He didn't answer me. "Because I almost killed him. I could never get in another car after that and take that chance again."

"*That's* why you don't drive? Are you kidding me?"

"Isn't it enough?" I snapped. "I used to think my father was invincible. Nothing could ever take down the mighty Planter Pierson. And then stupid little me came along."

"So that's why you're like this? Because you're afraid you're going to kill the whole world?"

"Like what?" I shouldn't have told him my secret.

"You don't drive, and you won't date me. Why? I know it's not because you don't like me. Is it because you're afraid that if you drive you'll run over everyone on the sidewalk? And if you fall madly in love with me, I'll die because I drive a race car?"

I couldn't look at him. "Can we just leave it alone for now? I've never told anyone besides Liza what happened. Can't you take that as a win?"

"No, we can't leave it alone. Because that means leaving you alone."

I looked at the table and pulled at my napkin.

"Piper," Colt said, "look at me. This is not over. I want to be with you. And if that means making you understand that living a full life and dying young is better than never taking chances and not really living, then so be it." He leaned back in his chair and grinned. "You watch." He raised his glass to me. "I'll make you see the world my way. And when you do . . . " He whistled. "Hold on to your hat because we'll have a hell of a ride."

8

It was high summer, and I couldn't remember ever being so happy. Colt was right. Being with him was freeing. I loved my job, and my box of fan mail got a little bigger each week. Mr. Matts had stopped by my cubicle a few times to compliment my work. Tack sent me to more and more races, and Colt and I were spending lots of time together.

I hadn't seen my parents in a week, so I was at their house for dinner. It was a Wednesday, and early, so some of the crew was still at the shop. I'd taken the back way in and saw Colt's car in the parking lot but didn't stop in.

"What's for dinner?" I asked. "Something smells good."

My mother was at the island, chopping celery. "I'm more interested in what's for dessert," she said.

I set my bag down on the counter even though I knew it made her crazy to have anything on it. "What do you mean? Was I supposed to bring something?"

"No, but I was hoping you'd make something here. I stocked the pantry for you."

"It'd be my pleasure," I said, unbuttoning the cuffs on my oxford and rolling up my sleeves. "What are you craving?"

"How about your famous black bottom pie?"

I checked my watch. It was four in the afternoon. "You got it, but you know that it has to chill in the fridge for three hours, right?" I pulled a bag of chocolate wafers out of the baking cabinet, put them in a bowl and began crushing them with a wine bottle to make the crust.

"That was our plan, little one."

My dad arrived through the garage door. With greasy hands and a stained shirt, I knew he'd been working on an engine.

"We want you to stay and hang out with us for a while," he said, walking toward the bathroom to scrub up and change clothes.

I was suspicious but didn't say anything. My parents were super smart people who lived in the spotlight. Therefore, they rarely did anything that wasn't well thought out, including asking their daughter to spend the afternoon at their house.

My father came back, and I asked him to chill a glass bowl for me so the whipped cream would get good and thick. He did as I asked, never taking his eyes off me. After another minute of melting butter, mixing it with the wafers and shaping it into a pie pan, I couldn't take it anymore. "Okay." I turned to my parents, wielding a rubber spatula. "Why are you being so weird? What do you have to tell me?"

"Can't we spend a few hours with our favorite child?" my mother asked innocently.

Growing up, I wanted a sibling, but my mom would respond that then she wouldn't be able to call me her favorite anymore. "You can. But that's not what this is about." I waved the spatula between them. "What's going on?"

My dad dipped his finger in the custard I had cooking on the stove. "You always were the smart one," he said. "Something is up. But I want pie first," he said. "So, we'll sit down and talk after you're done making dessert."

"Only you, Daddy. Only you could blackmail me into making

you a treat." I wiped my hands on a dishtowel, then flicked it at him.

"Blackmail is such an ugly word," my mom said, fitting the beaters into the hand mixer. "We just want to spend some time with our best girl and get something good to eat."

I finished making dessert, put it in the fridge to chill and cleaned up the kitchen. I washed and dried my hands and hung the dishtowel over the oven handle.

"All right, parents," I said, sitting on the couch adjacent to where they were. "Spill it."

They exchanged worried glances, and for an awful moment I thought one of them was sick.

"Your father and I love you very much," my mom started. *This is worse than an illness. They're getting divorced.* "And we want you to be happy."

"If you two are splitting up," I said, my voice on the edge of panic, "just say it."

They grabbed for each other's hands at the same time.

"Oh, good lord, no," my dad said. "I told your mom she should let me do the talking." He cleared his throat. "You know we're not going to live forever." I let out an involuntary squeak. *Maybe one of them is sick.*

"Enough with the preamble. Just say it."

"Fine." My mother smoothed her slacks. "We want you to reconsider joining us at Pierson Racing." I loved how my mother said *us.* She'd never worked for the team because she thought it'd blur the marital lines. She was happy to organize team dinners and entertain sponsors at their home. But she had no interest in doing the books or answering phones.

"That's what you wanted to talk to me about? Because the first thousand nos weren't enough?" I laughed. "I appreciate the offer. I do. But I'm happy at the newspaper."

"We know, sweetheart," my mom said, "and that's why we wanted to talk to you about it again. You have such natural talent and you relate so well to everyone you interview."

"That's what makes a leader succeed," my father added. "More important than experience or education is making people trust you. There's not one successful CEO of a large corporation who doesn't have people skills."

I had to make my parents understand why I'd never join them in the business. "Parents," I said. "I love that you have faith in me. That means the world. But . . . I can't do it. I won't."

My dad rested his head in his hands for a moment, then met my gaze. "Why, Piper?"

I sighed loudly. I was getting nowhere. "Do you love Mack?"

He cocked his head as if I'd suddenly started speaking a foreign language. "Of course I do. He's more of a brother to me than my blood brother."

"What about Birdie?"

"Our crew chief?" he asked.

"How many other Birdies do you know?" He wasn't going to make this easy for me. "Yes, our crew chief."

"Sure. He's been with us almost as long as Mack."

"And I assume you care about all the guys who work in the shop? The tire changers? And the engine builders? And the gas can catchers? And—"

"I get your point." His confusion was turning to impatience.

"I love them, too. All of them. Just like I love you and Mom. So why on earth would I want to make it my job to put them in harm's way every day?"

"Piper, have you been drinking the vanilla extract again?" my mother asked. "What are you talking about?"

When I was five years old, I helped her make a birthday cake for my dad. She asked me to add a splash of vanilla to the batter. It smelled so good that I drank it from the bottle, not knowing it was mostly alcohol. She didn't notice anything was wrong until I started talking nonsense and then vomited.

"Racing is dangerous," I said.

"It is," my father answered. "And that's the risk we all take. But we do it because we love it. I think if, God forbid, Mack was involved in a fatal accident on the track, that's how he'd want to go out. You can't live your life in fear every day."

"Don't romanticize this, Dad. Do you think Mack dying in the middle of a race would make Maggie feel any better about losing her husband? Saying 'At least he died doing what he loved, and he's in a better place now' are things we say to make ourselves feel better after we lose someone we love. You"—I pointed an accusatory finger at him—"almost died. And I would not have been okay if you had." My voice was shaking, and I was close to crying.

He got off the couch and sat next to me. "Is that what all this has been about? You're afraid of people you care about dying?" I nodded but couldn't speak. "Oh, Noodle, I could get hit by the milk truck going out to get the mail. Racing doesn't have anything to do with it."

"You keep telling yourself that, Daddy. But I'm not going to be the owner of a company who sends its employees out every weekend to get killed on a racetrack. Or watches as a car falls off the lift in the shop and crushes a mechanic. Or sits in the pits as our tire carrier jumps over the wall and gets run over by the driver behind us who missed his pit stall. It's too much."

We sat in silence for a moment, and I knew my parents were trying to think of something to say to make me feel better.

"I love that you want to protect the whole world," my dad said. "But accidents happen all the time. No one can predict what might occur from one day to the next. You can't stop living your life because you're afraid."

I walked into the kitchen. "I am living my life," I said, opening a cabinet and taking out three dinner plates. "I'm just not ready to live yours."

•   •   •

After dessert that night, my parents walked me outside. By
then it was well past dark; everyone at the shop had gone home.
My dad offered to drive me to my apartment, but I was afraid
he'd use the time to lecture me some more. I stood with my hand
on the cab's door, cold in my short jean skirt.

"It'll be okay, Noodle," he said, hugging me hard. "You go do
your reporting job and if you ever change your mind, just tell us."

"Thanks for understanding," I said, although I knew neither
of them would relent. "And thanks for dinner and the doggie bag."
I held up the plastic grocery bag my mother had put the leftovers
in, including most of the pie. "Liza and I have breakfast now."

I got in the cab and couldn't shake the feeling that despite what
they said, my parents were disappointed in me. The cabbie drove
a mile away from the house I grew up in, and I asked him to pull
over at a gas station. I went inside and called Colt. "Hey there,"
I said when he answered. "Any chance you're up for a visitor?" I
heard a voice in the background but couldn't tell if it was the TV.

"Um, sure," he said tentatively. "But it's kind of late to get a
cab from Charlotte."

I was not in a mood to be put off. "If you don't want me
there, just say so," I snapped. The clerk behind the counter was
eavesdropping and smirked when I caught him. "And not that it
matters now, but I'm coming from my parents' house."

"It's not that . . . " His voice trailed off. "My place is a mess.
Can you give me twenty minutes or so?"

Colt's house was never a mess. "Sure. Whatever. I'll see you in
a half hour." I bought a Dr. Pepper, a party-size bag of Fritos and
a Mad Libs. I sat in the parking lot munching for twenty minutes.

"Keep the meter running," I told the confused driver.

Finally, we headed out, turning out of the parking lot and
heading to Lake Norman.

Colt seemed out of breath when he answered his door. "What a nice surprise," he said, glancing over my shoulder into the darkness.

It didn't feel that way to me. "Thanks for letting me crash your party," I said, and let myself in.

"It wasn't a party."

"Who'd you need to get rid of?" I asked, suddenly understanding.

He stepped away from me. "It's not what you think," he said.

"I wasn't thinking anything," I said.

"Really?"

"Do you have a beer for me?"

Colt disappeared into his kitchen and came back with two beers. We sat on his leather sofa, and I noticed there'd recently been a fire in the fireplace.

"What's up?" he asked. "You sounded frazzled on the phone."

There was a soft throw on the back of the couch. I pulled it over my lap.

"Goddammit," I muttered, wiping my face on the blanket. While I had it against my face, I sniffed it. There was no remnant of expensive French perfume or the drugstore scent of the cheap stuff. No evidence of another girl. Just a woodsy, fireplace smell.

Colt brushed his fingers against my cheek. I pulled away from him, too late.

"Hey, are those tears I see? What's going on, Piper? Is something wrong?"

"I'm not this girl. I'm not this blanket-sniffing, jealous, needy girl." I took a sip of my beer and then put it on the coffee table. "We're not even a couple and—"

"Hey," he said. "That was your decision, not mine."

I dropped my head. "It's okay. Whoever she is, it's okay."

"She's a former girlfriend. And tonight was the first time I've seen her in forever."

"It doesn't matter who she is. You're free to date anyone you want."

I'd taken my shoes off and left them on a mat by the front door. Colt's house was so clean that I worried I'd track in dirt. Now I got up and headed to the foyer.

"Piper, wait." He jumped off the couch and followed me through his kitchen. "I want to date you. You know that."

I stopped by the refrigerator. "You spend your life on the road with screaming girls throwing themselves at you." The year before, I'd read an unauthorized biography of a racing legend. He claimed to have slept with almost a thousand women. He was fifty-three years old.

"Piper." He grabbed my wrist as I started for my shoes. "Stop. Let's talk about this."

I let him turn me around so we were facing each other. "Talk," I said.

"Why is this such a big deal? I told you my ex was still close to my family."

After I told him that I caused my dad's accident, I thought maybe that would be the start of something between us. "I don't know how to explain it."

"Well, try."

My conversation with my parents came rushing back to me. "I don't want you to die," I blurted.

"Die?" he asked. "Wow. I did not see that one coming."

"You have a dangerous job and—"

"And your dad almost died doing what I do."

"Yes."

"I'm not him." He held both my hands. "I'm not going to get hurt."

I barked a bitter laugh. "No offense, but you're *not* him. He's a legend. And if he can almost bite it in turn four, so can you."

He took both my hands in his, and I wanted desperately to

hug him. "Piper," he said quietly. "What happened in Tennessee was not your fault. It was an *ac-ci-dent*." He over-enunciated the last word. "I want to be with you . . . if you'll let me."

I was so tired. "It's so much more than me having a meltdown and driving my car into my dad's." He was still holding one of my hands and I squeezed it. "I had this perfect life. My parents are the happiest couple I've ever seen. And all I ever wanted was to be like them. That's why I started racing karts and then Daytona Dash cars. I saw how happy they were with each other and how much my dad loved racing. And I thought, *This is it. This is my life*."

"It still is your life. You know your dad would do anything to get you back in a race car."

"It's more than that."

He led me back to the sofa. "So tell me. Tell me what it is so we can fix it."

"There's nothing to fix. This is me. This is my life now."

He ran his hands through his hair. "What, Piper? I don't understand. Just tell me what you're talking about so I can help you."

All the therapy my parents made me have after the accident and the nights I talked to them and then eventually to Liza made me realize it was so much more than just the accident.

"After my dad recovered and came home, I was running out to pick up a prescription for him. I got in my car and backed out of the garage. Then I stopped and threw up. I thought I was having a heart attack. I sat in my own puke and laid on the horn until my mom came out. She called Birdie to come stay with my dad and drove me to the emergency room. They said I had a panic attack."

"Did they know what you'd gone through?"

"The whole world knew about the accident. But not that I was involved. The doctor told my mom to bring me home and let me rest. Said I'd be fine once I acclimated."

"To what?"

"My life."

"How do you do that?"

"Exactly. That's when I realized that my perfect life wasn't so perfect."

"I know it must have been terrifying—what happened with your dad. But he was all right and your parents still loved each other. And Mack kept winning. That sounds pretty perfect."

"I can't make you understand. I wish I could, but when I try to put it into words, all I see is—"

"What, Piper? What do you see?"

"You. Dead in a race car. And my parents taken out by cancer or a heart attack or the plague."

"The plague? Really? Have you heard about these nifty things known as antibiotics?"

I punched his shoulder. "Please don't mock me when I'm feeling sorry for myself."

He picked up my hand and kissed it. "All I can tell you is that I'm a good driver." He realized his mistake and stopped abruptly. "Not that your dad isn't. He was one of the best. But I can't get in a race car every weekend afraid I'll get hurt. That would kill my confidence." He winced with his word choice. "Cars and racing have gotten so much safer in the last couple of years. It's all good. I promise."

I wanted to believe him. "I think it's too much. I'm sorry." I took my hands back and stood.

He looked like I'd struck him. "What are you saying?"

"You know." I couldn't bear to speak the words.

"I don't know. Are you mad because I don't sit behind a desk for a living? By the way, do you know how many people die from paper cuts every year?" He grinned and it was all I could do not to kiss him. "I don't mean to be harsh, but you've known from day one what my job is. I want to be with you. And *only* you. But

I can't walk away from my career."

"I didn't ask you to."

He stepped toward me as I turned toward the foyer. "Piper, just give me a chance."

"To what? Make me change my mind?"

"To understand how wonderful life is. You are absolutely correct. I could die testing next weekend in Daytona. Or Liza could have a brain aneurysm and drop dead tomorrow. Or you could slip in the shower and that'd be that."

I had a flash of everyone I loved leaving me. "You're not helping."

"But I can. If you don't love anyone because you're afraid he'll die, and if you don't drive a car because you're scared something awful will happen, you might as well be dead. Because that's not really living. You have to love to live. And you have to live to love."

"Jesus, Colt. You sound like an inspirational saying."

"But I have a point, don't I?"

I touched his cheek. "You're hard to say no to. But I need some time."

"All you've had is time," he whispered.

"I'll call you." And then I opened the heavy mahogany door and stepped out into the night.

9

I was at the paper, writing, erasing and rewriting the same
sentence when Tack buzzed my phone and asked me to come
see him.

"What's up?" I asked after I knocked on his open door and
let myself in.

"I owe you an explanation. About the Tim Richmond article."

I'd meant to ask him why it wasn't published. "Oh, yeah. I
was wondering about that."

Tack scrunched his mouth tight, reminding me of my dad
when he was about to deliver bad news.

"Mr. Matts pulled it."

"What?" I stopped picking at a hangnail. "I thought he was
the one who wanted me to write it."

"He was." Tack picked up a pen and clicked the top. The
sound made me crazy. "But I don't think he was expecting you
to be so . . . thorough."

"What does that even mean?"

"I think he was expecting a recap of Tim's stellar career. You
know, a tribute to a lost brother."

"The man's not dead. But this sport has a short memory. So, I guess he might as well be."

I'd called Tim a few times since I turned in the article, but each time his mother said he wasn't feeling well and took a message. He never called me back.

Tack took a deep breath, and I imagined him counting to ten in his head, something my father swore kept him from ever saying something he'd regret.

"Both Jim and I thought your article was brilliant. You painted a picture of a great man who'd been wronged by the industry he loved so much."

"And that was my first mistake," I said. Why could no one say what they meant or be happy when I did what they told me to? "So, the next time I'm assigned to write about a living legend I should just report his rank and serial number?" I was already in a bad mood and feared I wouldn't be able to keep my attitude in check.

"Careful," Tack warned. "I understand you're disappointed and I don't blame you. But you're a reporter, not management."

"Aye aye, Captain." I saluted like a soldier. "Anything else?"

"Just keep up the good work, kid."

•   •   •

A few weeks after Tack nixed the Tim Richmond profile, Liza and I left the apartment we'd shared near school and signed a lease on one closer to Moorestown and Charlotte. Part of me was surprised that Liza wanted to live with me again. She'd met a guy at her job and spent so much time with him and at work, I hardly ever saw her. It was only a matter of time before she ditched me to go live with Teddy.

Liza moved in a few days before me. I was working on a difficult article about a driver who'd lost his wife to breast cancer, and I needed a quiet place to write. I'd been staying at my parents' guest apartment for three days and told Liza I'd catch up to her as soon as I was done. I still hadn't talked to Colt, and I wasn't over the sting of having my best work pulled, so I needed both the solitude and the distraction.

I unlocked the front door to our new apartment and threw my pillows and a pair of stilettos I had never worn into the living room. Something smelled odd. More specifically, I didn't smell something. Liza and I were not well versed in taking out the trash or throwing away takeout food. Even though she'd been there less than a week, I expected the dull odor of congealing beef in brown sauce and sweaty workout clothes to permeate the apartment.

"Liza?" I called. "Did the cleaning fairies come?" I stepped into the living room to find several bouquets of my favorite flowers—peonies, lilies, tulips and something kind of orange that I loved. I knew without opening the cards that they were from Colt.

"He doesn't go away quietly, does he?" Liza came out of the kitchen with her hair in pigtails and wearing sweats with *UCCH* written in block letters across the butt.

"Oh, he went away, all right," I said.

"Why aren't you hanging out with Colt?"

"I freaked out on him."

Liza and I had shared many bottles of Boone's Farm Strawberry Hill wine and boxes of Lucky Charms and watched mindless TV. But she was on Colt's side. She didn't get why I didn't drive anymore and thought I was wasting my life living like a nun. I opened a card. There was one word on it. *Understand.* I smelled a bouquet of lilacs and opened the card tucked among the bluish-purple flowers. *Live.* I continued around the room opening cards and tossing the envelopes on the floor.

"It's a freaking puzzle," I said, handing them to Liza. "Help me figure out what this bozo is trying to say."

"Okay," she said. "But let us not forget that you're the bozo."

We spread twenty-one cards on the floor and organized them into verbs, nouns and conjunctions. After fifteen minutes of rearranging words and still with a stack of leftover cards, I came up with, *Love Dies. So Does Everyone. Never Love.* Liza, who was a whole lot more optimistic than me, scooped up the cards and started over. She sat on the thick carpet in our high-rise apartment and shuffled the cards until she came up with: *Love Never Dies. Understand Everyone Must Love To Live.*

"No fair," I said. "You used more cards than me."

She rolled her eyes. "Would you please stop this nonsense and go call him before he changes his mind?"

"What's the point? I told you that I basically sent him away because of his scary-as-shit job. That's not going to change anytime soon. So why bother?"

She shuffled the cards like she did when we played poker and laid them out in a random order. "You did what?" she asked.

I shrugged.

"Um, sweetheart? Everybody you know has a dangerous job." She crinkled her nose like she smelled something bad. "If that's a deal breaker, you better run far and run fast to a place where people play board games on the weekends for fun."

I leaned against the back of a sectional couch. "But he's so cute." I plucked a linen-pink rose from a bouquet. Someone had removed all its thorns. "And sweet. And he makes our apartment smell so much better."

"Only you, sister P. Only you could send a boy packing for an entirely stupid reason and have him think it was his fault." Liza handed me the phone. "Now call him before he realizes you should be sending him flowers." She was still trying to decipher the shuffled cards on the floor. Now they read, *Piper Love is Life. Understand Me.*

I hugged her hard. "Thanks, L." I pulled myself up and brought the cards with me to my bedroom, completely unsure if I could handle watching Colt go 170 miles an hour every weekend.

Knowing he was getting ready for that weekend's race, I called his shop. Scott answered the phone. "Piper," he said, his tone cool. "What can I do for you?"

I'd missed Scott in the three weeks since Colt and I stopped hanging out, and I was taken aback by his lack of enthusiasm at hearing my voice.

"I was hoping to catch Colt before he heads to Indy. Is he around?"

"Yes, but I think he's busy."

It hadn't occurred to me that Scott would be mad at me, too. I thought only girls held grudges on behalf of their friends.

"Could you check for me?" I asked.

"Listen, Piper. Colt's been jerked around enough. Unless—"

"I'm sorry. But you don't know—"

"That's not what I mean," he said impatiently. "His last girlfriend was a train wreck. We thought you were different."

"We? I didn't know this was a group effort."

"What do you want?"

"Colt," I said, my voice small. "I just want Colt."

By the time Scott told Colt I was on the phone, I was expecting him to tell me to kiss off and that would be that.

"What's happenin', hot stuff?" he greeted as if it were the same as it ever was. "Did you get my flowers?"

I was so relieved I thought I would cry. "Yes, and they're beautiful."

"Cool." But he sounded unsettled, almost nervous. "Did you decipher the cards?"

"Liza and I are giving it a go." I'd spread them out across my bed. "Colt," I said at the same time he said my name. "I'm so sorry. I don't know how to fix this . . . how to fix me. But I want to be with you."

"That's funny," he said, although I didn't think it was at all. "I was about to say those same words to you."

"That you miss me?" I asked hopefully.

"You know I do. Listen, darlin', I wish I could talk, but I have to split to go see someone." I glanced at the alarm clock on my bedside table. It was almost ten.

"Okay. Good luck this weekend. Call me when you get home."

"Sure thing. See you soon."

I was screwed. *See you soon* were hardly the words of a boy who'd been missing me.

I heard Liza putting away pots and pans, but I wanted to lie with the thought of Colt a little while longer. Sometime later—I couldn't tell if it'd been an hour or three—I heard a knock on the front door and Liza talking to someone. I hoped it wasn't one of the cute boys from across the hall. I looked like crap and wasn't in the mood to drink beer and play Trivial Pursuit. When I peeked out my door, I saw Colt standing, palms up, facing Liza.

I walked into the living room. "Surprise," he said, dodging the stilettos and unpacked boxes. "I told you I'd see you soon."

"I don't get it. I thought you were leaving for Indy." Colt was now twenty-four years old, a superstar in the making, movie-star beautiful, but he rarely stayed out late during race weeks. "Don't you need to be home soon, sleeping?"

"A freak tornado came through Indy. Transporters can't leave till at least the day after tomorrow," Liza said, pointing to the weatherman on the TV.

"It was me," Colt said, grinning. "I politely asked Mother Nature to delay my departure so I could see you."

"Good." I grabbed his hand. "I know a few indoor games to keep us entertained." I led him to my room, closed the door and pushed two unpacked suitcases off my bed.

He undressed me slowly, kissing my collarbone as he unbuttoned my shirt.

"Piper," he murmured. "Are you sure? I don't want to rush anything."

"I don't have any idea. All I know is that I like you and I want to be with you. Can we enjoy tonight and figure the rest out later?"

He kissed me slowly. "I've been thinking. And I know how I'm going to make this better for you. You just have to let me tell you the deal."

I smiled. Every time a driver blew a tire or got wrecked by another car or ran out of fuel, in the post-race interview he'd inevitably comment that "*It was just one of those racing deals.*" As if that explained everything.

10

"Are you sure you can't get on a plane?"

"Colt, I'm in my pajamas. It's midnight. And the race starts in twelve hours. I'd never make it there in time."

"What if I beg? Will that change your mind?"

"I thought you liked smaller tracks. Why are you freaking out?"

"I don't know. Orange County is too far away, I guess."

"It's in New York, not New Guinea. Besides, you fly everywhere. Why do you care?"

"Listen, smart-ass. I have a bad feeling about tomorrow."

The digital next to my bed said it was almost one in the morning. "Well, you're in luck. It is tomorrow. And you're fine." I thought about the night he'd come over, right before the Indy race, and how we'd been together almost nonstop ever since. "Close your eyes and dream about me."

I said goodnight and promised I'd watch the race the next day. I couldn't sleep, thinking about what had him so rattled. He'd never sounded tentative about a race before, and I couldn't help but think that he shared my anxiety and knew something bad was going to happen. After an hour, I got up, drank a couple glasses of wine and got in bed with Liza.

• • •

As promised, the next day Liza and I watched the race on TV. Colt went out early with a blown engine. He was grumpy when he called, said he couldn't change his ticket to come home early and would call me the next night when he got back to Charlotte. So, I was surprised when the phone rang early Sunday afternoon and it was him.

"What's happenin', hot stuff?" I giggled, happy to hear his voice. But I couldn't understand what he was saying because he was crying so hard. My mind rewound to the moment his engine blew. He didn't hit the wall. There was no accident. He just coasted slowly to his pit stall.

"Oh God, Colt, what's wrong? Are you okay?" My heart pounded. Over the years there had been a few fatal accidents that initially hadn't seemed that bad. Could Colt have gotten hurt the day before but not known it until now? This was exactly what I'd been afraid of when I picked that fight with him earlier in the summer. What looked like nothing at all could kill someone in this sport.

"Tim died," he told me.

"Tim Richmond?" My stomach turned. "Oh, sweetheart, I'm so sorry. I know how close you two were."

I thought back to the article I'd written and how much Tack had loved it, and how when I threw it in my father's face that he'd been right and the big big boss put the kybosh on it, my dad sat me down and said he was proud of me for standing up for what I believed in. It was as if he'd never summoned me to his house to try to talk me out of it.

"Pipes," my dad had said. "You are the picture of integrity. I'm proud of you, little one."

"I can't believe he's gone." Colt's voice brought me back to the present.

"I'm so, so sorry." I didn't know what else to say. "I'm sorry I never got a chance to visit him with you." Colt and I had called Tim and asked if we could spend a weekend with him. But he was too sick by then and didn't want to see anyone.

"It's already started," Colt said, his voice still shaky.

"What has?"

"A press release was sent out saying Tim died of heterosexually-transmitted AIDS. God forbid those good ol' boys should be associated with a homo."

In the years since AIDS had become a national epidemic, it was widely believed that it was only obtained through homosexual sex or intravenous drug use. A few weeks before, Tim released a statement of his own admitting he slept with every groupie he could. That he got AIDS from a girl was unspoken but implied. I'd wondered then what made him speak publicly for the first time in years, and make such a bold statement, at that. But now I understood. He must have known the end was near and what the bigwigs would say after he died.

"Maybe something good will come of this," I said. "Tim was famous around here. Maybe his death will mean something and people will be more careful from now on."

"Jesus, Piper. Could you get off your soapbox? My friend just died and you want to make a public service announcement? You're just like the rest of them. Any angle for a good story."

His words stung even though I knew he didn't mean them. "Colt," I said, trying to keep the hurt out of my voice. "I know you're sad. I was just looking for something positive."

He sighed loudly. "I know. I'm sorry. I just miss him so much."

We talked for another minute and Colt said he had to leave for the airport. I told him to come straight to my apartment when he got back—if he wanted. After we hung up, I couldn't help but feel a bit relieved. At least now I knew his bad feeling about the weekend had nothing to do with racing.

•   •   •

It seemed like everyone in the state of North Carolina said they were going to Tim Richmond's memorial service. I asked Colt if he and his parents wanted to come with us. The state police issued a statement that they were going to cordon off a block in downtown Charlotte. Parking by the cathedral was going to be a nightmare, and I figured Colt would want to carpool.

"I don't know if that's a good idea," he told me.

"Why not? You're one of us now. Just because you're not officially a member of Pierson Racing doesn't mean you're not family. The entire team will be with us. Mack, Birdie, the pit crew, everyone who works in the shop, the secretaries. There'll be a herd of us."

We were on Colt's boat anchored on Lake Norman. He stood behind me and pressed his finger into my shoulder. "Ooh— you're red." He reached in the console and grabbed a bottle of sunscreen. "It's not that. This is a stupid thing to say, but I feel funny being around Mack."

I twisted around so I could see him. "What? Why? He's such a sweet man."

He rubbed a blob of lotion between his palms and massaged it into my shoulders. "I know. That's kind of the problem."

I put my hand up to block the sun. "I don't follow."

"Mack has driven for y'all since you were a little kid. He's won five championships with your daddy. And in three months he's going to be out of a job. Because of *me*." He dropped his head and let it hang.

"Hey now." I held his cheeks between my hands. "Mack's not out of a job. He's retiring because he's won more races than any other living driver and has a terrible disease that's taking his muscle control. And he's not really retiring. He'll still work in the shop as a general manager of sorts. He just won't be able to race."

Colt kissed my hand. "I didn't mean to upset you. I can't imagine how hard retiring must be for Mack. I just feel like maybe Mack would have held on for a while longer if I hadn't signed a deal with your team."

Mack had passed his monthly physical the week before, but I was worried about him. I noticed him having trouble holding his coffee mug at the race shop. I hadn't said anything to my father because I didn't want to worry him. But the thought of Mack still racing terrified me.

"That's a sweet thing to say. But, to tell you the truth—it's a huge relief to Mack that you've come on board."

"How so?"

"We were at a party in April and Mack had one too many shots of whiskey. He gets a little emotional when he drinks. He told me that he would have quit already if he knew my dad had someone to replace him."

I remembered leaning against Mack's arm out by the fire pit and feeling so sad with the thought of him retiring one day. I never imagined Colt Porter would make our driver's wish a reality so soon.

"The point of my story is that Mack, like the rest of us, is very grateful to you."

Thunder rumbled across the lake and clouds moved in along the horizon. Colt went to the bow. "A storm's coming. Let's get out of here." He pulled up the anchor, opened a hatch and stowed it. "I appreciate the offer to go to the funeral with you, but I still feel funny about it. I'm sure I'll see you there."

• • •

I didn't bother to hide Colt from my parents. My mother could sniff happiness on strangers walking down the street, never mind her own kin. Drivers and crew were like a legion of spies and big brothers who regularly reported my whereabouts and nocturnal activities to my parents. And then there was the fact that Colt was going to be driving for us in Winston Cup. Even if we could have hidden our relationship from my parents, there was no way that was going to happen come February.

My dad had taken Colt aside at the October Charlotte race and kept him in our motorhome for almost an hour. I killed time with two of our pit crew playing Crazy Eights. My father could have been giving Colt pointers on how to handle the turns on super speedways. Colt had a hard time in places like Daytona, Michigan and Charlotte because he didn't brake enough coming into the turns and would often get loose. Once, he got so loose he slid into a Winston Cup driver. It was an honest mistake, but one that cost the veteran driver the race.

Instead of brushing it off as *one of those racing deals,* the more seasoned driver acted like a two-year-old having a tantrum. He threw his helmet at Colt's car, told a reporter to fuck off, then refused to come out of his motorhome. Winston Cup drivers used Busch races as practice, and a chance to win easy money. Officials had been tossing around the idea of changing the rules to put an end to legitimate Cup drivers collecting points in Busch races. Until that happened, true Busch drivers never had a chance of dominating the lesser series.

When Colt emerged from our motorhome after my dad summoned him, I could tell from his sheepish expression that he'd been given the *you hurt my daughter and I'll hurt you* speech. It seemed a little late and a bit redundant for my dad to have the talk with Colt five months after showing up unannounced in Georgia, but I knew it meant that he could tell just from watching me how much I liked Colt.

• • •

As predicted, Colt and Brent Austin battled each other for the Busch Grand National Championship that fall. It came down to the final race in Martinsville the last weekend in October. As long as Brent didn't win, all Colt had to do was finish fifteenth or higher and he'd become the youngest person ever to earn the title. Knowing there was a good chance he'd win the points chase, my parents and I had already made plans to fly to the track and watch from the pits. I hadn't told Colt yet, as I wanted to surprise him.

I had to go to the race anyway. Tack thought it fitting that since I began my career at his newspaper with an article about the camaraderie, friendship and competition between Colt and Brent, I should cover the final race between the two. Brent would stay in Busch come the new season, and Colt would move up to Winston Cup—with us.

"I don't think this is a good idea," I told Tack. We were in his office and I felt like he was only half listening. He had a draft of an article from a senior writer laid on his desk in front of him and was madly marking it up.

He waved away my concern. "Just go, Piper P. Stop being modest and telling me that someone else could do it better. You've been here six months, kid, and you haven't failed me yet."

"It's not that."

He put down his pen and looked up at me. I had about five seconds to explain myself before he'd get bored and start proofreading again. "Then what is it?" he asked.

"Amy said something to Ken about how pissed she'd be if I got sent to cover the last race of the year. She thinks I only get the good stories because I'm sleeping with all the drivers."

He let out a long, aggravated breath. "And how exactly do you know this?"

"I was in the break room and she was right outside. She didn't know I was in there."

"Clearly," he muttered. "Fine, I'll talk to her and tell her to share the sandbox."

I had an image of two cats both pooping in a giant litter box all the while hissing at each other. "Please don't," I said quickly. "She already hates me. She doesn't need to think that I tattled on her, too."

"You're hard to help." He capped the marker and set it on his desk. "What, pray tell, would you like to have happen?"

"Send Amy to Martinsville. Let her have the story."

He rubbed his temples as if he was thinking about my proposal, or maybe I'd given him a headache. "Do you remember what I told you the day you came in for your interview?"

I thought back to that hot afternoon and wondered if Colt and I would be where we were if I hadn't gotten this job. "Um, not really."

"I called you an odd duck."

"Quack?" I honked in my best duck voice.

He laughed. "I said it then and I'll say it now. You're an odd duck. This is a cutthroat business and I've never had a journalist try to give away stories."

"I'm just trying to do the right thing." I hadn't advertised the fact that Colt and I were dating, and Tack hadn't asked. But sooner or later, we were going to have to talk about it. I remembered from an ethics in journalism course I took in college that reporters weren't supposed to have any personal connection to their subjects.

"Have it your way. I'll ask Amy if she's up for the assignment."

"What does that mean?"

"She's been out sick a bunch lately."

"Oh. I just thought she'd been away covering stories. Anyway, let me know if she can do it. I appreciate it." I left his office feeling a little guilty that I hadn't told him the whole truth. Sure, I was tired of Amy making snide comments about me. But I also wanted to spend the whole weekend with Colt being his cheerleader, not having to worry about deadlines and quotes and the ethical dilemma of writing about my boyfriend.

11

The week before Martinsville, I went home to visit my parents. When I let myself in the front door and no one answered when I called out, I walked to the race shop. Parked in the driveway was Colt's car and another I didn't recognize. I ran my fingers through my hair and patted my front pockets for lip gloss, but I didn't have any. Then I stepped into the waiting room. If I'd known Colt was going to be there, I would have worn something cuter than boot-cut jeans and tennis shoes.

"Dad?" I called out. "You here?"

My father came out of a conference room followed by my mother, Colt and his parents. "Noodle, is it six o'clock already?"

"It's actually almost seven," I said. "I got caught up at work." I hugged Meri and Doug Porter. Since running into them at Sandwich Construction, I'd spent a bunch of time with them at races. They seemed as committed to Colt as my parents were to me.

"What a lovely surprise," I said. "Will you be joining us for dinner?"

"Oh, no, we wouldn't want to impose," Meri told me. "We were just wrapping up a little meeting. So sorry to keep you from your family."

"Nonsense," my mother told her. "I made a casserole this morning. There's plenty for everyone." She glanced at her watch. "I had no idea how late it was; otherwise I would have invited you already."

My mother would rather have walked around all day with toilet paper stuck to her shoe than come across as a bad hostess.

"Are you sure?" Doug asked. He didn't seem as self-assured as he was the last few times I'd met him. I wondered if my dad intimidated him.

"Come," my father said. "The business portion of our night is over. Let's open a good bottle of whiskey and have dinner."

I hadn't said anything to Colt, and we both hung back until everyone else was out the door and walking up the hill to the house.

"Hi. Looks like you all had a meeting of the minds."

He kissed me in the dark. "Hi yourself. What a nice surprise."

I wasn't so sure that it was. My parents knew I was coming, and I wouldn't have put it past my dad to intentionally schedule a team meeting knowing I'd be home.

"Everything okay?"

"Oh sure. We were just talking about Martinsville."

"Are you excited?" A light in the house went on and people moved around in the kitchen. I slowed so we could have another minute alone.

"It's just another race," Colt said, stepping on twigs, making them snap. That was so Colt. He was about to make history as the youngest driver ever to win the Busch Grand National Championship, and he wouldn't allow himself any glory.

"Sure it is," I teased. "If you don't mind me asking, why were you talking about Martinsville? You know we'll be there, right?" As much as I'd wanted to surprise Colt at the race, I wanted him to know I'd be there to watch him make history.

"I need to talk to you about that." He stuffed his hands in his pockets and toed the ground. We'd gotten to the deck and my father opened the door, holding a tray of crab puffs.

"Get your hind ends in here and have an appetizer," he commanded, resting his free hand on Colt's shoulder.

"Later," Colt mouthed to me as the three of us walked inside.

My mother and Meri were by the fire, drinking red wine and talking about books, and Doug had come to the doorway to join my father, Colt and me. My dad handed Colt a whiskey, but he asked if he could have a soft drink instead. I didn't know if he was nervous or trying to make a good impression, but I smiled at the thought of him sipping a Diet Mountain Dew all night.

"We have about twenty minutes before the casserole is done," my mother called from the living room. "Why don't you four join us over here?"

I sat next to my mom on the loveseat, even though there was an empty space next to Colt. He frowned and I stuck my tongue out at him.

"This is a happy coincidence," I said, although I didn't believe it. My father rarely did anything without considering all possible outcomes. I was dying to know why he wanted me there at the same time as Colt's parents. "It must be kismet," I said, turning my head in my dad's direction. "Or like someone arranged it."

My dad cleared his throat. "What did you make us, Poppi? Something smells delightful."

My mom put her wineglass on a coaster and got up. "Speaking of, I better check it. It's my famous chicken pad thai," she said. "I hope everyone likes spicy."

"The spicier the better," Meri said, getting up to help her. I often went to the bathroom at the same time as my friends when we were at bars. I wondered if I'd go into the kitchen with them at dinner parties when I was older.

"Tell the truth," Doug said to my dad. "What's going to be the most challenging part of next year?"

My dad sipped his whiskey and held it in his mouth for a few seconds before swallowing. "The toughest part for me or your boy?"

I kept my eyes on Colt while his dad answered. "I didn't think there were any tough parts for you anymore. There's no one in this sport more successful than you. I was talking about Colt." Doug tapped Colt's shoe with his. "What kind of tangles do you think he'll get himself into?"

Colt was one of the cleanest drivers I'd ever seen race. My dad wouldn't have hired him otherwise. He said racing was difficult and dangerous enough without having some hothead intentionally wrecking other cars because he was pissed or mouthing off to the press because he didn't win. If anything, Colt had gotten even more respectful since signing with Pierson. He always tucked in his shirt, called everyone sir or ma'am and was the last to enter restaurants and conference rooms because he was holding the door.

I reflexively opened my mouth to defend Colt, but the look in his eyes made me stop. My dad spoke up.

"There will be no tangles for Colt. He's made it through three years of Busch races without any significant incidents. Winston Cup won't be any different. But I do think his biggest obstacle will be convincing himself that he's good enough."

"Confidence has never been Colt's problem," Doug interjected.

Even the most talented Busch drivers faltered their first year in Winston Cup. They started the season in Daytona cocky and confident. They'd all spent plenty of time testing Cup cars and had raced at the storied track plenty of times before. But none were ready for the reality of driving a race that was 500 miles instead of 200, or how much more skilled and competitive the veteran drivers were. It was only a matter of time before Colt put his car in the wall or accidentally rubbed panels with someone who needed to then teach him a lesson.

By the middle of March, every Winston Cup rookie was visibly humbler. The peacock strut of the young and confident was replaced with hushed tones and slouched shoulders. That's when the best team owners became invaluable. For the most part, new drivers were young like Colt—just kids, really. And they needed a father figure to convince them they'd made the right decision by moving up. Colt wouldn't stumble and stutter—as long as he had Planter Pierson by his side.

I thought my dad would set Doug straight and explain to him that Colt would get knocked around both in his car and mentally, but my dad just said, "Whatever trouble comes our way, we'll handle it together. Because that's what family does."

Just then my mom came out of the kitchen. "Hope everyone's hungry," she said. "Dinner is ready."

My dad, Doug and Colt got up and helped carry food to the dining room table. I filled a water pitcher that had long ago been a trophy and set it on a sideboard. After we were seated, my dad raised his glass and we all did the same.

"To family," he said. No one moved, waiting for him to speak again. But he took a sip of his drink, ending the toast.

We passed our plates around the table filling them with homemade biscuits, casserole and sautéed zucchini. I was starving, but no one had started eating, so I waited.

"I just want to say," Meri began, smiling too much, "that you both are so sweet to agree to allow Colt's tire changer and friend, Scott Stephenson, to move to your team next year."

Is that what their meeting was about? Staff changes? It hadn't occurred to me that if Scott was coming on board, we'd need to find a new position for Dave Reynolds, Mack's right-front-tire changer. Colt told me early on that he'd told my dad and Cal Thompson that he and Scott were a package deal. My father told me later that Colt was willing to give up a seat at Pierson Racing's table to ensure he stayed with his friend. That made him respect Colt even more. "That Porter kid has an old man's values," my dad had said.

"It's our pleasure," my dad told Meri now. "Scott's the best at what he does and we're honored he'll be a part of our team next year." He talked like there was a camera on him.

I filled everyone's water glasses, topped off my mom's and Meri's wine, and got Colt another can of Diet Mountain Dew.

When I returned to the table, my dad and Doug were still discussing the pit crew—who would stay in their current position, who would move to a new one, and if the two of them thought anyone needed to go. My father was fiercely loyal to his staff. He never asked anyone to get to work before he did or stay after he left. His dedication was rewarded with twelve guys who'd been with him for more than a decade. The average lifespan of a crew member with any one team was less than three seasons.

I didn't have much to contribute to their conversation, so I cleared the dinner plates and got the key lime pie I'd made the night before and stashed in the fridge. I cut it into eight pieces, put six slices on plates and carried them two by two to the table. I ate in near silence, watching Colt watching his father. Doug seemed to be studying my dad, who was in the middle of a monologue.

"You need to make them feel like you have their backs no matter what. Even if one of my guys makes a mistake, I stand by him. If employees feel like they're going to be punished for making an error, they will never take a chance and do something brilliant."

Although my dad usually cleaned up if my mom or I cooked, I cleared our dessert plates so he could keep dazzling Colt and his parents. As per my mother, I rinsed the dishes in the sink before I put them in the dishwasher, a task that offended me. Washing plates before putting them in the dishwasher was like cleaning the house before the cleaners came. I shut off the water and started to load the plates when I heard my father say, "Well, our marketing department is solid. But if you'd like, I'll ask around and see if any other teams are looking to hire."

Who were they talking about? And why was Doug Porter in my parents' living room trying to hustle a job for someone? Doug spoke, his voice low. I stopped loading the dishes so I could listen.

"She's been through so much and she's like kin to us. The team she works for got sold and the new owner's son is taking her job. We'd really appreciate it if you could find a place for her next year. If not on your team, then maybe with another. Anywhere would be fine."

They were talking about a *her*? *Colt's her?*

I tried to catch Colt's eye, but he just stared at the carpet, rubbing his temples. He seemed sad or guilty. Finally, he raised his head and looked just like I did when my mother caught me using her eye makeup without asking. *Oh no. No . . . no . . . no!* Things had been going so well for Colt and me that I'd almost forgotten about his ex.

Everyone had moved into the living room. I turned and glared at Colt. He'd been watching me and dropped his eyes. He'd known exactly what they were going to meet about and never told me. I decided it was time Colt told me the whole story about his ex-girlfriend. I picked up the coffee pot and brought it to the living room.

"Would anyone like a refill?" I asked. I had no takers, so I put it back in the kitchen and then took my spot on the couch. "What are we talking about?" I asked the room.

For a moment, no one spoke. "Oh, just personnel changes for the upcoming season," my dad said.

"Oh yeah? Do we have new team members, other than Scott Stephenson?" I gave Colt an annoyed smile, the same one I used when my mother was trying to take my picture, only I had to hold the pose because it took her three minutes to figure out how to work the camera. But no one answered, so I drank my coffee even though Colt motioned toward the kitchen like he wanted to talk.

Perhaps sensing the tension, Doug said in a loud, cheery voice, "Martinsville ought to be quite a race. I'm so thankful we'll all be there to celebrate."

Suddenly the last thing I wanted to do was go to the race I'd been looking forward to all summer. "I'm not sure I can make it," I said suddenly. "My boss just gave me a big assignment and I might have to stay home and work on it."

My father startled in his seat. "Piper!" Only he could say my name and make it sound like an admonishment. "Of course you're going. Piersons support their teammates. That's what we do."

I felt Colt staring at me, but I wouldn't meet his eye. "Yes sir," I said. There was no disobeying Planter Pierson. "I suppose I can work from there."

Doug Porter leaned forward in his seat. "Don't scare us like that. We're going to make history at Martinsville and then again next year when Colt wins the Cup rookie title." He smiled when he said it, but somehow his tone sounded menacing.

"Dad," Colt said softly, almost whining. "I told you I just want to drive my best and make Mr. Pierson proud. I don't care if I win the rookie title or not. There are lots of other great Busch drivers who will move up with me. It's far from a done deal."

I felt bad for Colt in that instant. I could see a lifetime of his father pressuring him to be the best at everything.

"Planter, son," my dad said. "And you have exactly the right attitude. My mentor used to tell me that form follows function. You try your hardest and good things will come to you."

"Thank you, Planter," Colt said. "I'll do my best every time I get in one of your race cars. That's a promise."

"Now that that's settled," Doug said, "I want to invite all of you to our team dinner next Friday night. You'll be our guests."

I glanced at my dad to gauge his reaction. It almost sounded like Doug was inviting us to the race, which would have been ridiculous. My father belonged everywhere he went. Even though he wouldn't have a team at Martinsville, people would have been surprised if he wasn't there.

"Thank you, Doug," I said, just to fill the silence. "That's very kind of you."

I didn't need an invitation from Doug Porter to show my pretty face at Martinsville. Nor did my father. But I appreciated his offer. Colt's dad was clearly trying to reciprocate my family's hospitality.

"We'd be honored to be your guests next weekend. Isn't that right, Daddy?" I could already see the battle between the men about who would pay for dinner. It'd be a fun spectator sport.

I checked my watch. "I have an early staff meeting tomorrow. Can I crash here?" I looked at my parents. Their house was closer to my office than my apartment, and thanks to my dad and his survivalist instincts, I kept a go bag there.

"Of course," my mom said. "I changed the sheets this morning."

"We should get going, too," Meri said, standing up and looking behind her. "Oh dear, I think I left my wrap at the race shop."

My father had always been adept at reading people, and he understood Meri's intent.

"It's a nice night for a stroll," he said. "Why don't the four of us walk down together to get it." He turned to Colt. "Would you mind staying for a few minutes and keeping Piper company?"

Colt waited till they disappeared; then he hugged me hard. "Can we talk?" he asked. When I didn't answer, he said, "I should have told you that she works for a team and I still see her around." I found it odd that I'd known about her existence for almost half a year and I still didn't know her name.

I pulled away from him. "It's fine."

"Let's go out tomorrow night and I'll tell you everything."

The last thing I wanted to do was waste a night with Colt talking about another girl.

"No, let's go out tomorrow night and do anything but that. You can tell me your race strategy for Martinsville."

He exhaled. "I'm so glad you changed your mind. I couldn't imagine going to that race without you."

His naiveté annoyed me. "Grow up," I said. "How would it look to the press if your new team owner and his family weren't there to watch you set a record?"

"Oh. I get it. You're going for the good press? That's cool."

"I'm going for you," I said at last. "We both know that."

12

Liza and I went shopping for my weekend at Martinsville. It was going to be a big deal, and I had to look good when Colt made history.

Silly rules prevented me from wearing anything I had in my closet that showed off my best features—super toned arms, long legs and pink toenails. At least there wasn't a no-cleavage law. I saw it coming down the pike, though. There seemed to be a subtle shift to clean up the sport a bit, to make it more family friendly. To sort out the riffraff, I suggested to the round table of my dad's weekly poker buddies that anyone who passed through the gates on race day—fans and drivers alike—had to take a quiz with questions such as, *When was the war of 1812?* and *Who is buried in Grant's tomb?* Maybe even a real brain twister such as *Which word is always spelled incorrectly?* My dad laughed and said he'd pitch the idea at the next owners' meeting. One of his friends, the general manager of another Cup team, kept calling out commonly misspelled words, and a crew chief glared at me.

"*Incorrectly* is always spelled *incorrectly*," the crew chief finally said.

. . .

I showed up at Martinsville in hotter-than-hell black, shimmery pants and a see-through blouse with a tight, low-cut camisole underneath. I couldn't remember the last time I'd dressed like this—and it felt good. Liza had spent an hour and a half curling the ends of my hair so I had a carefree, tousled appearance as if I'd been on a windy beach. It took me twenty minutes to get from the front gates to Colt's transporter because every pit crew guy I'd ever known stopped me to chat. Most were well educated, well spoken, and well dressed when they weren't in their fire suits. All of them were the nicest men I'd ever met. Sometimes I thought everyone was exceedingly kind to me because I was Planter Pierson's kid.

Somewhat akin to the mafia, in racing everyone watched out for their friends—especially their friends' kids. If one of my garage-area playmates ever got fresh with me, there was a long line of brawny guys waiting to kick some ass.

Slung over my shoulder and clashing with my outfit was my messenger bag. Tack had given the assignment for the championship story to Amy, but a few days before I left for the race, he called me into his office.

"Piper P," he'd said, his tone unusually flat. "Amy is . . . well, she has . . . " He rubbed his temple as if he had a headache. "Amy's sick again. So I need you to go to Martinsville."

"Of course, anything I can do to help," I told him, secretly happy I'd have a reason to drop in on Colt whenever I felt like it.

Tack looked at me, puzzled, no doubt expecting me to fiercely object as I had before. This time I had an ulterior motive.

"So, you're good with this?"

"All good," I said. "But is it a problem? Colt and me?" I couldn't look him in the eye. "I probably shouldn't be writing about him."

"Well, the race is in two days. So we don't really have a choice. But we'll talk about it when you get back."

"Okay," I said quietly, opening the door.

"Hey, Piper?" Tack said to my back.

"Yeah?" I made myself meet his eyes.

"I'm happy for you."

•   •   •

My five-by-seven notebook with the fluffy kitty on the cover was my shield. As long as I was on assignment, I had a reason to be in Colt's transporter and spy on anyone who might be in there. Although I decided after dinner at my parents' house that it was time to have the talk with Colt about what was going on with him and his ex, we hadn't gotten around to it yet. And I didn't think it'd be fair to have the conversation at the most important race of his career.

Colt hadn't told me much about her. I didn't know how old she was, if she was pretty, how they met, or what kept him so tied to her. I assumed she was attractive. Colt bordered between adorable and handsome, depending on his mood, and he was a race car driver. In North Carolina, that was better than being Mick Jagger or one of those boy band people.

I knocked on Colt's navy-blue motorhome, thinking how understated his was compared to some of the others. A lot of these drivers were barely out of their teens, living on their own and had more money than most of the world had ever dreamed about. Unfortunately, they had neither the maturity nor the common sense to responsibly manage their lifestyles. Maybe it wasn't so bad that Doug Porter seemed to control most of his son's life.

"There she is," Scott said when he opened the door. "We've been waiting on you." His tone was entirely genuine, but his bug eyes and plastered smile told me *she* was there.

I winked at him and pushed him two steps backward into the transporter. I kicked the door shut with one high heel. "I'm here!"

Colt gaped at me. I couldn't tell if he was surprised that I sounded so happy even though the girl sitting next to him must have been his ex, or if he was taken aback by the way I was dressed.

"Piper," he said, weakly. "You look so . . . not you."

I touched his cheek. "What can I say? I'm finally feeling like myself again. Must be the company I'm keeping."

Twice during the fall, Colt had gotten me to sit in the driver's seat of his street car. The first time I cried. The second time I didn't.

"You're Piper?" the girl next to Colt gushed. "It's so nice to finally meet you." She hugged me hard before I could stop her. "Colt talks about you all the time." So, she was a crafty vixen—reassuring me that Colt talked about *me,* but also letting me know they still spent time together.

I wouldn't have expected anyone but Liza to pick up on her intention, but Colt jumped in. "Yes, we run into each other at prayer services sometimes." I squeezed his hand, letting him know it was okay. We were okay. Poor guy looked like he was going to barf on his shoes.

I took a step back so I could study her without staring. She was so bubbly that I feared her giddiness might be contagious and that I'd start talking like I was twelve. She was cute in a way that I never would have noticed if we'd been at the same bar or store, but she wore way too much makeup. She was skinny but didn't have a great figure. Her hips were slim, and she had no butt or boobs. I'd never seen a pair up close, but I was certain she was wearing mom jeans, high-waisted and kind of shapeless. With lace brocade across the top and puffy sleeves, her peasant blouse would have been cute if she were eight—and it was 1782.

I heard Colt talking, but I wasn't paying a lick of attention to him. I was too enthralled with her. She had nice eyes, greenish brown, but a little on the small side. Her hair was her best feature, long, thick and a beautiful reddish color. Not redheaded-stepchild red, but a soft auburn.

When I got done sizing her up, I was thoroughly confounded. She looked a good ten years Colt's senior. Maybe this was a Mrs. Robinson fantasy. I was younger and prettier than her. *Two points for me.* But he still wouldn't let her go. *A million points for her.*

I stayed long enough to ask Colt a few questions for my article and for Mr. and Mrs. Porter to come in and remind me that tonight was their team dinner. They said they'd just come from my parents' motorhome and had received the bad news that my mom was studying for midterms and wouldn't be able to attend, so my dad was going to stay in and keep her company. He'd never leave my mom alone in a hotel room so he could go socialize with other people. Family meant everything to him. It was also a convenient excuse for him not to allow another man to pay for his meal. And since Whatshername was still there, the Porters invited her, too, and she was more than happy to accept.

•   •   •

That night, as we filed into Ruth's Chris Steak House, I made sure I sat at the other end of the table from the Porters and Colt. Scott started to sit next to Meri but took a seat on my left. He leaned into my shoulder and whispered, "What's up, Piper? Why are you down here all by your lonesome?" He smelled of mint and fresh air.

"Oh, you know." I nodded toward Colt. "I like to people watch."

Scott scoffed. "I get it." We watched the redhead sit next to Doug Porter. "This has got to be weird for you."

I reached for my water. "When Colt and I first started dating, he told me he had an ex who was still close to his parents. I guess he wasn't kidding."

"Doug is like the patron saint of lost souls."

"What's that mean?" I asked. I wanted to hate this girl, but with her big hair and sweet smile, she just seemed so . . . eager.

"That whole family is very protective of her."

"Protective? Why?" *Dammit!* I should have asked Colt to tell me their backstory. But I'd been living with this fantasy that if we didn't talk about her, she'd magically go away.

Scott slung his arm around me and leaned in close so he wouldn't be overheard. "Colt never told you? Her ex is crazy."

"Crazy like he's not playing with a full deck or crazy like he'd boil a bunny?" Almost every driver I knew had had a run in or two with an obsessed fan. Most were harmless.

"Crazy like he put her in the hospital once."

We shouldn't have been talking about this at a table with twenty other people. I was sorry I'd brought it up. When I noticed the woman on my right was eavesdropping, I straightened a little and said in a normal voice, "Why yes, I do enjoy working at *NASCAR Weekly*. It's very fulfilling."

I flashed Scott a look and he seemed to understand that we were being observed. I purposely dropped my napkin between us, and when I reached for it, I whispered to him, "I wish I'd known. I feel like an asshole now."

"All you had to do was ask," he said.

"I didn't even have to do that. Colt's been trying to tell me about her for months."

He leveled his gaze. "Piper, it was bad. I was at Colt's the night it happened. She called, hysterical, couldn't even get the words out. So we went to her house and there she was—a black eye and a broken arm. We took her to the hospital and the doctor said he had to call the cops. But she refused to press charges."

"Brilliant," I said, eyeing her.

He poked me in the ribs. "Don't get all catty on me. I'm just trying to make you understand that what that poor girl has lived through is serious."

"Now I really feel like an asshole," I said. I glanced down the table at her. The waiter had delivered appetizers, and she was happily picking apart a fried octopus platter.

"So what happened?"

"She said she loved Colt too much to put him in the middle, so she broke up with him." Scott took a sip of water and wiped his mouth with a napkin. "Honestly, I think she was afraid for him. Didn't want him to get hurt, too."

My stomach felt like there was a boulder in it, and I pushed my plate away. "So, nobody fell out of love or cheated. It was just two people who loved each other trying to protect one another. Great. How am I supposed to compete with that?"

"Piper." Scott's tone went from sympathetic to cold. "This is not about you. Colt's crazy about you. But he still cares about her."

"Did she go back to the guy? After he busted her up?"

A pretty waitress filled our waters while two others delivered salads. I watched the redhead at the other end of the table stuff the last of an appetizer in her mouth before a server took her plate.

"Let's not talk about it now," Scott said. "We should be cheering Colt on, not whispering to each other." He picked up three warm rolls and juggled them. "Now you know their deal." He stopped juggling and put two of the rolls on his plate and one on mine. I picked it up, slathered it in butter and took a bite.

"I suppose I could talk to her this weekend," I said quietly. "She seems like she could use a girlfriend." She and Meri were chatting, Doug and Colt's crew chief were drawing diagrams of tracks on a napkin, and Colt was walking around saying hello to everyone.

Someone at the other end of the table must have ordered wine because the pretty waitress came back with a prettier friend, and they went around asking us if we wanted red or white. Scott held up my glass for red, then handed it to me. "Shut up and drink. Enough talk for tonight."

I took the glass from Scott and said a pouty thank you. "I just want him to love me best," I said.

"He does, you idiot."

I couldn't hide my smile. "Thanks for saying that."

"I only speak the truth."

Despite Scott's reassurance, all through dinner I couldn't stop studying them and strained to hear their conversations. Colt never called her by name or even a nickname, something that seemed incredibly impersonal to me. He was constantly calling me Pipes and Pierson and P., shortening my name the way we do when talking to people we're close to. I may have been reading too much into it, but it gave me hope and frustrated me because I still didn't know her name. And now that we'd officially met, it was too late to ask.

Colt's mother was cordial to her, including her in whatever conversation she was having. But Meri Porter seemed like the kind of woman who would go out of her way to make others feel comfortable. A few times I thought I caught Meri checking out her outfit. She wasn't badly dressed. She wore a simple, tea-length, off-white dress with long, capped sleeves and a shiny pair of pink pumps. She seemed so simple in her slightly ill-fitting dress that I felt badly for her.

My parents had been married by the time they were my age. Until recently, I had wanted to be alone. Didn't want to risk loving someone and losing him. But this girl seemed desperate in her longing to fit in with Colt, his friends and the team.

We ate and drank as if Colt had already won the championship. Meri and Doug Porter told stories about Colt as a toddler sitting on their laps steering the family station wagon around the driveway, and as a teenager driving his go-kart to school when he missed the bus.

"In my defense," said Colt, "my mom told me if I missed the bus one more time, I was going to have to find my own way to school. She never said *how* I was supposed to get there. I thought I deserved bonus points for not even being late."

"Imagine our surprise when Trooper Dunaway brought Colt and his go-kart home an hour later," Colt's dad said. He put his arm around his wife while she was still holding hands with their son. *What a happy, perfect family,* I thought. I belonged to a happy, almost perfect family. Why couldn't I belong to his, too?

"There's something to be said for growing up in a small town." Colt raised his glass and we all cheered him. "It miraculously never showed up on my record."

"You were a handful," Meri said kindly. "A handsome, charming handful." I wondered if his mom knew that some things never changed.

"Well, what about you two?" Colt pointed between his parents. "Remember the time you locked yourselves out of the house in your pajamas?"

His dad spit out his drink. "I'd totally forgotten about that. There we were, Meri in her short nightie and me—"

"In your boxers and no shirt," his wife finished for him.

"So how did you get back in?" I asked, watching Whatshername, trying to gauge if she'd heard this story before. I didn't want her to know more about Colt's family than me. She leaned forward in her seat, anxious as I was to hear the end of their tale.

"Lucky for them," Colt spoke up, "their neighbors were home and had an extra key." He grinned like there might be more to the tale. "Their very strict religious neighbors. Their neighbors who believed all skin except for the face and hands should be covered. The family who didn't even allow their children to say things like *holy cow* because it mocked religion."

"Oh, you should have heard the lecture we got," Doug said.

"We stood on their stoop," Meri interjected, "while Mr.

Troyer explained the importance of modesty. I wanted to explain the importance of brevity because the whole time he was making me feel like a teenager who got caught with the neighbor boy, I was freezing my butt off."

"Eventually we got them to give us our spare key and conveniently forgot to give it back," Doug said. "Now we're the proud owners of one of those fake rocks that you use to hide keys."

"If you don't mind me asking," I said, wiping my mouth with my napkin, "what were you doing outside in your jammies?"

Doug and Meri looked at each other. "Oh, we'd forgotten to check the mail that day and we were waiting for a magazine to come." I was immediately sorry I'd asked as I could only imagine one type of publication that would get them out of bed at night.

The Porters filled lulls in our dinner conversation with more charming and corny stories. It was clear that they were holding court and this was their night. I asked funny questions and gave witty answers, but for the most part, they had the spotlight. Whatshername was quieter than I wanted her to be. She answered questions with a sweet smile and a soft voice. But she rarely made eye contact, and she didn't speak unless spoken to. This was not what I had hoped for. I wanted her to get sloppy drunk and make a fool of herself, spill red wine on Meri's white linen pants or pick a fight with Colt for flirting with the waitress, even though he didn't. At the very least, I wanted her to drink enough to get chatty with me and confess why she didn't marry Colt.

Other than being introduced to an exquisite pinot noir from Australia, I didn't learn much that night. Colt gave equal attention to everyone at the table, never giving the impression that anyone was more important than someone else. He also excused himself from the table to pee more times than a drunk college girl. Every time he squeezed behind my chair, he touched my shoulder or tangled his fingers in my hair. I thought about following him and maybe getting frisky in a bathroom stall, but

I couldn't, knowing his parents were fifty feet away.

Scott and I both tried to chip in for dinner, but Doug wouldn't hear of it. "Don't be silly," he told us. "Scott's been our second son for more than half his life. And now we have you in the fold." He squeezed my shoulder.

"Well, thank you for including me," I said graciously. "You and Mrs. Porter are great storytellers." We walked into the night and stood on the sidewalk.

"Call me Meri, darlin', please." I hadn't seen her come out of the restaurant. "You are a little ray of sunshine. I'm looking forward to seeing more of you in February, if not sooner."

Scott and I stood in the parking lot waiting for Colt to come out of the restaurant. It was earlier than I thought, not even eleven. Amazing how slowly time went when I had to eat dinner across the table from the girl I'd spent six months pretending didn't exist.

"How was your lobster?" Scott asked.

"You should know—you kept stealing bites off my plate." I jabbed him in the ribs. A couple nodded at us as they entered the brass-handled front doors. No doubt they thought we were together. I stepped away from him. I liked Scott too much to give him the wrong idea.

"Hey," I said. "Where's Sasha? I can't believe she's not here."

I heard Colt's voice behind me. I turned to see him come out of the restaurant alone. "My sister had a late exam today," he said. "I couldn't convince the goody-goody to skip class. She'll be here in the morning."

Knowing I'd have her to hang out with in the pits made me smile. Sasha and I had become good friends and got together even when Colt wasn't around. We'd gone to the movies a bunch of times and joined the local gym so we could play racquetball. We got through one and a half games before I hit her in the face with the ball, gave her a bloody nose, and that was the end of that.

"Okay then," I said. "Thanks again for dinner. We'll see you tomorrow."

Colt was staying in his motorhome at the track, and Scott and I were at the same hotel, so we'd come together.

"Wait," Colt called, his eyes pleading. "It's so early. Let's take a stroll on the Heritage Trail." He looked upward. "It's such a beautiful night. We can walk from here." The redhead had come out of the restaurant and was standing next to Colt. I felt a little sick until both she and Colt handed separate tickets to the valet.

I turned to Scott and whispered in his ear. "Please don't make me stargaze with them."

He squeezed my shoulder. "I think we're going to pass," he said. "Early morning."

Colt's expression went from hopeful to sour. "Yeah, that's probably a good idea. I need to be on top of my game tomorrow." We said goodnight, and Scott and I got in his car to go back to the Marriot. I closed my door a little too hard.

13

In the last race of the 1989 Busch Grand National Series, there were eight caution flags for forty laps. Twice Colt pitted under green, only to have the yellow flag fly as he was pulling back out on the track, sending him to the back of the thirty-two-car field. Another time a lug nut got stuck and Brent Austin and several other drivers beat him out of the pits. It seemed like for as many times as Colt had the race and the championship wrapped up, fate conspired against him.

"I don't think I can watch any more of this," I told Sasha. I checked my notes. I had all the information I needed to write the article. I loved that I wasn't stuck in the press box when I was working. Wandering around the track and observing pit crews gave me a much better vantage point.

We'd been in Colt's pits for almost three hours, and I was too nervous to sit still. I turned my back to the track, and saw Whatshername coming toward us. "Shit," I said, loud enough for Sasha to hear me over the roar of the engines. "I hate to ask you this, but—"

She followed my gaze. "Good God, woman," Sasha interrupted. "Yes, Colt is crazy about you. No, he's not getting back together with her."

"Thank you for saying all that, but I was going to ask you what her name is."

Sasha pointed at her. "Candice? How do you not know that? Do you and my brother talk at all?"

Now I felt stupid for being so belligerent every time Colt tried to tell me about her. "Can we talk about this later? *Candi* is right there." I said her name mockingly.

"Sure," Sasha said. "But a word to the wise. Her name is Candice. She says Candi makes her sound like a stripper and she hasn't met many strippers who were high school valedictorians."

"Duly noted," I said as Candice joined us in the pit.

"Hey, *Candice*," Sasha called. "Where've you been hiding?"

Candice opened a small notebook, then said loudly, "If Colt doesn't move up in the next seventeen laps, he might not win the championship." She ran her finger down a page filled with math equations. "I've been calculating every possible scenario for Colt to end up first place in the points and I'm starting to go a little cross-eyed." Maybe she was brighter than I'd thought. "Do either of you want to take a break and get a coffee?"

I checked the leaderboard behind us. There were eighty-seven laps left, and Colt's car number wasn't listed in the top ten. The last thing I wanted to do was to sit here helplessly watching his year go to shit. "It's way too hot for coffee," I yelled over the din of the engines. "I'll hang here with Sasha." It was almost ninety—unseasonably warm for Virginia this time of year.

Sasha jumped out of her director's chair. "Iced coffee, my friend," she said to me. "Best thing ever."

I hadn't known how much I wanted Colt to win the championship until it seemed like he wasn't going to. Sitting in the pits, with no respite from the sun, I couldn't stay still any longer. I was afraid if I went to our motorhome, even for a minute, something would happen to him. Stupid as it was, I secretly believed that as long as I was watching from the pits, he'd drive a good, safe race. That magical thinking had worked since my dad's accident.

"I guess I could use a sweet tea," I shouted over the noise. I tugged on Sasha's sleeve. "Come on."

"I was hoping you'd bring me back something cold," she yelled back. I flashed her a wide-eyed, panicked look. She mouthed *good luck* and pulled the brim of her straw hat over her eyes.

Candice walked with me to get the drinks. I ordered three sweet teas and pulled out a twenty to pay. "Hold up there, little lady," the vendor said, waving off my gesture. "You must be your daddy's girl."

"Yes sir," I said. My Southern upbringing kept me from sarcastically pointing out the obvious.

Mr. Vendor Man apparently realized his mistake and belly laughed. "You must be Planter's little girl." I was almost five foot ten and old enough to drink. "You look just like him."

"Yes sir," I repeated.

"Well, that settles it," he said. "No kin of Planter Pierson's pays for drinks at my restaurant." *Restaurant* was a strong word for his eight-by-fifteen-foot trailer.

"Thank you. You're very kind." I put the plastic cups in a cardboard tray and carried it to a small bar with sweeteners, sugar, lemons and milk. I put it down and handed Candice her drink. She took the top off and squeezed the juice from a lemon in and then mixed it. I waited for her to throw away a wooden stirrer and then we turned toward the pits.

"I'm glad we have a few minutes alone," Candice said, walking to a picnic table and sitting. "I want to talk to you about something."

I sat and took my drink out of the tray, then fanned myself with a paper plate someone had left on the table. "What's up?"

"It seems like you've gotten to be pretty good friends with Colt."

I shrugged. "He spends a good amount of time at our race shop, so I see him pretty often. Why do you ask?"

"I was just wondering." She paused and shook her drink, watching a lemon seed float to the bottom. "Do you know if he's dating anyone?"

I almost choked on my tea. "I've never seen him with anyone." That wasn't an untruth.

"And you? Are you seeing anyone?"

She was not making conversation. She was fishing. I was bored and hot and wanted to go back to the pits. "I think we should get back," I told her. "I don't want to miss any more of the race." We stood up and began weaving our way through tables.

She put her hand on my shoulder from behind me. "I just want him to be happy," she said. I couldn't help but think she was mocking me. I stopped and turned toward her. "You know, we talked about having a life together. Adopting a dog. Spending the off season on the water. Getting married."

I was terrified of water but never told Colt so he'd keep taking me out on his boat, and I hated dogs. Still, those were things I should be doing with him.

"So, what happened?"

"I got spooked. It seemed so perfect. And I guess I got scared."

"Wow," I said, as we both started walking again. "That's too bad. He seems like a great guy." I felt a bit guilty for not fessing up that Colt and I had been dating since August.

• • •

As the racing pundits had predicted, Colt won the Busch Grand National Championship. Doug was Colt's spotter, so he spent the entire race on the tower above the grandstands with thirty-one other men telling their drivers where the wrecks were and whether they needed to go high or low to get around them. And Meri was the backup scorer, which meant she sat in an air-conditioned section of the suites with a herd of other heavily made-up women marking lines on paper every time their driver crossed the start-finish line. Officially their jobs were to keep track of who was on the lead lap in case there was a power outage and the electronic scoring system failed. Unofficially, it was a temperature-controlled room with never-ending food and drinks that gave fussy girlfriends and bored wives something to do.

The Porters graciously invited me and just about everyone else at the race to a party later that night where they were expecting the standings to be officially calculated, confirming that Colt had become the youngest driver ever to win the Busch Grand National Championship.

I'd been to enough victory parties, consolation parties and *we want to get drunk and screw, so let's have a party* parties to know what to expect. Everybody would want a piece of Colt. Reporters, photographers, fans and crew would literally stand in line to have his attention for a minute or two. Yet, somehow, I was still surprised when I shuffled through an impromptu receiving line consisting of Sasha, Colt's parents, his crew chief, team owner, a few ElectroAde big wigs and finally Colt.

I envisioned how he'd handle his five seconds with me. I pictured him pulling me into a tight hug and sticking his tongue in my ear, or him whispering four different ways he was going to violate me when we were finally alone. I checked my watch when I got in line behind the wife of another driver. She talked to me about white-gold versus yellow-gold jewelry for twelve minutes and fifty-seven seconds before I got to Colt. If my parents had been with me, at least I would have had someone to talk to while I waited. But they congratulated him at the track, and my dad made a speech about how proud he was to call Colt the newest member of the Pierson Racing family, and then they split so my mother could finish studying. Once they left, I sat with Colt, his parents, Cal Thompson and their crew chief and took notes while they talked about what it took to win the championship. I hadn't planned on that being my official interview with the Busch Grand National Champion, but I was glad to get it out of the way before that night's festivities started.

"Hi there," I said to Colt when I finally reached the end of the line, feeling foolishly, stupidly like the world had stopped and it was just us. I opened my arms and waited for him to grab me tight or whirl me around.

"Thanks so much for coming." He shook my hand, kissed me on the cheek and sent me toward the bar. And that was it. All night. Not a glance. Not a message delivered by Scott telling me to meet him in the bathroom. Not a quick ass grab on his way to the crudités. Nothing. Every time I tried to join the conversation with whomever he was talking to, it seemed like someone else came and pulled him away. There was always a photographer or a fan waiting. I'd already gotten all the quotes I'd need to write the article Amy was supposed to.

I thought I should ask Colt a few more inane questions, just to be near him. But I didn't want to use work as an excuse to make him talk to me. So, I did the only thing any self-respecting girl could do. I got drunk.

Scott found me half asleep, or maybe I was closer to being passed out, under the condom machine in the men's room. Ever the good friend, he wiped my mouth, gave me a few breath mints and snagged a small bottle of hairspray from the ladies' room to fix my updo.

"Please take me to the airport and push me out of the car when we get to departures," I told him. A nasty headache had already set in, which made me want to start drinking again. There was something to be said for that hair-of-the-dog philosophy.

"No such luck, my prettiest Piper. You already signed away your rights to go home. We're guests of the great state of Virginia for one more night." Scott pushed the button for the elevator and leaned against the wall while we waited. "Now do you want to tell me what's going on?"

"Did he ignore me all night because of *her*?"

"He was *busy* all night because he just won the Busch points race." He hesitated for a moment, as if trying to decide what else to say.

The elevator doors opened, and Scott got on without waiting for me. Just before they closed, leaving me drunk and alone in the lobby of this swanky hotel, I turned sideways and scooted in. "You could have held it for me," I said, pouting. Scott's hands were clenched into fists. He pressed the number for my floor, but still didn't speak. I couldn't stop.

"I thought I'd be enough."

"You know her ex-husband hit her." He said it with such hatred that I stumbled away from him, against the back wall of the elevator. "Why can't you just let them be friends? Are you really that selfish?"

I'd never heard Scott talk to anyone like this before, never mind me. He was forever telling me I was the coolest girl he knew. "I . . . I can. They can be friends," I sputtered. "I'm sorry, Scott."

The elevator chimed with each floor we passed, and I hoped no one else would get on. "Colt loves you, Piper. And he's doing the best he can. Cut him a little slack."

• • •

When I got up the next morning, I rang room service and asked for a sliced cucumber, a bucket of ice and as many strawberries as they could find. A bellhop, whose nametag read *Christopher,* knocked on my door and called me ma'am when I opened it. I must have looked worse than I thought. I soaked myself in a hot bath with cucumbers on my eyes and ice on my face and ate strawberries until the water became tepid. I'd almost fallen asleep when I remembered that I'd forgotten to tip the boy who delivered my stuff. I climbed out of the tub significantly less puffy but still feeling like shit.

Makeup had forever been my friend, and I hoped it wouldn't fail me now. I slathered concealer under my eyes until the purplish color was almost gone. The only lipstick I had with me was great for victory parties but, as my dad would say, made me look like a two-dollar tramp. I wiped it off and settled for clear lip gloss. It felt like my brain was bouncing off my skull every time I took a step. I gathered my party dress and undies, threw them in my suitcase and eased myself into the hall. Somehow, I got to the first floor before I had to throw up in the lobby bathroom. I rinsed my mouth out in the sink, searched for a mint in my purse but couldn't find one, and looked both ways as I stepped into the hall. Then I ran into Colt's mother.

"Oh, Piper, it was good to see you last night." *Holy shit, her voice is loud.* "You left so early. Were you okay, hon?"

"Thank you for asking, Mrs. Porter. I had to finish my article for work," I lied. "Sorry I missed the festivities." If she was in the lobby, Colt couldn't be far behind. "Thank you so much for including me in the celebration. It was a great way to end the year and begin Colt's partnership with us."

I'd spent my entire life with my parents at press conferences and standing in the background as my dad gave radio and TV interviews. There was so much more to our sport than drunk fans and cars turning left at 180 miles an hour. It was a political game of always thanking sponsors, never speaking badly about another driver, and pretending our well-rehearsed words were spontaneous and sincere.

"Please tell Mr. Porter and Colt I said goodbye and thank you. But I've got to get home and submit my article." The truth was, I still had to write it.

"Hi," I said to the front-desk clerk. "A nice gentleman delivered some things to my room about an hour ago and I forgot to tip him. Can I leave money here with you?" I took a twenty out of my purse. "I was in room 1320."

He struck a few keys on the computer in front of him. "No problem, Ms. Pierson. Who helped you out this morning?"

I had to think about it for a second. "His name was Christopher." My father rarely got angry with me, but he never tolerated me forgetting someone's name. He said it was disrespectful and showed I wasn't paying attention. Since eighth grade when I stumbled on the name of a substitute teacher who we'd run into at the grocery store, I made up a saying when I met someone to help me remember their name. *Christopher carefully carried cucumbers.*

"Ah yes, Christopher Fox. One of our best employees." He took the cash from me. "I'll make sure he gets this right away."

"Thanks so much," I said. As I walked away, his name suddenly reminded me of the mix-up with the dead fox being sent to Colt's house the summer before. I'd meant to call the taxidermy shop myself and ask if they'd been expecting a delivery. But Colt assured me someone screwed up the towns, and that was all.

14

Mack Marlin won his sixth Winston Cup championship with Pierson Racing three weeks after Colt secured the Busch championship. My parents threw a *congratulations you won again and we're going to miss you and here's our new driver* party the week after the season ended. Colt had been vexed to see Mack at Tim Richmond's funeral, and I wondered how he'd feel about attending a joint party with him.

I hadn't seen Colt since his victory party as I was still mortified by my behavior. Thanks to Scott, Colt never knew how drunk I was and why I got that way. But, still. They were best friends, and if it'd been me and Liza, I would have told her everything.

My dad was keeping Colt plenty busy, and I spent a lot of time with my mom, proofreading papers and helping her study for finals. Colt called to ask if I'd had fun at his party and why I left so early. I gave him the same practiced speech I laid on his mother.

After much discussion about whether to have the party for Mack and Colt at the Ritz-Carlton or the Omni, my parents decided to host it at their house, a place they'd named Boulder Camp for no other reason than they liked the way it sounded.

Liza and I came early to help my parents set up. Since announcing his retirement, Mack had said he was going to buy a couple horses and keep them at his house and join the rodeo. But we all knew he wasn't going anywhere. He'd stay on at Pierson Racing as our chief strategist, a position I thought my dad invented just so he could continue to hang out with his best friend.

Knowing how much Mack loved horses, my parents transformed their rec room into a rodeo. When Liza and I walked in that Saturday morning, there were four mechanical bulls and six clowns that looked like giant Weebles. They tottered back and forth when we pushed them, but they never fell down. Lengths of lassoing rope hung on the walls in intricate patterns spelling out *Congratulations Mack on #6*. The party planners had even brought a few miniature horses and threw them flakes of hay. They were content to munch on their food and stay in their corners. There wasn't much for Liza and me to do, but we helped put condiments in small glass serving bowls and dumped bags of ice into muck buckets for the drinks.

Thirty minutes before guests were scheduled to arrive, the caterers put out hotdogs and hamburgers, big piles of homemade relish and sauerkraut, and macaroni and cheese. Liza came up behind me and put her hand on my shoulder.

"This is so sweet; your parents are serving all of Uncle Mack's favorite foods." Everyone called Mack Marlin *Uncle Mack*. "Aren't you worried the ponies will eat everything?"

I untied an apron I'd found in the pantry and slung it over my shoulder. "I asked the caterers the same thing. But they said horses are vegetarians and they've never known one to eat pasta or cheese."

She leaned in to me, and I could smell whiskey on her breath. "What happens if they have to poop?" she whispered.

"They're potty—" I saw Colt walk in dressed in pressed jeans, shiny cowboy boots, a black cowboy hat and a white oxford, and I completely forgot what I'd been saying. I pressed my teeth together and opened my lips so Liza could see if I had spinach dip anywhere it shouldn't be. She gave me the thumbs-up and I looked down at my outfit. The heels on my boots were too high, my jean skirt was too short, and my blouse was unbuttoned one too many holes. It was a new look for me, and I loved it.

"What are you going to say?" Liza asked. "Have you seen him since Martinsville?"

I was already walking toward Colt.

He was standing with his parents and Mack, so I hung back a couple feet. Doug Porter saw me, and his eyes brightened. "Well, if it isn't the prettiest little filly at the rodeo." He pulled me into a hug. "Come over here and say hi to us."

Meri Porter gave me an air kiss. In all the times I'd talked to her at races, she never made skin-to-skin contact. I suspected she was a germaphobe. She touched the end of my curls.

"Your hair always looks perfect. Perhaps when we're together every weekend next year, you can tell me some of your beauty secrets."

I made small talk with them for a few minutes, congratulated Mack again and told Colt it was nice to see him. He gave me a one-armed hug, but we didn't really talk. Mostly we were caught in the mix of well-wishers, of Doug asking Mack what his post-racing plans were and Meri complimenting me on how beautiful the house looked, as if I had anything to do with it. I was telling the Porters how the night was my mother's brainchild and I thought she should have been a party planner rather than going to school for an undergraduate degree in biochemistry or dead languages or whatever she was interested in this week. She'd finished her finals earlier in the week and kept a spreadsheet of her grades on tests and papers. She anticipated receiving As in all three courses.

"My mom aced all her exams, but I'm telling you, she's wasting her—" I heard Liza shriek, and we turned around to see one of the miniature horses on its back legs, eating guacamole off a table. A server ran over and shooed the black-and-white pinto away. It took its time getting down, and as it trotted away, it licked green off its muzzle.

"Okay, maybe the ponies weren't her best idea." I excused myself to help clean up the mess.

I told the server I'd take the guacamole in question and throw it away, but after she turned her back, I took it to the corner, sat on the floor with the pony and held the bowl in my lap. He took a few tentative steps toward me and reached his nose out to mine. He sniffed the air, then stuck out his tongue and licked my face. I held the bowl up for him and he dug his lips in and began slurping up the avocado mix.

"I let you out of my sight for five seconds and another man is kissing you." I raised my head and saw Colt standing over me. "Mind if I join the party?" I patted the space next to me and he sat.

"Have you met Oreo, my date?" I patted the pony's neck.

"He's a little short for you, don't you think?" The pony didn't have shoes on, and he kept slipping as he tried to lean into the bowl for more food. I took my hand away from his neck and it was covered in hair.

"And probably a little too furry. You know how I like men who wax."

He unbuttoned his shirt a hole so I could see his smooth chest. "At least I'm doing something right."

I put my hand on his leg. "You do everything right. I'm the idiot."

"I heard you had a rough night at my party."

So Scott did tell on me. "I think Scott had a worse time than me. He had to take care of me."

"Shit, Piper," Colt said softly. "I wish I could have spent more time with you. But you know how those gigs are. They're all about kissing babies and shaking hands."

I groaned. "You know that wasn't what was bothering me. I've been to a zillion of those shindigs with my parents. I didn't expect or want you to babysit me."

He reached for my hand. "Was it because Candice was there?"

It was the first time he'd said her name aloud to me. The pony had finished the dip and was sniffing around for something else to eat.

"I heard you and Scott talked a little about it."

"We did, and I'm sorry. For what it's worth, she and I talked at Martinsville and I like her."

Colt sat up against the wall. "She talked to you? Really?" He sounded incredulous. "About what?"

"Mostly you and if you're dating anyone. Then she asked why I'm single."

"Do you think it's time we come clean about us?" He squinted at me and the scar by his eye was even more pronounced.

"We're not not telling people. We're just not announcing it."

He held my hand. "Maybe we should."

Originally, we kept our relationship private because we weren't sure how my father would feel about a soon-to-be employee dating his daughter. But when it became apparent that he knew and approved, we just never felt the need to advertise it.

I glanced around the room and spotted my parents holding hands talking to Colt's mom and dad. "I know I'm the one who never wanted to talk about Candice and what she meant to you. But I always got the feeling that you were more than happy to not let her know about us. Like she might go all *Fatal Attraction* on me."

He picked some black and white horsehair off my skirt. "You're not wrong. But it's time. She needs to know. And even more so, I want the whole world to know."

"Are you sure? How do you know she doesn't want you back?"

"We're just friends. But like I kept trying to tell you, she depends on me . . . because of what she went through with her ex."

"Why didn't she file a police report or something?"

He slid the ring on my pointer finger from side to side. "I'm going to say something and then we are going to change the subject. Okay?"

"Sure."

"He's a cop."

"Oh."

"Yeah, oh. Now what are we going to talk about instead?"

The words fell out of my mouth before I could stop myself. "Are you still sleeping with her?"

He snapped his head back as if I'd slapped him. "Of course not. I wouldn't do that to you. I love *you,* Piper. And only you."

That was the first time he'd spoken those words to me.

"Really?"

"Head over heels," he said plainly. "Forever and ever."

"That's pretty cool."

"Is that all you have to say?" He poked me in the ribs.

"Yeah." I shrugged and he huffed out a breath. "Oh, and this. I've loved you since the moment I walked into your motorhome in Georgia."

A woman who I recognized but couldn't name stumbled by us, sloshing her drink out of her cup. I thought I should get up and clean her mess, but I was enjoying having Colt all to myself.

"The idea of you with another girl makes me crazy."

He picked up my hand and kissed it. "I can't have you going schizo on me, can I? I guess I'd better tell you right now that you're it." I felt like we were somehow getting engaged without the words, like he was going to bust out a promise ring or give me his varsity jacket.

I glanced at my parents, who were now talking to Mack and his wife. "Thank you," I told him.

"For what?"

"For letting me come clean about all my crazy and not giving up on me."

"Darlin', I don't know if you know this, but I'm never going to quit you. There's nothing you could say that would scare me away."

"I love that you're not scared. But I am. Still. So much."

The party had been going on for more than an hour, and I felt guilty not being a part of it. This was Mack's big send-off. My parents had spent months planning it, and I'd been hiding in a corner with my boyfriend and a pony. My mother caught my eye and gave me a little *get up* wave, but I pretended I didn't see her.

Colt put his arm around me and pulled me to him, then kissed my temple. "I know. And I hate that for you." He jumped up and offered me his hand. "Come on, I have an idea."

I let him help me up. "Where are we going? We can't just leave. Not now."

He tugged on my hand and I followed him toward the door. "Yes we can. No one will even miss us."

I tried to catch Liza's eye to signal to her that we were leaving, but she was flirting with a driver. "Okay, but if my parents yell at me, I'm blaming it on you."

"Who are you kidding?" Colt said over his shoulder. "Planter and Poppi have never yelled at anyone a day in their lives."

We snuck up the stairs, through the kitchen and into the yard. It was littered with cars and two valets who were leaning against a big oak tree, talking.

"Where are we going?" I asked. It was dark but warm, and the sky was full of stars.

He pulled his keys from his pocket and I flashed him a look. "I never let a valet park my car."

I groaned. "Oh, are you one of those kinds of guys? God forbid your beautiful baby gets a scratch?" Colt's Busch cars were made by Pontiac, so he drove one in his everyday life. It was the least glamourous car around.

"What?" He stopped. "No. I just don't like letting other people do things for me I can do for myself."

My mind flashed back to the day we'd met in Braselton and how he'd cooked for everyone. Most other drivers had chefs travel with them or hired caterers.

"Sorry. I should have known." We weaved through rows of perfectly spaced cars until we got to the edge of the property where Colt's dark-blue sedan was parked by itself under a tree. He opened the passenger door for me and waited till I got in. Then he closed it and walked around to the other side.

"Where are we going?"

"I'm going to drive and talk. And you're going to listen."

I could tell from the way his mouth was a straight line that he was trying to be serious, but there were creases around his eyes like he was trying not to smile.

"Let's do it." I put on my seatbelt and stretched out my legs. "Are we going somewhere specific or just enjoying the night scenery?"

"The Moorestown High School is just a mile or two from here, right?"

"Yes," I answered tentatively. "Why?"

"Because it has a big parking lot and it's empty now." He turned left out of our road and headed toward the place I'd graduated from years before. We drove in silence for a few minutes, and when we got to the school's parking lot, he put the car in park and let it idle.

"Piper." Now his voice was serious. "I have a dangerous job." I opened my mouth to agree with him, but he stopped me. "And I'll be honest. The few wrecks I've been in have scared the shit out of me."

"If you're trying to help me get over my fears, you're failing miserably," I said. I rubbed my hands together. My palms were sweaty.

"Just listen. Racing on a good day can be scary. These cars go so fast. And there are thirty other guys on the track who all want to be in front. You must remember that fear and exhilaration from when you drove the Dash cars. But you did it because you loved it. And that's why I'm a driver. There's nothing more freeing than finishing a race and knowing I've driven my best."

I crossed my arms. "That's probably what my dad thought, too. Right up until I almost killed him."

"I know I could die every time I get in a race car. But I could also bite it running out to the grocery store. Or my plane could go down. *Or. Or. Or.* And somehow, most of the world magically keeps living every day." He held my hands tight. "Don't you get it, Pipes? It's that tiny voice in the back of my head that tells me that today could be my last that sets me free. I love my life because I know each day is a gift."

I pulled away and leaned against the door. "Did you read that on a coffee mug?" I was getting mad at him and I didn't know why.

"Come on. Don't be like that. You know I'm trying to help you. And I have helped you. I can tell."

"Oh yeah." My voice was tight. "How?"

He held up his hand to tick points off on his fingers.

"One. You have fun with me. According to Liza, that's something you haven't done in a very long time. Two. You went from wearing baggy jeans and tennis shoes when we first met to things that have been in the back of your closet since high school and actually make you look like a girl. Three. You laugh a lot more than you used to. Four. You don't scream out in your sleep anymore. Five." He held up his thumb. "The first time you sat in the driver's seat, you cried. The second time you didn't. The third time, you put your hands on the steering wheel and closed your eyes like you were remembering something delicious." He stared at me. "Do I need to keep going? Because I can."

"You seem to know an awful lot about me." I played with the rings on my fingers.

"That's because I love you like crazy, Piper. Do you understand that? Like, really truly get it that I'm not going anywhere? And it kills me to see you so unhappy?"

"I'm not unhappy," I snapped. "How could I be when I have you?"

"Bullshit. You're unhappy every day that goes by and you're not driving a car. I'd say it'd be a win if you'd just drive a street car again. But that's not enough for you. You won't truly be happy until you're racing again."

The truth made me dizzy. "You don't know what you're talking about."

"Don't I? Look me in the eye and tell me you don't want to drive again."

I stared at the floorboards. "I can't."

"Then my work here is done. Let's go back to the party."

Suddenly it clicked why he'd brought me to a deserted lot.

"Now? But we're here." We'd been doing laps around the sprawling brick building. "And there's no one here for me to hit."

"Exactly." He grinned. "I want you to remember how badly you wanted to drive tonight. I want you to taste it. Dream about it."

•   •   •

The following week, Colt and I were at the race shop, painting his office.

"I've been thinking about what you told me at Mack's party," Colt said.

"What's that?" I answered. "That I want to climb on top of you and—"

"Eh hem," my dad said from the doorway.

"Hello, Father," I said, not meeting his eye.

"Daughter," he said, then kissed me on the forehead. "Colt." He shook Colt's hand and I could tell from the way Colt winced slightly that my dad had gripped it too hard.

"Did you come to help us paint?" I asked. I scratched my nose and Colt pointed to it. I tried to wipe it, and I could tell I'd smeared bright blue paint, Pierson Racing's signature color, on my face.

My dad sat on the edge of Colt's desk. "No. But it is work related."

"I'll go grab a coffee," I said, not wanting to get in the middle of their business. My father often did things like this. He'd start a conversation about racing or the team in front of me but with someone else, knowing I'd have something to say. I was sure it was his way of trying to suck me into working with him.

"It's okay, little one," my father told me. "Stay. We could use your input."

"Yes, Daddy." I rested my paintbrush on the lid of a gallon can of paint and wiped my face with a rag. I closed my eyes and started humming a Georgia Satellites song. I didn't want to be a part of this conversation.

My dad flipped through the notebook he was carrying. "I think there's been a mix-up. I called a few buddies and found your friend"—he scanned a page—"Candice a job with the 99 team, but when I called her office to let her know, they said she'd moved."

"No mistake, sir," Colt said. "She's leaving town and moving in with her sister. She'll be gone before the start of the new season."

I couldn't believe what I was hearing. "Really?" my father and I asked at the same time. I opened my eyes and Colt was grinning at me.

"Really," Colt said. "I guess it was time for a fresh start." He looked at me. "For everyone. Come the first of the year, I'll be one hundred and fifty percent dedicated to team Pierson."

I was so happy I felt like crying.

My dad looked from Colt to me and back to him. "Are you sure?" Was there anything that man didn't know?

"Absolutely. All that I ask is that Scott comes with me, and you and I have already talked about that. So, I'm all good. And Mr. Thompson knew when he hired me that Scott and I were a package deal. He goes where I go." My dad gave him a wry smile. "Only, only if that's okay with you, sir," he stuttered.

My dad stepped toward him and messed his hair. "Of course. I'm just giving you a hard time." He took in the progress we'd made painting the room. "I'll let you two get back to it. It's looking good in here."

I waited till my dad closed the door behind him before I spoke.

"Does this mean what I think it does?" I asked Colt.

"That depends on what you're thinking."

I stepped into his arms and kissed him. "Is it just you and me now?"

"It's always been just you and me," he said and kissed me back. "How about we go out tonight and celebrate?"

"Sounds great," I said. "Where to? Sandwich Construction?"

"I was thinking someplace a little fancier. How about Dressler's in Charlotte?"

•   •   •

Dinner at Dressler's never happened. Colt came to my apartment so I could grab a dress, and then we went to his place to shower and change. But, when we got there, there was an inch of standing water in his kitchen. "What the hell?" he asked, his hand still on the garage door.

"Did a pipe burst?" I guessed.

"Doesn't it have to be winter in Maine for that to happen?" Although it was December, the temperature hadn't been below freezing. It'd been a warm fall and was supposed to be a mild winter, too.

"Let me call my dad," I said. "His buddy Hank is a plumber. I'm sure he'll come right over and fix whatever's broken."

"My floors," Colt said sadly. "I love them." He was the only twenty-four-year-old guy I knew who would even notice that he had floors, never mind grow attached to them.

I called my dad, who called Hank, who showed up twenty minutes later. As soon as he got there, I went in the other room to order pizza and take a shower. When I came back, a shop vac was sucking up the water in Colt's kitchen, and Hank and Colt were in wet shoes drinking beer.

"This doesn't look like good news," I said, putting the pizza box on the counter and pulling three plates out of a cabinet.

Colt groaned. "It's not. The pipes are a mess."

My dad's parents had retired to Massachusetts and bought a farmhouse built in 1709. Everything in it broke all the time.

"Is this house old?" I ran my hand down the painted wall as if it might crumble with my touch.

"A whopping seven years," he said.

Hank answered my question before I could ask. "In very rare cases, the lining of the pipes can react to compounds naturally found in water, causing the pipes to erode prematurely."

I'd never heard of anything like that in my life, but I knew nothing about plumbing. "You'd think that they'd test for high levels of whatever," I said.

Colt and Hank exchanged a look. "They do," Hank said. "That's what makes this even weirder. I can't think of a logical explanation for this, other than a substance seeping into the soil."

"Like acid rain or something?" I asked. Colt's property was peaceful and secluded. "Hardly seems like there'd be a pollution problem here."

"There's not," Hank told us. "Or at least there hasn't been.

But you never know. With more and more people moving to the area every year, there's no way to know what people are dumping in the lake."

I glanced at the dress we'd picked up from my apartment. It was hanging on the back of a door. "I'd much rather eat pizza with you two than have to talk quietly in a stuffy restaurant," I said. The truth was, I didn't care where we ate that night or even if we ate. I was just so happy to know that Colt and I were finally in the clear.

15

Colt called a week before the Busch Grand National Championship awards banquet. I was at home and had been working on an article but getting nowhere. I'd foolishly thought the off-season would bring me less work.

"Hey, good lookin'," he sang when I answered the phone. "Whatcha doing?"

"Um, I was trying to write a piece about a dirt track crew chief whose record says he's one of the best out there, but rumor has it that he's battling a nasty drug addiction. I won't give in to gossip or speculation, but—" I realized Colt probably didn't care what I was working on; he was just being polite. "Oh, it's nothing. What's going on with you?"

"Finish telling me," he said. "I know a bunch of guys in that series. Can I help you with anything?"

I didn't think it was possible to love him any more. "You are so freaking sweet. I'm fine. I'll figure it out. What's up?"

"I wanted to talk to you real quick about the Busch banquet next week."

I'd bought my dress as soon as Colt won the points race.

"What about it? Pierson Racing has a table, but I already told my parents I'll be hanging out with you for most of the night."

He exhaled. "That's what I wanted to talk to you about. I feel terrible that we'll be sitting at different tables."

"Don't be silly. You sit with your team and I'll sit with mine. And when no one's looking, we'll make out like bandits."

He laughed. "I love it."

"Besides, we can still go together." I saved what I'd been working on and shut off my computer. "And more importantly, leave together."

The phone went quiet, and I thought we'd gotten disconnected.

"Do you want the good news or bad news?"

"Hit me with the bad, so we can end with the good."

"I have to be there about three hours ahead of time for photos and interviews and such."

For as many times as Mack had won the Cup championship, I should have remembered that the winning driver was chained to the hotel for the entire day. "Ugh. That's right. What's the good news?"

"I'm sending Scott and a limo to pick you up."

"That is good news. But is he okay with that? Doesn't he have a date who'd rather be alone with him?"

"Nope. And he's looking forward to hanging out with you."

I opened the fridge and a wall of stink hit me. Liza and I might have forgotten to empty it before we went to my parents' for a week to get ready for the holidays. Now it smelled as bad as our across-the-hall neighbors' fridge did when the power went out during the last storm and a pound of salmon went bad. I put on a pair of pink, polka-dotted rubber gloves. "I'm a lucky girl to have a faux beau who will hang out with me when my rock star boyfriend is busy with the paparazzi."

"Pierson, you're the coolest."

"But?" I asked.

"Damn. Beautiful, fun, and you know me so well."

I opened a tub of tapioca and nearly gagged. "Out with it."

"It's no big deal. I just wanted to let you know that Candice will be there. We're not going to hang out or anything," he added quickly. "I probably won't even talk to her. I just didn't want you to be surprised."

I started to say something but stopped. "You're sweet to let me know. But it's fine." I opened a carton of milk and sniffed it. I dumped it and it came out in chunks.

"There are no words for a girl like you. I'll get with Scott and we'll figure out what time he needs to pick you up."

"Are you sure this is okay with him? What if he wants to bring a real date? I see him talking to the scorer from the Clorox team all the time."

"Don't you worry about him. I got it all handled."

"You always do."

"But I do have a question. And you're not going to like it."

Crap. "What's on your mind?"

"Remember when you gave me this whole spiel about how Pierson Racing employees aren't allowed to cavort with one another?"

"I don't recall ever using the word *cavort*. *Frolic*, maybe. Perhaps even *gambol*." I was showing off. "If you're worried that my dad might break your face, he loves you. Besides, I'm not an employee."

"I take it your parents still approve?"

I took a carton of eggs from the door and tossed them one by one into the trash. "Your legs aren't broken. What do you think?"

"It's gonna be a good year. You, me and Winston Cup."

●   ●   ●

I believed Colt when he told me Scott volunteered to take me to the Busch banquet, but I wanted to be certain he was okay with it. "It'd be my honor to escort you," Scott told me when I called. "I love hanging out with you."

"Are you sure? If there's a cute girl waiting for you to call, I don't want to stop you."

"A cute girl did call me. Just now."

I'd suspected a few times that Scott may have had a crush on me.

"You're sweet. But I'm serious. If there's someone else you want to take, you should take her. This is a big deal. Your driver won the championship."

"It *is* a big deal," he said. "Which is why I want to spend the night with my favorite people."

He was making it hard for me not to feel guilty about going with him. "If you're sure," I said tentatively.

"I am."

"Then thank you. It will be a great night."

"In other news, I hear congratulations are in order," Scott said.

"For you, yes. Colt has said in every interview he's given since Martinsville that he wouldn't have won the championship without his pit crew."

"Thanks," he said. "But I meant for you and him. I hear you're officially official."

"That's what I hear," I said. I felt myself smiling.

"You know what this means, right?"

"That you'll have to break up with me?"

He chuckled. "That too. But you, my friend, are now the lucky owner of Colt's heart."

That was such an un-guy thing to say.

"You flatter me so. But let's not get ahead of ourselves. All that's happening here is that Colt's finally down to one girlfriend. It's hardly a marriage proposal."

"You say that now," Scott said. "But let's have this conversation again in six months."

I hung up and was entirely too happy to continue cleaning moldy food out of the fridge.

• • •

"I think *I* want to have sex with you," Liza said. It was a week later, and she was helping me get dressed for the Busch banquet. "Look at you." She turned me toward the full-length mirror in my bedroom. Knowing most women would be wearing black, I went for a backless, shimmery silver wrap dress with a slit in the front practically up to my belly button. In my strappy heels, I was over six feet tall.

"This is so not me."

Liza took my hand and led me to the kitchen. She opened a bottle of champagne and poured two glasses. "This"—she motioned to my outfit—"is the real you. The one I see in pictures of you from high school. The confident rock star racing girl."

I took a sip and the bubbles tickled my nose. "That girl's been gone a long time."

Liza waved me off. "Think of it like this. You are Aurora Rose and—"

"Who?"

"Just listen," she scolded. "And your dad's accident is the evil witch who put you to sleep."

"I get it now. Sleeping beauty. How'd you know her real name?"

"Never mind. And stop interrupting me." She blew me a kiss. "You snoozed for a really long time until Colt came along."

"Does that make him Prince Philip?"

"Yes, whatever. Aurora was the only name I could remember. So now you're awake and remembering how entirely awesome your life used to be."

A few minutes later, Scott knocked on the door. He was leaning against the frame in an Armani tuxedo with martini glasses on his bowtie and cummerbund. I was a little turned on with how well he dressed up. He could have found a real date, some cute chippie who would hang on him all night and put out in a VIP suite. No matter what he said, he was making a sacrifice taking me. I wanted to show my appreciation for him giving up yet another night to babysit his best friend's girlfriend.

The week before, a bunch of us were at his house roasting marshmallows at a bonfire on the edge of Lake Norman. I climbed the hill of his backyard under the pretense of having to pee and snuck into his bedroom closet. When I unzipped the black jacket bag and saw the playful motif of his tux, I knew what I was going to get him.

"Colt's a lucky son of a gun," Scott said, taking me in. He handed me a huge bouquet of winter flowers. I felt a little like I was going to the prom. "Piper, you look good." He dragged out the last word, exaggerating his already thick Southern accent.

I twirled for Scott, then did a little curtsy. "I do, don't I? My daddy always said it ain't bragging if it's true." I opened the door wider. "Come in; I have something for you."

Liza had filled a third glass with Moet and gave it to him while I ran to my room to get his present. I came back and handed him a small silver bag stuffed with dark-blue tissue. I drank a second glass while he opened his present.

"I love surprises," he said, methodically removing the tissue paper. "But what'd I do to deserve this?"

I covered my mouth to burp. "We both know you could be going to this shindig tonight with someone who'd have sex with you afterwards."

He covered his mouth in mock surprise. "You mean you're not?"

I punched him in the shoulder. "Open your present so we can get a move on."

He reached into the bag and pulled out a pair of silver martini-glass cufflinks. "Ah, kiddo, I love them."

"I helped her pick them out," Liza called from the kitchen table. She had on a pair of silk boxers and a camisole.

I helped him attach them to his cuffs, put our glasses in the dishwasher, and we set out for a night of epic fun. My night would not be all pleasure, as I agreed to cover the award ceremonies for *Weekly*. Tack loved my strategy article from Martinsville so much he asked me to write a piece for the awards banquet.

An hour after Scott arrived at my apartment, we strolled arm in arm through the front doors of the Adams Mark Hotel in downtown Charlotte. We greeted a few people whose names I couldn't remember, then found our way into the ballroom. I laughed out loud when I saw the dinner tables. Each had a bucket of cold Busch Beer for a centerpiece, and every place setting was adorned with a packet of Goody's Headache Powder, a contingency sponsor for the series, and a bottle of ElectroAde Sports Drink. I heard Colt before I saw him. He was behind me talking to Amy from the newspaper. I'd forgotten that she was going to be at the banquet, covering another story Tack had assigned. I approached a waiter with a tray of champagne so I was in front of Colt. He stopped midsentence and stared at me before turning his attention back to her. He was either pleased with what he saw, or my dress was tucked into my underwear.

Colt made his way to me. "Good evening, Ms. Pierson. Don't you look smashing." He took my hand, pulled me to him and kissed both cheeks. His lips were soft as velvet. He whispered in my ear while his mouth was pressed against my skin. "I've never loved anyone the way I love you."

I ducked my head in false modesty. "Why, Mr. Porter, you flatter me so."

"Hey," he said, his eyes lighting up. "Porter. That would be perfect."

"Perfect for what?"

"Planter Pierson. Poppi Pierson. Piper Pierson."

The drinks I'd had with Scott and Liza were catching up to me and I had to pee. "Yes, you've established you know the names of my family."

"Piper Porter. How happy would your dad be?"

•   •   •

Cocktails flowed, egos grew, and people got very drunk. By the time Dave McClellan, a well-known TV commentator, started making announcements asking guests to take their seats for dinner and the awards, I was happily buzzed. I knew myself well and had already gotten all the quotes I'd need to write a good recap of the evening. So, I left my recorder in my bag on the table and set out to find Colt. After his victory party in Martinsville, I reminded myself that this night was all about him and I was one of a thousand people who'd be vying for his attention, so I wasn't surprised I hadn't seen him in a while.

He wasn't at any of the bars, and Scott said he didn't know where Colt was. I waited outside the men's room until a man came out, and I described Colt and asked if he was in there. The man said he knew exactly who Colt Porter was and told me if Colt had been in there, he would have asked for his autograph. I found a circle of people surrounding Cal Thompson, Colt's Busch team owner, discovered that Colt wasn't with him, and kept looking. Sasha and her boyfriend, Dan, were at their table, but she said she hadn't seen her brother in the last half hour.

Finally, I remembered that the winner's sponsor always had a private suite where its VIPs could have a quiet conversation or grab a drink without having to wait in line. It was easy enough to find. There was a sandwich board sign in front of the door designating it as such. The ElectroAde VIP suite was devoid of reporters, executives and brownnosers. For a second, I didn't see anything but hors d'oeuvres and ice buckets filled with champagne. Closing the door behind me, I stepped toward an amazing ice sculpture of Colt's car, a fruit-and-cheese platter big enough to feed three pit crews, and Colt and Candice kissing on the couch.

I grabbed the door handle to keep myself upright and opened my mouth, but no words would come out. I started to back out of the room, but the door squeaked, and Colt looked up and saw me.

"Piper!" he yelled, his voice weird and wonky.

I stopped at three bar stations on my way back to the ballroom and did as many shots as I could before each bartender sent me away. Already a little wobbly, I wished I wasn't wearing heels. I wanted to take them off and spike them through Colt's forehead, but they were my mother's. Scott found me in the lobby asking the concierge to call me a cab.

"There you are," he said. "Just in time for the salad."

"Screw the salad. I'm getting the hell out of here." I couldn't control my tongue, and I felt a line of spit hanging off my bottom lip

He pulled an old-fashioned monogrammed handkerchief out of his breast pocket and gave it to me. I didn't recognize the initials.

"Piper Piper Pumpkin Eater, that's a great idea." He put his hand on my back and urged me forward. "Let's go get some coffee and pie somewhere. Banquet food is never good."

"I'm leaving. *You*"—I stabbed my finger into his chest—"have to stay here with boy wonder. Have a good night." I pushed myself away but stumbled badly and he caught me.

"Come on, Piper," Scott whispered. He put one arm around my waist, and I leaned all my weight against him. "I can't let you leave by yourself. Let's go back in that room and get through the night."

Even holding onto him, I had a hard time keeping my balance. "Fine," I said, "but we better not have missed dinner. I'm starving."

"You're always starving."

"*Ha* freakin' *ha*."

Servers were already clearing glass plates of arugula and mixed greens and setting down entrees when we got back to the ballroom. I leaned over someone's shoulder and stuck my pointer finger in a steak. It dripped with a pinkish-red juice.

Scott gazed at me for a long moment, no doubt trying to decide what to do. Without a word, he escorted me to my table and poured me a glass of water. I picked it up and heard a few people clapping. As I turned toward the applause, Colt and *Candi* came through the entrance closest to the VIP suites. Like the time I saw a fatal bus accident on Highway 16 with multiple bodies on the road, I tried to look away, but I couldn't. Colt kept his gaze on the floor. Candice caught my eye and smirked. Scott saw the pair emerge as well and grimaced, shaking his head.

"I'm so sorry Colt did this to you," Scott whispered in my ear. His breath smelled of garlic and whiskey. "But it's not like you didn't know this could happen."

Liza's dad had died second semester of our freshman year. He'd been sick with ALS for most of her life. I flew to Boston with her for the funeral, and as I stood next to her at the wake, someone who worked with her dad said how sorry he was. Then he patted her back and said, "But it's not like you didn't know this would happen." What an asshole. I vividly remembered wanting to kick that guy in the nuts. Now, I wanted to do the same to Scott.

"What does that mean?" I growled. "Does Colt get a pass because he's famous? I don't know if you know this, but my father was ten times the driver Colt will ever be and he'd never do anything like this. Never."

"I didn't mean it like that. I just meant—" He buttered a roll and put it on my plate. "I don't know what I meant. I'm sorry, Piper. I'm not trying to make excuses for him. But I promise that he loves you more than he's ever loved anyone else."

•   •   •

Colt stared at me during his acceptance speech and made vague references that only I understood. "A reporter asked me what it's like to be so young and so successful." That *reporter* was me. "I told her I wake up every morning and say a prayer, so the big crew chief in the sky knows how thankful I am for all that we"—he motioned to his crew and owner—"have accomplished." That was true. He did pray every morning, and it always started the same way: *Dear Lord. If this is my last day on Earth, I have no regrets. Thank you for letting me live like everyone should. Full throttle and full of love.*

"During another interview, I was asked what my secret was to be able to concentrate for three and a half or four hours in a hundred-and-fifty-degree car. I explained that I use relaxation techniques before races start to help me stay focused."

That was also a shout-out to me. When he wanted to be alone with me at races, he'd make noisy proclamations to his crew about having to relax and concentrate before the race. Then he'd ask everyone to clear out of his motorhome for an hour.

Colt rambled on about the amazing engine builders, his elite crew and generous owner. He talked about his favorite super speedways, the challenges of road courses and the skill required to handle a bunched-up field of cars on a short track. Cal Thompson and a rep from ElectroAde were onstage with him, and when he was done speaking, they made emotional speeches. Then Colt, without notes, thanked his parents and sponsors, and then named all fifty-seven people who worked at his race shop. He got a standing ovation. When the music started playing, a subtle cue telling him to get off the stage, he held up his hand as if he had one more thing to say.

"Lastly, I need to thank the people who really made me successful." He paused to build suspense, then finished his sentence in his charming, boyish way. "My fans are the reason I'm standing up here." A cheer erupted from the audience, and I envied how loved he was. "I owe everything to them. Especially my number one fan." At Richmond, I'd sent his crew to lunch on me and waited for him in his rig wearing nothing but lace panties that said *number one fan* on the butt.

His well-disguised apologies made no difference. As I watched him go down the stairs leading off the stage, I noticed his uneven gait. I thought maybe he'd had too much to drink, but he hadn't sounded drunk during his speech. His voice wasn't labored, and he didn't slur his words the way people do when they're intoxicated. But something was off—like when he said my name in the suite.

Colt was crowned the Busch Grand National Champion, Most Popular Driver, winner of the most races and the most poles. Seven times he broke away from the crowd around him and tried to approach me. And seven times I turned my back and placed my hand on whoever was nearest me, as if I was engaged in some enthralling conversation. After a full meal and a few cups of coffee, I had sobered up enough to get through the night.

I was chatting with the wives of a few of Colt's crew when I overheard him tell his dad that he was going back to his room for a few minutes before going to the after-parties. Not thinking through what I was about to do, I excused myself from my conversation and found Scott.

"There's my handsome date," I said.

"Oh no." He put down his glass of whiskey "You have evil in your eyes. What's going on?"

I draped my arm around his waist. "What kind of question is that? I'm ready to party."

"Uh, sister, you've been partying. Your liver is probably failing as we speak."

"I left something in Colt's room. Will you come with me to get it?"

"You haven't been to Colt's room. Have you?"

I waved him off. "I'm telling you, I left something up there."

"Something?" he asked, not believing me. "What kind of something?"

"Uh, um, a girl product." No guy wanted to know about tampons. On our way to the elevators, several crew from other teams high-fived Scott. At first, I thought they were celebrating Colt's win, but then I realized they saw Scott taking a pretty girl to his room.

"How do you know I have a key to his room?" Scott asked while we waited for the elevator to arrive.

"Because I know you," I said. "And Colt. He probably gave you his extra key as soon as he saw you and told you to make yourself comfortable. You know, as long as he wasn't getting busy up here with—"

"Okay, Piper. I get it. You know us both *so* well."

Once inside, I had second thoughts about doing something so cruel. But fury and alcohol got the best of me. I fumbled in the dark for a few moments pretending to search for my unmentionables when I lost my balance and landed on the bed. "Uh oh," I groaned. "The room is spinning. Scott, come here and make it stop." When he sat next to me, I pulled him down on top of me.

"Piper," he shouted, sitting up. "What are you doing?"

"Trying to have sex with you." My original plan was to screw Scott in order to screw Colt. But then I thought that maybe I should date him for real.

"Sex? With me?" He scrambled to the edge of the bed. "Why?"

"Really, Scott? You're going to ask me that? Does it matter?"

He took my chin in his fingers. "I'm flattered. Really I am."

I put my hand on the bulge in his pants. "I can see that."

He shifted away and crossed his legs. "As much as I would love to take you up on your offer, you're my best friend's girlfriend."

"Not so much since your best friend was last seen getting busy in the ElectroAde VIP room."

"Ah. The truth comes out. You're mad as hell and want revenge."

"I am still a bit buzzed. And mad. But I'm also attracted to you. We all knew Colt and I weren't going anywhere. It was just for fun." The sound of my own words pierced my eardrums like a jet engine. "Kiss me, please?"

We kissed gently for thirty seconds, and I had glory in my mind thinking about Colt's reaction when he saw me getting it on with Scott. Against my will, I kept picturing what it'd be like if I walked in on Liza and Colt. I'd never survive him sleeping with my best friend. I couldn't give a shit if I hurt Colt. But I couldn't be responsible for ruining their friendship and hurting Scott in the process. The two men might as well have been brothers.

I bolted up. "Oh God, Scott. This is so wrong. We have to get out of here. If Colt sees us together, he'll never forgive you. Right now I hate him, but I love you and I can't get in the way of your friendship because he's a wanker and I'm stupid."

I didn't give him a chance to respond. I straightened my dress, grabbed my shoes and ran for the door. I opened it to see Colt fumbling for his key card.

"Fuck!" I yelled, startling us both.

"Piper, what are you doing in my room? I've been looking everywhere for you." He stepped forward and touched my face. I backed away as if he had slapped me.

"Well, you giant asshole, I lured Scott up here with the hopes of seducing him and having you walk in on us." Colt peered over my shoulder, scanning the room. "But Scott being the saint that he is turned me down flat. At least there is one decent person among us."

I scooted under his arm and into the hall. As the elevator doors closed behind me, I heard them both yelling for me to stop.

Once downstairs, I had nowhere to go and no one to go there with. It was after midnight, and the party was all but over. I wandered into the empty ballroom and, as a preemptive strike, took a few packets of Goody's powder from a table. Sooner or later I was going to have a headache that would make it hurt to open my eyes. Colt and his friends swore snorting the medicine made it work instantly. But the thought of putting anything up my nose made me gag, so I picked up a random glass of water and ingested three packets. I sat for a moment, took off my shoes, then decided I should go back to my original plan and call a cab to take me home.

As I was slinking toward the lobby, the president of ElectroAde blocked my path. I only recognized him from presenting Colt with an award on stage.

"You're Planter's girl, right? Pepper, is it?"

"Piper." I tried to casually straighten my dress and tuck in my bra straps.

"The man of the hour seems to be on the lam. But we're having one hell of an after-party. The only thing we're missing is a beautiful girl. Would you do me the honor?"

He held out his elbow, and I hooked my arm through it. "I would love to go to your party, sir. Thank you."

He blatantly checked out my backside as we walked. "No, no. Thank *you,* sweetheart."

He led me back to the scene of the crime, and I was amazed to see the ice sculpture was still intact. I thanked Mr. ElectroAde for the invite, plucked a flute off a tray and filled it from the champagne fountain I hadn't noticed earlier in the night. Colt and I were over, and Scott probably hated me. What else was there left to do but drink?

"You don't want that piss water, honey," my escort said. "Have you ever done a lemon drop?"

I knew champagne. I took a sip. If I had to guess, I'd say this piss water had Krug bloodlines. It certainly wasn't a seven-dollar bottle of Andre flowing out of the mouth of a little cherub. "I confess," I said. "I've never even heard of a lemon drop."

He took the glass from my hand and placed it on a table near the sculpture. "Now listen here, little lady." In any other part of the country, that would have been offensive. But in the South, well, that's how we talked. "It's a lot like doing a tequila shot. Lick the sugar off your hand, gulp the vodka and put that there lemon in your mouth and suck like you've never sucked before." I had a flashback to the night Colt and I met and was reminded of all the tequila we drank.

Mr. ElectroAde settled me on an expensive black leather couch and excused himself for a moment. We'd already been introduced twice since the party started, and I still couldn't remember his name. My fallback of *darlin'* would have to do. I doubted he could recall my name, and I was quite sure neither of us cared. He returned with a tray carrying a ceramic bowl of cut lemons, sugar, two shot glasses and a magnum of Nuage, whose main ingredient was grain alcohol.

"Here we go, sugar," he said. He poured us each a shot and handed me a lemon. Then he licked the top of my hand between my thumb and pointer finger. I was glad I'd washed my hands after I'd gone to the bathroom. With a silver demitasse spoon, he sprinkled sugar on my wet skin. "Bottom's up." We clinked glasses, licked the sugar off our hands, and I tossed my shot far back into my throat. I hated vodka. Then I sucked on that lemon for a good twenty seconds.

My new friend and I drank, chatted some, invited a small crowd of other tuxedoed men to join us and drank a little more. Someone suggested a friendly game of strip poker. It was not lost on me that I was the only girl in the group. But it would take many rounds before they got a peek of the banana-shaped birthmark on my left breast. I'd played the game in high school enough to know all the tricks. Jewelry and hair accessories came off first. There were at least fifteen bobby pins holding my updo together. Both ears had four earrings each. These guys would be going commando by the time I got around to taking off my shoes.

I lost the first hand on purpose, asked last year's Busch champion to unzip me and slipped my dress down my body in one motion. To hell with the bobby pins and earrings. I wanted to give these boys something to look at. I guessed Liza had been right. I was awake now and finding my way back to the girl I used to be.

In black bikini underwear, thigh-high stockings and a push up bra, I slowly crossed the room, holding my dress. I found a coat closet and carefully hung it up. "What?" I asked innocently. "I can't have this pretty girl getting any wrinkles." I stroked the dress as if it were a purebred cat. Everyone watched me take my seat.

Someone had started dealing the cards again when the door opened and I heard my name being yelled. "Goddamn, Piper! Put your clothes on." Sasha and Dan came rushing at me, Dan ripping off his jacket and covering me the best he could. He guided me to the door while Sasha fetched my dress, all the while apologizing and bidding the room goodnight on my behalf.

"What are you doing here?" I asked Sasha as she tried to ease me back into my dress. It was tight and uncomfortable, and I didn't want to put it on. I wriggled left when she tried to straighten it and shimmied against the wall when she went to zip it. A favorite expression of my dad's came to mind: It was like trying to nail Jell-O to a tree. She finally gave up, yanked it up as far as she could and buttoned the jacket around me.

"Colt and Scott sent us to look for you. We've all been worried," Sasha said.

"Why aren't those wankers looking for me themselves?" The night appeared in my mind like out-of-focus snapshots.

"Colt is going room to room in the hotel and Scott is canvasing the bars."

The elevator came, packed with other drunk partygoers. We got off on the sixteenth floor, and Sasha guided me to a room and led me to an unmade bed. She helped me get undressed while her date fetched a bucket of ice and a bottle of water. "This isn't my room," I said. Sasha wrangled me into a pair of boxers and a T-shirt and reminded me that I didn't have a room. Scott and I had come together, and I was going to stay the night with Colt.

"This is my room," she said. "You're staying here tonight." Sasha's boyfriend returned with water and several packets of Goody's headache powder. I mixed them in my drink like they were Alka-Seltzer and chugged it. He squeezed my shoulder as a way of saying goodnight and quickly kissed Sasha.

She gave me a few more sips of water, then covered me with blankets. "I hate him," I said, on the edge of what would be a restless sleep. "I really hate him."

"I know," she soothed, stroking my hair. "I know."

•   •   •

Never being one to sleep well after being so drunk, I was awake and out of the hotel before the sun came up. I put on my dress, but no shoes, and swiped the same jacket Sasha had wrapped around me the night before.

In the hotel lobby, I asked the concierge to hail me a cab to Moorestown. "That's not a short ride," he said.

"I understand that. But I still need to get home." I was anxious to get out of there before I saw anyone I knew. The helpful man got me a new town car with no upgrade fee and exchanged a look with the redheaded driver. I let myself in the back seat for a long, dehydrated, head-throbbing ride home. Almost an hour later, I got to my apartment, took a thirty-minute shower, slinked into bed and left Scott a message saying how sorry I was for the night before. When Liza got home late that night, I pretended to be sleeping so I wouldn't have to speak out loud what had happened.

16

Colt called me three times a day for a month, but I refused to speak with him. What was there to say? I was embarrassed by my sideshow more than I was mad. But I needed to face facts. Once you walk in on your boyfriend fooling around with another girl, you're pretty much done.

Both the Winston Cup and Busch Grand National seasons were over, and there wasn't much racing news to report. Since the piece about the drug-addicted dirt car crew chief, I hadn't had much to do. And the assignments Tuck did give me left no doubt that I was low man on the newspaper totem pole.

I covered a story at Charlotte about them switching from triangle-shaped pizza slices to square ones. Apparently, people were attached to their crusts and had been angrily protesting the food trucks. Another article focused on whether it was more politically correct to say "Drivers, start your engines" rather than "Gentlemen, start your engines." There was something to be said for tradition, and unless a random girl qualified for a specific race, I thought we should leave it alone—even though once upon a time I had dreams of being such a force in the series that they'd have to change it. I included my say in the article, and Tack sent it back to me with a sticky note explaining that it wasn't an op-ed piece. In other words, I was supposed to sit down, shut up and report just the facts.

Liza was in Boston visiting family for a week. Work was slow, and I was bored and lonely. Even worse, Colt was officially employed by my father, so he was constantly at our race shop, which meant I couldn't even go home. I hid in my apartment, wrote most of my pieces in my pajamas with a roll of cookie dough on the nightstand next to me, and waited for Liza to come back.

When she got home, grossed out by how little I'd cleaned and my lack of showering, she told me to get off my ass and do something fun with her. *Fun*, for her, was hot yoga.

We made the twenty-minute drive to Yoga One, me in my short shorts and extra-tight running shirt that I had never once worn for a run and Liza in baggy shorts and a tee. She warned me to wear loose-fitting clothes, that the heat would make spandex feel like it was strangling me.

I opened the cedar door to the yoga room and a wall of heat hit me dead on. This wasn't hot yoga. It was *boil your organs from the inside out, sweat in your eyes, too hot to move* yoga. Liza was some high priestess of the Bikram branch of this type of torture, which involved twenty-six postures and two breathing exercises. I'm quite sure Gumby or Elastigirl or any other cartoon superhero couldn't have done the things that she was trying to make me do. But I was never one to get left on the porch while the big dogs were out playing, so I sucked it up, pretended it wasn't killing me, and bought a package of ten sessions.

It certainly did its job of getting my mind off Colt. Every morning at eight thirty when Liza and I escaped the ninety minutes of unbearable pain, it was hard to walk, never mind mope over a boy. But as soon as we got outside, where the winter air was cool, I'd go back to it.

Was what he did so terrible? Was it any different than a guy having strippers at his bachelor party a week before his wedding? Could I forgive him? Could he forgive me? With time to ponder everything that had gone wrong between Colt and me, I couldn't stop myself from harping on it as soon as Liza and I left the gym every morning. She'd listen to me recount every sweet, apologetic, please-take-me-back message he'd left over the past month. She must have been growing weary of hearing the phone ringing, unanswered at all hours, and the accompanying messages.

"For the sake of all that is good in this world, turn off the damn ringer," she pleaded one night as we sat on the couch eating Hagen Daaz from the container and watching mindless TV.

"No can do," I said, digging out a hunk of frozen cookie dough with my spoon. "I don't want to talk to him, but I want to know he's still calling."

"That's either the stupidest or sweetest thing I've ever heard." She scraped the bottom of the ice cream container. "I get it. You've got to torture the bastard." As if said bastard were listening to our conversation, the phone rang. When the machine picked up and it was Colt's voice, I smiled and tossed the phone on the coffee table. Liza held up a spoon with a blob of ice cream on it, ready to flick it at me.

I held my hands up in surrender and said, "When do you think he'll stop calling?"

"Not soon enough," she muttered. "If you're not going to talk to him, I wish he'd get the hint and move on. I dreamed last night that we pulled the phone out of the wall and it kept ringing. It's getting a little creepy."

•   •   •

The day after Liza told me about her dream, she got her wish. It took exactly one month after the banquet for Colt to stop calling. There were still a few weeks before Daytona, so maybe my dad had sent him to some tropical island with no phones to rest up before the start of his rookie season. Or maybe he was skiing in Tahoe or windsurfing in the Caribbean and hadn't taken my number with him. But a week went by, then ten days, and it seemed like my phone hadn't rung at all.

I was running late for work. With the start of the season so close, the stories were getting more interesting, and my workload was increasing. The phone rang as I was closing the door. Something in my gut told me it was Colt. And this time, not only would I answer his call, but I'd take him back as if nothing had ever happened.

"Hi there," I said into the receiver.

"Goddamn, Noodle, you're still alive. Why haven't I seen you lately?" I hadn't told my father anything about the night at the banquet.

"Hey, Daddy. I'm late for work. Can I call you back from the office?"

"Do me one better and come see me tonight. Colt and I were just talking about you. Wondering where you've been. You haven't gone off the grid now, have you?"

Colt. He'd been here all along and had officially stopped calling me. "Hardly. You called me at home. And I answered."

"Then what's your excuse?" I heard voices in the background and wondered if one of them belonged to Colt.

I'd never lied to my parents before. "Nothing, Daddy. It's just been so cold and rainy that I haven't been going out too much. I'll stop by and see you soon, I promise. But now I really do have to get to work. Tack hates it when people are late."

"Look on the bright side," my dad said. "If he fires you, you can come back to where you belong and start the year off by Colt's side."

I was already late for work. A few more minutes wasn't going to make a difference.

"Speaking of Colt, how are things going?"

"Why are you asking me?"

"Uh, because you're his boss?"

"I get that. I meant, why haven't you asked him how things are going?"

Crap. I should have known this wouldn't be easy. "I have. I just wanted to get your take on it."

He was quiet for a moment, and I imagined he was trying to decide if he should believe me or not.

"Well, we went into this marriage knowing there was nothing else for him to win or prove in Busch. So, we're staring down the barrel of a clean slate. Whether he wins the rookie title or never has a top-ten finish, he's still the best young driver that ever was."

My dad was quoting an ESPN sportswriter who'd interviewed Colt after we made the official announcement that he was joining our team in the new decade. "And like that guy said, Colt's ready for the big time and Pierson is the team to get him there."

I wasn't going to coax info from my father. "Okay, well now I probably am going to get fired. I'll talk to you later, Big D."

"Sure thing, Piper P." I started to hang up when I heard him still talking. "One more thing," he said.

"What's that?" Nothing happy ever followed the phrase *one more thing*.

"Colt's been dragging his ass around the race shop for the better part of a month and you're nowhere to be found. It doesn't take a genius to figure out that you all are having problems. So just tell me now if I need to have a talk with that boy."

"Thanks, Daddy. It's all good," I said and then hung up.

• • •

The week before Daytona, I spent an evening making gooey raspberry pastries. I wrapped them individually in waxed paper and packed them in an insulated bag. I stopped the next morning to pick up Tack's favorite blend of coffee sold at a shop that was close to neither my apartment nor work.

"So," I said, standing in Tack's doorway with the pastries in one hand and his coffee in the other. "May I come in?"

He sniffed the air and came around from his desk. "Only if you let me help you with those." He took the bag and the cup from me and nodded to a chair. "And by help, I mean eat."

"They're all for you." I looked around Tack's office. Every time I entered, it seemed like he'd done something more to make it his. Today, there was an embroidered pillow on his couch. It had intricate stitching on it, but it was too far away for me to read.

He opened the bag and took a bite of a danish. I'd heated them in the oven before I left for work, and warm raspberry goo oozed out of the center onto his desk. "You have a much better chance of getting what you want if you ask me while I'm still eating."

"Are there any drivers, crew chiefs or tire changers who need interviewing next week?"

Daytona was the Super Bowl of racing, and the two most senior staffers were already there covering qualifying. That morning I'd purposely picked out a black dress that came to mid-thigh. I sat on the edge of my seat and crossed my bare legs, not that it would do me any good. Tack was the one guy who never seemed to even notice I was a girl. But I needed to get to Daytona, and I wasn't above trying to use some skin to get me there.

He wiped his face with a paper napkin and extended his hand across his desk. "I'm Tack Richards, editor-in-chief. Nice to meet you."

I pretended to shake, even though he was much too far away. "Very funny. Are you going to send me or not?"

He kept up the act. "You bear a striking resemblance to a feisty girl I hired last summer. But she made a big fuss about wanting to fly under the radar and not get any special treatment. Are you her twin?"

He caught me. "Racing's in my blood. I can't not go to Daytona."

"Funny you should mention that little ol' race team your dad owns. Don't you think he can sneak you in the gate?"

Damn these smart Yankee boys. I had no choice but to tell him the truth. Kind of. I pulled down my dress and sat up straight.

"When I'm at the races with my dad, I might as well not have a name. I'm Planter Pierson's kid. His feisty kid." I puckered my lips. "But still his kid. I've known these boys my whole life and they still think I'm eight years old. No one takes me seriously."

He wiped at his eyes with balled fists. "It must be so hard being famous."

I took a hair tie off my wrist and snapped it at him. "Come on. You know what I mean. I feel like when I have that press credential hanging around my neck, it gets me some respect." I fluttered my eyelashes at him. "Is that such a bad thing?"

He took a sip of his coffee and closed his eyes like he was remembering something wonderful, a juicy steak or a first kiss.

"I'm going to level with you, kid." Tack was only seven years older than me, but I kept my mouth shut. "I imagine being the daughter of Mr. Racing has its advantages. You must get the best tables in restaurants, there's not a cop in North Carolina who would dare give you a speeding ticket, and every guy under the age of fifty probably wants to date you."

"But?" I asked.

"But some of my senior staffers have complained."

I half snorted. "About me? Because I've been getting all the good stories lately? Like the piece you had me write last week about how lip gloss with sunscreen doesn't really work any better than the regular stuff?"

"Hey now." He was trying to sound serious. "Wouldn't you want to protect your kisser if you could?"

"Did you ever make Ken or Amy write pieces like that when

they were newbies? Or am I the only lucky one because I made a stink about being like everyone else?" I made a dramatic show of turning around and peering out his office door. "Oh, well would you look at that! Ken and Amy aren't even here." I tapped my nose with my finger as if I were thinking. "Oh, that's right. They're at Daytona."

He smiled and shook his head. "I don't think it's a good idea."

"It's Amy, isn't it?" He nodded. "Does she know I tried to give her the lead for Martinsville last fall? It wasn't my fault she was sick—again."

"It is Amy, and no, she doesn't know. And I don't think you should tell her. Go to the race with your parents. Be a spectator. Have a good time. Don't worry about writing. And you can pick up where you left off when you get back. I actually have an idea for a series piece that wouldn't take anything away from your more experienced colleagues, but would send you to a lot more Cup races this year."

"Thank you," I said. "So, can't that series start with the first race of the year?"

He cast his eyes downward. "I'm afraid not."

"I'm a good writer," I said defensively. I turned in articles that readers wrote fan mail about. I got calls from other publications wanting me to freelance for them. "I deserve the assignments you give me."

"You're a great writer. It's not that. You know some of our journalists have been here for ten years or more."

My stomach tightened. I thought everyone at *Weekly* liked me. Well, everyone but Amy.

"Oh. I get it. They think you're giving me work because I'm a Pierson?" I grew up in a man's world. I could outdrink any guy I knew. I didn't cry. Not in front of anyone, anyway. I shot a mean game of pool. I was as tough and as good as any guy, and any other writer, out there. "Never mind then. Thanks anyway."

"Piper, wait," Tack called to my back. I stopped at the door and turned to him. "Try to see it from their point of view. Ken, Amy and all the others have spent years covering the races no one wanted to go to—Hickory, Orange County and South Boston. They worked their way up to Daytona and Talladega and Atlanta. They've all taken turns gathering intel for the gossip column, Bits from the Pits. And then along comes Piper Pierson who I immediately send to Braselton, Michigan and the Busch Grand National awards banquet."

I thought about the articles I'd written about sunscreen and the shape of pizza slices. I most certainly did not shoot to the top. I worked for it. "I get it," I said, more hurt than I'd thought I'd be. "They're accusing you of favoritism because my dad is a big shot owner. I guess that's why Amy cornered me in the parking garage last week and said the only reason I get good stories is because I'm bagging all the drivers." If only she knew I wasn't bagging any of them anymore.

He took another bite of pastry and had a glob of raspberry stuck to the side of his mouth. But I was in a bad mood, so I didn't tell him.

"I'm sorry, Piper. It'll get better, I promise."

"Don't worry about it," I said, then let myself out of his office. "I've never missed a 500. I thought it'd be more fun if I was there working, but I guess I'll just have to hang out in the garage area and see who I can get to buy me drinks at night."

Missing that race would be like missing the Oscars if my father had been nominated for an Academy Award. It was the first race of the year, and our team had a hot, new driver. We were favored to win the pole. Or at least the outside pole. I'd never told my dad, but I hated it when our drivers were on the pole. It was a hex. A curse. Hardly anyone ever won when they'd qualified first. There was a driver a few years before who had a record number of poles and hardly ever finished a race, never mind winning one. Other than the five bonus points received for starting the race in the first position, poles meant nothing.

• • •

I'd thought I was well liked at *NASCAR Weekly*, so it smarted a bit that some of my co-workers thought I was a spoiled little girl pulling strings to get what I wanted.

"Screw 'em if they can't take a joke," Liza said. We were home in our apartment, phone in hand booking a last-minute flight to Daytona to go be groupies.

"I already told my dad I wasn't coming. It'll be impossible to get another hotel room, and if we don't want to be in the pits with Colt, we'll be risking our lives in the stands." I was painting my toes an outrageous orange. Too bad I couldn't wear sandals at the races.

"Was Daddy Pierson furious when you told him you weren't going?"

I blew on my toenails to dry them. "He was more hurt than angry. He actually cried a little. Said he couldn't make it through a race without his Noodle. I've never missed a 500."

"You made your father cry? That's so low." She took the polish and painted it on her thumbnail. "Think how happy he'll be when you tell him you changed your mind. By the way, what excuse did you give him for not going? You didn't fess up about Colt, did you?"

"I kind of told the truth. I said I have a lot of research and writing to do and I don't really have the time to take the weekend off." I kept seeing the look on my dad's face when I told him I was skipping everyone's favorite race.

Liza gave me a sideways glance "Pants on fire."

I held up my palms. "Do you know how many kinds of toilet paper there are? How am I supposed to know which one fans prefer?" I opened a bottle of clear topcoat nail polish. "I guess this BS article will let the senior staffers know I am, in fact, a peon."

"You sound a little grumpy."

I shot her a look. "Wouldn't you be?"

"Well, yes. *I* wouldn't take it well. But *you* said there are no small articles, only small minds."

I grabbed for the phone and flopped on my bed. "Thanks for reminding me. Now let's book our flight so I can call my dad and secure our spots on the motorhome couches."

We called the travel agent Liza used when she went north to visit her mom and got two overpriced tickets to Daytona. Then I called my parents.

"Hey, Daddy," I said when he answered. "Liza and I decided we couldn't miss the 500. We'll be there Friday morning. Any chance we can crash in the motorhome?"

Liza had dated a guy in college who was a sailor. Every September he'd do an overnight regatta. The first year he went, he and Liza got in a huge fight when he told her he'd be gone for four days. The Daytona 500 was like that regatta. The race itself took about four hours, but crews, owners and drivers were in Daytona for almost three weeks. The qualifying races, the Twin 125s, took place the week before Valentine's Day, and everyone went several days in advance to set up the cars and practice. So, when I called my dad with the good news, he'd been in Florida already for fifteen days.

"Noodle." He sounded exhausted. "Nothing would make me happier than if you and Liza got your pretty little selves on an airplane, but you might want to check the Weather Channel first. Looks like a storm front is moving in." My father was always predicting a weather Armageddon. He'd probably brought enough flashlights with him to illuminate the entire state.

"Settle down, Dad." I rolled off the bed and peered out the window. "Nothing but blue skies here."

"Do me a favor," he said. "Go turn on the TV and call me back in five."

I did what he asked. Liza had gotten in the shower, and as soon as I heard the water turn off, I called to her. "You gotta see this," I yelled through the bathroom door.

She came out wrapped in a towel, her hair dripping water on the floor. "Is it the cute new weather guy?" she asked when she saw what was on.

"Not exactly. It's a not-so-cute storm moving in. My dad was right. I don't think we're going anywhere this weekend."

My stomach had been in knots since Liza and I decided to go to the race. I couldn't imagine spending three straight days with Colt and the team, eating, sleeping and frolicking together like one big happy family. But now, knowing I might not be able to get down there, I felt sick at the thought of missing his first race with us.

"Shit, Piper," Liza said, sitting on the bed next to me. "That's a big ass storm."

A rapid drop in barometric pressure was creating a monster storm that might turn into a rare winter hurricane.

"I have an idea," Liza said when the crawl on the bottom of the TV started listing airports that were already canceling flights. "Let's get in your car and drive. How long can it possibly take? Nine hours? All we need to do is stop at the Crown station for gas and all the potato chips they have, and we'll be there before curfew." My father insisted that everyone be in their rooms, with the lights out by ten.

"Liza," I said, jumping up, pulling a duffel bag from under my bed, "are you sure? You'd have to do all the driving. That's a long ride."

"Don't be mad," she said. "But Colt told me he's been working on getting you to drive a car again."

I dropped the bag. "You've been talking to Colt?"

"Good god, no. Before you two split. He told me he really

wants you to drive again."

I could feel my fingers wrapped around the leather steering wheel. "I sat in his car . . . once." She gave me a disbelieving sideways glance. "Okay. Three times. That's a long way from actually driving."

We both knew if I'd stayed with Colt, I would have done anything he asked. Including driving a car.

"Oh, who cares about that right now. If we get up super early, we can make the drive all in one day. As long as you promise to bring amazing mix tapes and fill the whole back seat with junk food, I'll drive."

I picked up my bag and remembered that I had to call my dad back. I knew he'd only be in the transporter with access to a phone for a few more minutes. "Give me one sec so I can call Big D. and tell him we're coming."

"Absolutely not," my father said when I shared our plan with him. "You'll be driving into the eye of the storm. And what happens if it does turn into a hurricane? You'll end up in the middle of the Atlantic." For a guy who had risked his life many weekends for a lot of years and almost died doing it, he was a big chicken.

"Come on, Dad. The rain is not supposed to start until tomorrow."

"Then why has Charlotte already started canceling flights?"

I should have known he'd check. "We'll be fine. I can't miss this race. I've never not been there for the 500 before."

"Lucky for you, your old man knows what he's doing. I'll be fine. Colt will drive a good, clean race, and you and Liza can have a hurricane party."

No one argued with Planter Pierson—especially not his daughter, and never about my safety. "Yes, Daddy." I felt like I was going to cry. "I'm so sorry I'm going to miss my first 500 ever. Please be safe and wish Colt good luck for me."

"Will do, Noodle. I'll call you tomorrow."

• • •

The storm shifted its path, dumping the most rain and wind on Atlanta, making air travel impossible, and my father had already forbidden us to drive. It missed Florida, so the race was never affected. Being stuck at home with nothing to do but work, I called fifteen tracks asking what kind of toilet paper they used, then Liza and I went to the grocery store and bought every brand mentioned and tested them. No wonder fans were upset. Using the cheaper brands was like wiping my butt with pebbles.

I turned my article in early and asked Tack if he had anything else for me to do. He told me no and suggested I spend the weekend like the rest of North Carolina, watching the Daytona 500 on TV. If I couldn't be there in person, I didn't want to suffer through watching it on TV where I couldn't hear our scanners or see the expression on our crew chief's face. That always told me more than track position.

Liza didn't know it, but I kept track of how many messages Colt had left me after the Busch banquet. Ninety-seven. He hadn't called in more than a month, and I didn't blame him. No returned calls after that many messages made a pretty loud statement. Liza also didn't know that I'd been planning on using Daytona to talk to Colt. I missed him so bad that I was starting to think just being friends would be enough.

With no plans for the weekend, Liza and I donated fifty-four rolls of toilet paper to the Boys and Girls Club of Charlotte. The woman whose job it was to catalog all donations commented on it being an odd gift and wondered a little too loudly why each pack was missing one roll.

Still bummed about my father and the storm putting the kybosh on letting us travel, Liza and I drove home in sulky silence. Neither of us wanted to be home this weekend.

"Let's go to Sandwich Construction to watch the race," she

said after we got back to the apartment.

"You know we'll have to pretend we're at a Stones concert and sleep out to get in, right? And then we'll be subjected to three hundred drunk people crowding around four TVs."

Growing up in racing gave me a different perspective than the fans who piled into bars, waiting for a wreck to take out ten cars at once or a fight between two drivers. I hated the conundrum of what attracted most fans to our sport. When the thirty or forty cars on the track drove a clean race and there weren't any accidents or caution flags for debris, it wasn't that exciting to watch. At least not for other people. It was when a driver tried to squeeze between the car in first place and the outside wall and couldn't quite fit or when a driver was taken out by a rookie's mistake and let his temper get the best of him that most fans thought racing was fun.

It was human nature to be fascinated by destruction.

I didn't want to go to Sandwich Construction or any bar because I hated the cheers that rose up when someone hit the wall or an angry driver threw his helmet at the car who'd put him in the garage area. That wasn't racing for me. I knew things that the girl wearing the number 3 shirt couldn't possibly understand. Like how most of the drivers were treated for dehydration after almost every race because it was about a hundred and fifty degrees in a car and once a driver ran out of water, he could only get more during a pit stop. I also understood that no matter what they admitted, even the most experienced drivers hated going blind into the smoke of an accident where they couldn't see anything and had to rely solely on their spotters to get them safely through the carnage. My dad and his buddies had told stories about driving down the entire length of a superspeedway functionally blind because they couldn't see the car in front of them through all the smoke.

I knew that most drivers believed in God and prayed to Him before every race to keep them safe. Over the years, I'd had a few disagreements with non-fan friends who said racing wasn't a sport and required no skill or athletic ability. They argued that everyone over the age of sixteen could drive a car. A couple of times I'd gotten so mad that I'd taken them behind the shop and had them drive an old clunker of my dad's with no power steering while I put the heat on full blast. Every time, after five minutes or so they were exhausted and had to stop. Then I'd politely ask them to envision doing that for four hours at a hundred and seventy-five miles an hour with a car an inch in front of them and one an inch behind them. I always won those arguments.

So no, I had no desire to go sit at a bar and listen to people bellyache that a safe race was a boring one and cheer when someone I cared about got hurt. But I didn't want to stay home by myself, either.

• • •

The next day, Liza and I dressed in everything not allowed in the pits and headed out to meet friends at the Crown station on Old Concord Road to carpool to the bar. I was still sad and feeling sorry for myself and didn't want to eat soggy, microwaved nachos with Liza in our apartment while she pretended to care about the race. They piled in Liza's Blazer and we got about a mile from Sandwich Construction on Route 49 before traffic came to a halt and a nice state trooper told us we'd have to park in the commuter lot and take a shuttle.

"Officer," I said, leaning across Liza, making sure he could see my cleavage in the racetrack-prohibited sleeveless minidress I was wearing. "Would it be okay with y'all if we tried our luck at getting into the parking lot?" I found the thicker my accent, the better chance I had of getting what I wanted. "My friend bartends at Sandwich and he said he'd save us a spot."

He stared down my dress for several seconds. "I think the parking lot attendants are trying to figure out how to stack cars on top of each other, but if you want to give it a whirl, go ahead."

I giggled and touched his arm. "Oh my, you are too kind." Thank God I hadn't worn a bra.

A few minutes later Liza turned in to the packed lot and pulled up next to a dumpster where there was a big No Parking sign. Liza and I jumped out and knocked on the kitchen door. Two bouncers I knew came out and told us to get back in the car. They directed us to the side of the building where several spaces were cordoned off with yellow crime scene tape. It paid to be nice to everyone and tip well.

My friends and I ate hot wings and drank beer at Sandwich Construction with 300 other race fans. It was impossible not to think about Colt. We met at a race. I counted at least twenty girls wearing football-style jerseys with his car number and name on the back. Pieces of his race cars were on the walls next to some of the greatest Winston Cup drivers in history. He drove for my family's team now. I couldn't get away from him And even though I was still mad, I didn't want to be away from him anymore. We weren't married or engaged. If he wanted to have one last romp with his ex, it probably wasn't as big of a deal as I had made it.

"I know what you're doing," Liza whispered. She reached in front of me and took a handful of napkins from the metal dispenser. "And you need to stop it. There's nothing you can do now. He's in a race car and you're here. So stop looking longingly at all the reminders of him and put on your happy face." She dropped the napkins on the table and pushed my mouth into a smile with her fingers.

Every time I thought about Colt, I took a sip of beer. I downed a pint in less than ten minutes, and it still wasn't working. I thought of the Rolling Stones song "Honky Tonk Woman." *I just can't seem to drink you off my mind.* I wondered what finally worked for Mick Jagger. Drinking cheap beer out of a plastic pitcher wasn't getting the job done, so I squeezed between a hundred people and came back to the table with a round of shots.

As far as races went, this one wasn't terribly exciting. Dale Earnhardt dominated, leading 155 of the 200 laps. There were only three cautions, and no serious accidents. Normally, that was the exact kind of race that I loved the most. But I wasn't sitting in our pit, a few feet from the track, and I couldn't see Birdie's expression when he was on the radio, and I wasn't listening to our scanner and hearing my dad and Colt talk about where he should go high and which cars to avoid.

About halfway through I understood why most race fans lived for the excitement of crashes, and I was bored enough to want to go home. I had to abandon my game of *Think of Colt, drink a Colt 45* after I'd finished three beers in half an hour. I'd gotten stupid drunk too many times because of him. And I did not want to be hungover at work the next day. Much to my chagrin, I couldn't leave. So I ate, drank a Shirley Temple and called our apartment every few minutes to see if I had any messages on the answering machine.

Walking back from the payphone by the bathroom, I heard one of the announcers mention Colt's name. I looked up to see an in-car camera focused on Colt. It was impossible to read his expression through the shield of his helmet, but I swore by the way he was gripping the steering wheel up high that he was nervous. There was no way he couldn't be. It didn't matter that he'd raced at Daytona a bunch of times in his Busch car. Winston Cup was entirely different.

I stood by the bar as the camera angle changed and now showed Colt's car in the middle of the lead lap. The car in front of him faltered for half a second and I shouted, "Do it, Colt." Probably no one in the bar could see what I did. The driver of the 16 car hesitated just long enough to give Colt a chance to get around him.

Colt dove to the outside, and I grabbed the man standing next to me. "Sorry!" I said when I realized what I'd done; then I turned my attention back to the TV. "Don't let up," I said as if Colt could hear me. "There's room."

The whole maneuver lasted no more than a few seconds, but it felt like slow motion. When the 16 car let off the gas, Colt took a shot to get around him on the high side. It wasn't a move that many drivers used, simply because it wasted real estate. But if everyone was going low, the path to go high would be clearer. My dad had taught me that when I first started racing karts.

But Colt did what I'd done, what every rookie—hell, what every driver had done more than once. He used too much force and jerked the wheel a bit too hard, causing his tail end to spin to the inside, sending his car into the wall at turn four.

I covered my mouth and yelped. The caution came out, and the other forty-one cars on the track managed to avoid getting caught up in Colt's wreck. Suddenly Liza was next to me, her hand on my back. "He's fine," she said. "He's fine. He's fine. He wasn't even going that fast." I looked at her. "Okay, he was. But he's fine. He'll drop his window net any second now. Just watch. Before Fire Rescue even gets there." But her voice faded into the noise in the bar and constant hum of the cars on the TV.

An ambulance parked behind Colt's car as a tow truck pulled around it and backed up to its hood. "Liza," I finally said. "Why isn't he getting out?"

She held me tighter. "He will. He will." We watched. And waited. "He has to."

Two paramedics approached the car as Colt's net came down and he pulled himself out. "Oh God. Oh God." I turned to Liza. "He's okay, right?"

"Look." She lifted my chin with her fingers.

Colt had taken off his helmet and was waving to the crowd. When the camera zoomed in on him, he smiled and gave a thumbs-up. The announcer came back on and said they'd take a commercial break while they cleared debris. Just before the screen went dark, I caught a glimpse of Colt's car. On the left front quarter panel, written in white cursive, was the word *Piper*.

By the time the race came back on, Colt's car was behind pit wall, and the announcer mentioned he was getting checked out at the infield care center but appeared to be fine. I didn't realize Liza was talking to me until she touched my arm.

"Honey," she said. "Do you want to take off? You look a little green."

"Do you mind?" I asked, and we went to find our friends.

• • •

When my parents called that night, I made sure Colt wasn't hurt and then asked my dad if Colt was disappointed with finishing his first Winston Cup race almost forty laps down.

"That boy's something else," my dad said. "He apologized for letting me down and promised he'd drive a harder race next weekend in Atlanta. I told him he did no such thing and these deals happen. But the poor kid looked like he was going to cry."

That made two of us.

• • •

The next day I realized I left my leather jacket at Sandwich Construction. It was buttery soft, somewhere between milk and dark chocolate in color, and Colt had given it to me for no reason other than he saw it and thought I would like it. I called the restaurant to see if they'd found it, and Adam the daytime bartender said he'd hang on to it until I got there.

Despite turning to soda toward the end of the race, I'd still drunk enough that now I was hungover, sad, and looked like poop. The parking lot was almost empty. No sooner did my cowboy boots echo in the dining room than I heard the voice that spoke to me almost every night in my dreams.

I walked up behind Colt as casually as I could and stuck my hands in my pockets to keep them from shaking.

"Hey, stranger. What's it like in the big leagues?" He was alone at a table.

He dropped his fork when he saw me. "Piper." He studied me for a long time. "You look amazing." It was and it wasn't true. I had lost some weight since the Busch banquet, but I hadn't showered that morning, nor had I bothered to brush my hair. If Tack noticed at work that morning how bedraggled I looked, he'd been kind enough not to say anything.

"What are you doing here? By yourself?" It struck me as oddly sad that Winston Cup's newest rock star was eating lunch by himself. As quickly as my concern for him arose, a flash of the Busch banquet extinguished it.

He got up from the barstool, brushing his fingers on my cheek. I thought I would melt.

"I called you a million times, wanting to apologize. I needed to explain what happened."

"I took sex ed. in ninth grade. I figured it out."

He shook his head sadly. "Nobody deserved to see that, especially you."

I couldn't muster the strength or maturity to forgive him, as much as I wanted to and as much as I missed him.

"It's nothing but a thing, Colt," I said. I was going for breezy, but thanks to my high, squeaky voice, I was coming across as borderline hysterical. "It's not like we were going steady." I tried to laugh but made a honking noise.

"I didn't sleep with her," he said quietly, desperately.

Across the room, Adam held up my jacket. I nodded to him and he tossed it on a stool. "It was nice to see you," I said to Colt. "Good luck with the run for the rookie title."

Wishing him well for the entire year sounded so final. This was the breakup we didn't have after the Busch banquet. I touched his shoulder, grabbed my jacket and said goodbye to Adam. I let myself out the front door, sat on the front step and sobbed into my hands. The concrete was cold through my jeans.

Months of missing Colt bore down on me. I did not hear him open the door behind me.

"God, Piper, look what I've done to you. I am such an asshole." He offered his hand, but I didn't take it. I had snot and tears and last night's makeup smeared on my face. After a moment, he sat beside me. It was almost noon when I got to the bar, and the lunch crowd would be there soon. "*Piper . . . Piper . . . Piper*. What can I do to make this up to you?"

I answered without thinking. "You can tell me why you did it."

"I've been asking myself that every day for two months."

"And?"

"I honestly don't know, Pipes." I loved it when he called me that. "One minute I was watching you from across the room and the next she was handing me a glass of champagne."

"Can't you just admit that you were drunk and stupid?"

"I was definitely stupid. But I swear to you, I wasn't drinking. At least not then. I knew I'd have to make a speech and I was so nervous. I was afraid if I even had one drink that I'd say something stupid."

"But you did drink. You just told me she brought you a glass of champagne."

"She did." I was so thankful he didn't say her name. "I told her I didn't want it, but she whined that we had to celebrate. I figured one glass wasn't going to hurt me, so I took it. And then another. Next thing I know, you walked in and I freaked out."

"Please don't lie to me." I started to get up, but he grabbed my hand. "Just tell me the truth. You wanted to sleep with her and that was that."

"But that wasn't it," he said. He was still holding my hand. "I don't know, Piper. I guess the excitement of the night and the drinks and everything else got to me and I made the worst decision of my life." He pulled me to him. I took that opportunity to wipe my face on his crisp, white Jewel Petroleum polo shirt. With a new race series and new team came a new sponsor.

"All I can do now is tell you how madly in love with you I am. Never felt this way before. Will never feel this way again. Stupid, helplessly in love with you. I've loved you since the day you walked in my motorhome asking me ten-thousand questions for your article. Any girl that can drink more tequila than me has a place in my heart."

I couldn't not smile. "Oh that's nice. You like me for my high tolerance for alcohol?"

"No," he mused, "I love you for that." He pulled me to him again and kissed me. I had almost forgotten how much I missed that. How much I missed him.

"I love you, too." I took a breath and kissed him again.

"Does this mean what I think it means?" he asked.

I knew what he wanted to hear. That all was forgiven, and we could start anew.

"I want to forgive you, Colt. I want to be with you. Forever. But you need to give me a little time and tell me that it didn't mean anything to you. That she doesn't mean anything."

"I don't even remember it," he said. "Maybe I did drink too much. I just don't know." I rolled my eyes. "But that's not an excuse. I just wish I could give you a better answer. I meant everything I said about telling her that I found someone I wanted to be with forever." He wiped his eyes with his hand. "I've been going crazy these last two months without you. I need you to forgive me, Piper. Please. Please tell me you forgive me."

We were both crying. "I didn't tell my dad," I finally said. "Next time you hurt me, I will."

"And he'll kill me."

I leaned my shoulder against his. "Yup."

"So I guess this means I'd better not hurt you ever again."

I wanted to kiss him and have that be that. But I needed to know. "Is she gone?"

"Yes. I haven't seen or talked to her since that night. I called Mr. Thompson to make sure that she didn't go back to his team. He told me he wrote her a recommendation for her new job. She's doing PR for a soccer team in Wilmington. I promise you that it's just you and me."

I'd seen so many of my friends in college never let their boyfriends forget when they screwed up. Eventually the guys couldn't take it anymore and would leave. I didn't want to be like that.

"Clean slate," I said, pretending to erase something. "Let's let 1990 be the best year ever."

17

A month after Colt and I started dating again, he had an off weekend between the Atlanta and Darlington races, so he invited a few friends over to watch *St. Elmo's Fire* and *The Breakfast Club*. I'd been avoiding the race shop so I wouldn't have to see Scott, and I suspected Colt orchestrated movie night so I'd have to talk to him.

"Hi," I said when Scott came through the front door. "Can I get you a drink?"

He followed me to the kitchen, and I handed him a beer from the fridge. "So," I began, looking at the ceiling. "I'm really sorry."

He hugged me hard. "You're lucky Colt's my best friend. Otherwise, your ass would have been mine."

"I could do worse." We clinked our bottles together.

I jumped up on the counter and he pulled out a chair from the kitchen table and sat backwards on it. "So, I take it everything is good with you two now?" he asked.

"I think so." I thought about the last month and how easy it all had been.

"What does that mean? From what Colt tells me, I expect to see a ring on your finger any second now."

I'd been thinking the same thing. "No, things are great. Really great. And I guess that's the problem. I keep waiting for the other shoe to drop."

He laughed. "Didn't the other shoe smack you in the face at the banquet?"

I took a long sip of my beer. I'd hoped that when Colt graduated from Busch to Winston Cup he'd start buying something better than Busch beer. At least he hadn't started smoking Winston cigarettes.

"Yeah, I guess it did. I don't know. Things are good with Colt. He's sorry. I'm sorry. And we love each other."

"And . . . what? You don't think it's going to last?"

"Would you? We're so young. And he's this rock star in the making."

"You two are David Bowie and Iman." He stood and kissed my forehead. "Settle down and enjoy it. That boy isn't going anywhere."

●   ●   ●

In a *NASCAR Weekly* staff meeting the following week, an intern brought me a stack of letters. "They wouldn't fit in your mailbox." I thanked him and leafed through them. They were all hand addressed.

"Nice work, Piper," said Ken Dilaurentis. "You're putting us all to shame." He winked.

I caught Amy's glare. "It's nothing," I said. "It's just because I'm new. The novelty will wear off."

"You're too modest. You made an article on the track that doubled the number of trashcans interesting. Who knew that was even possible?" Ken tipped an imaginary hat to me.

"They did a lot research," I said. "Duplicated Disney World's model on how many steps people will take looking for a garbage can before they'll just drop their trash. It was actually pretty fascinating."

Amy pretended to sneeze and said, "*Kiss-ass*" when she covered her mouth.

"Excuse me?" Tack asked.

"It's fine, Tack. Just a joke," I said.

"What was the name of that town?" Ken asked with a fake grin as if he were trying to defuse the tension. "East Nowhere?"

"West Nowene," I told him. "But it felt like East Nowhere."

"Back to work," Tack said. He put a stack of rough draft articles on the table. "Everyone find yours and read through my comments. Let me know if you have any questions."

Amy grabbed the papers and walked around the table, passing out our work. She threw mine on the table in front of me so hard that it slid onto the floor. Ken reached down and handed it to me. "Nice," he said, but I didn't know what he was talking about until I turned it right side up and saw what was in the upper left-hand corner.

After the meeting, I sat at my desk peeling off the gold star Tack had stuck to my article about a new manufacturer of fire suits that was actively challenging the established brand that virtually every driver in NASCAR used.

"Do you not like being the star pupil?" Tack asked, walking to my desk.

I startled. "Hi. No . . . I mean, yes." I glanced over my shoulder. Amy's chair was empty. "I don't want anyone to think I'm bragging."

Tack followed my eyes to Amy's desk. "Good thinking. I should have considered that. Things have been a bit tough for her since she got out of the hospital the last time."

I'd never asked Amy what illness had caused her to miss Martinsville, but judging from how much weight she'd lost and how pale she was, it must have been something bad. "No more stickers for you." He winked. "Next time I'll just tell you what a great job you're doing."

"You do that anyway."

I was so happy at *Weekly*. Ever since I'd taken an intro to journalism course my freshman year, writing was the only job I'd wanted, and I loved what I did. According to fan mail, I showed a rarely seen side to drivers. They went from being hotheads with big egos to intelligent men with real concerns and emotions.

Tack rapped his knuckles on my desk in quick succession. "Since we're on the topic of your stellar abilities, I've got another piece for you." I spun around in my chair and sat up. "You got so much positive feedback when you did those two articles last year on Colt Porter and Brent Austin that I talked to Jim Matts about giving you a series." The newspaper rarely ran series.

"What do you want me to write about?"

"Well, originally I wanted to you keep track of the rookies for this year. I thought it'd be fun to keep tabs on all the up-and-coming hotshots."

"That's a lot of ego for one article. My parents invited all five of them for dinner a few weeks ago. They all think they're the second coming of Richard Petty."

"Well, good news or bad news, I can't let you write about them."

Amy sat at her desk, and I watched as she opened and then closed a drawer a bit too hard. "Let me guess—you're giving the piece to a more seasoned employee?"

"I'm giving the piece to a more *single* employee. Our whole *don't ask, don't tell* method of pretending you weren't dating Colt Porter worked for a while. But now that he's driving for Pierson Racing and you two made it into *Bits from the Pits,* you can't even put his name in print."

A late-night trip Colt and I took to my favorite ice cream shop, the Big Dipper, made it into the gossip section of *Weekly*. "I've been thinking about that and wanted to talk to you. Last season I only covered Busch, so none of my stories were remotely related to Pierson. But this season, it sounds like you might give me some

Cup stories. Would it be easier, or cleaner, if you left me in Busch?"

"Yes. But I'm not going to. You're a good reporter, so I'm going to use you where I need you. But I need you to write like everyone is watching. Not a word about Colt, Pierson or the 20 car. Got it?"

I'd lived my whole life like everyone was watching. "Got it. So what's the series?"

"I want you to predict who's going to win the Cup championship this year."

"I'm sorry?" I coughed. "I'm not sure I can even make an educated guess. Especially if I can't consult the smartest person I know."

"Planter?" he asked. I appreciated him not calling him my father while we were at work.

"I'm sure he already knows who's going to win both the championship and the rookie title. He's freaky good like that."

Tack pulled up an empty chair and sat. "Well, let's see how good you are."

"This could get me in trouble with some of my fath—" I stopped myself. "Is this a test? To prove I can be unbiased?" His expression told me I was correct. "Well then, I guess I better do my homework. I'll make you proud," I told him. "But why now? We're four races in." I'd spent hours trying to calculate every possible outcome for Colt, who was leading the rookie chase. Only thirteen points separated the five newcomers. But I'd hardly paid attention to the leaders of the series.

"Nah. It's getting interesting now. Just do what you do. Put together a monthly installment after you've interviewed the top five or seven contenders and come up with a stream-of-consciousness piece for each driver and his strategy. Then put your magic touch on them."

I blinked at him several times and cocked my head. "Why, Mr. Richards, I don't know what you're talking about," I said in an exaggerated Scarlet O'Hara accent.

He smirked. "Yes you do. I've heard about your crazy algorithm."

We lived in a small world. Fired crew chiefs took up camp in someone else's pit. Terminated drivers joined the garages of men they previously hated and now smiled with for photo ops. Someone told Tack that in the past I'd predicted with decent accuracy which of the new crop of Winston Cup rookies would make a go of it and which would run out of money and talent in the first half of the year. I'd correctly chosen the Rookie of the Year the last five seasons running. Even my dad thought I had some kind of magical power. But I'd never tried to do it for the champions.

"If you must know," I said in my regular voice, "there's nothing to it. Everyone knows each other. I've grown up with these boys. It's not that hard. I research the rookies' racing records from their days in karts and on dirt tracks and then I add a few bonus points for good names or good looks. I suppose I could try to figure out the leaders of the series."

"Well, whatever you do, keep on doing it. Because your first article will list your predictions, and then whatever happens at the end of the year, you'll write a recap explaining how close or how far off your choices were."

•   •   •

On the plane on the way home from the June race at Michigan, I was making notes for my series when my dad unclipped his seatbelt and scooted around my sleeping mother. Colt and I were sitting together, and my dad plopped down in an empty seat across the aisle from us.

"What's shakin'?" my dad asked as he opened a package of peanuts he pulled out of his breast pocket.

Colt slid his headphones around his neck. "Honestly, sir, I'm just relieved I finally gave you a top-ten finish. I promise it will be the first of many."

My dad reached across the aisle and patted his shoulder. "Of that, I am certain," he said.

"I know Winston Cup cars are much more powerful than Busch, but I tested a bunch of Cup cars last year. And I just can't handle them on the smaller tracks." My dad looked like he wanted to say something that would make Colt feel better, but he let him keep talking. "It seems like I go too fast on the short straights and lose control in the turns." He'd put four cars in the wall throughout the season, but I wasn't about to start counting for him.

"Don't even think about that," my dad told him. "Short tracks are always harder for rookies. Look how well you did this weekend on a super speedway."

A commentator had said that exact same thing during the race.

"A lot of good that will do me. We race on more short tracks than super speedways."

My dad spoke as if he'd been anticipating this moment. "So, what do you need to do?"

"Drive better, I guess."

"You drive so much better than you give yourself credit for." My dad finished the peanuts and put the empty wrapper back in his pocket. "What you need to do is imagine every short track is a super speedway. Or at least figure out why the bigger tracks are easier for you."

"That's simple. I have more time to back off the gas without having to brake before I get to the turns. Like when we were at Talladega in May." Alabama was home to NASCAR's biggest track at 2.77 miles. It was there that Colt showed his fans, our team and other drivers glimpses of the powerhouse he was in Busch. He had no wrecks and drove a good, steady race. I watched the race at Sandwich Construction with Sasha and Liza. Even the commentators thought he'd break his freshman slump and finish in the top ten.

"That's right," my dad said. "That was a great race."

"Not great enough. Eleventh is no top ten."

"Look, Colt. No one expects you to win a race your rookie year. The boys at Jewel Petroleum love you."

The team's new sponsor sent reps with portly bellies pushing against their starched, button-down shirts to every race, and they totally backed Colt.

"You know you have a home in my stable for as long as you want. This is a warm-up year. You're dipping your foot in the pool. Next year you'll go swimming."

I'd been quiet long enough, leaning over Colt trying to hear my father. For such a big man, he was very soft spoken, and he never handed out false compliments or hope.

"You're leading the rookie chase," I said. "Settle down and enjoy your first amazing finish running with the big dogs."

My dad stood. "Listen to your girlfriend. She's a smart cookie."

18

The following week, we celebrated Colt's birthday with Scott, Liza, Sasha, their boyfriends and some guys from his crew. After dinner at the McNinch House in Charlotte, we went back to Colt's place, sat on the deck and drank until the sun came up. I couldn't help but imagine that he'd spend the rest of his birthdays with me. We were so young, too young to think about marriage and babies and a life together. But my mom was younger than me when she got married. And my parents rarely spent a night apart. If they could make it work so young, so could we.

The morning after Colt's party, he rolled over and slung his arm across my chest, waking me up. "Oh good," he said. "You're up."

I wiped the sleep out of my eyes. "I am now."

"Sweet. Throw some clothes on and let's go." He jumped on the bed on all fours like a dog waiting to be let out. When I didn't move he poked me in the ribs. "What are you waiting for? Time's a ticking."

"Why are you so happy?" I rolled over and looked at the digital—6:15 a.m.

"Because today is the day."

In my gut I knew what he meant. I ran to the bathroom and threw up.

An hour later, I'd thrown on a pair of yoga pants and a Pierson Racing sweatshirt and we were driving to Moorestown High School. Colt pulled in the parking lot, unbuckled his seatbelt and held my hand.

"You can do this." He leaned over, and I thought he was going to kiss me. Instead he unstrapped me, then reached across my lap and opened my door. "It's time."

I crossed my arms over my chest. "*No. No,* it's not." My mouth watered. "Please don't make me do this."

He got out of the car, came around to my side, opened the door wide and knelt beside me. "Pipes. You're the coolest, strongest girl I know. There's nothing you can't do."

I took a breath and held it as long as I could. "I'm not saying I will drive, but if I do, I don't want you in the car."

"Why?"

I realized how crazy I sounded, but I couldn't stop myself. "If I hit the gas instead of the brake and go flying into a brick wall, I'm not going to risk hurting you."

He picked up my hand and kissed it. "Oh, Pierson, were you not there a few weeks ago when I did go flying into a wall? Granted it wasn't brick, but at a hundred and ninety miles an hour, it might as well have been." He stood up and ran his hands down his body. "And look at me. I'm as good as gold."

I got out of the car and hugged him. "You make being a petulant fraidy cat hard when you talk like that."

"Then I'm doing my job." He stepped away and lifted my chin so we were looking at each other. "Pierson. I need you to listen to me and listen good. You may be the only journalist here, but I did my research, too. I remember you. Racing with you." I remembered it too. So many times we'd split a one-two finish. I used to keep track of how many times he beat me, but after a while it was pretty much fifty-fifty. "*You're* the reason I'm as good as I am."

"Me?" I'd been trying hard not to look at him, but now I did. "How so?"

"To borrow your daddy's phrase, 'It ain't bragging if it's true.' You were the only driver in the Dash series who could give me a run for my money. You pushed me to be better than I thought I could be. So now I'm pushing back."

"Oh, Colt." I couldn't catch my breath and it was hard to speak. "I don't think I can do it."

He took my hand and I let him lead me to the driver's side. "We'll do it exactly like we did last time. Just sit in the seat and hold on to the wheel."

I wiped my nose. "That's all?"

"Whatever you're comfortable with. Let's just start there."

I got in the car and shut off the radio. Even the low din of the soft rock station Colt had chosen was too distracting. He walked to the other side and knocked on the window, motioning for me to put it down. I put the keys in the ignition and my breath caught in my throat. I pressed the control and Colt slid in through the window as if it were a race car. I couldn't help but laugh.

"Smooth," I said.

"It made you smile, didn't it?" He licked his finger and held it up as if marking a board. "Score one for Colt." He put his hand on the key. "I'm going to turn the engine over now, but the car is in park. We're not going anywhere."

I started to slap his hand away, but he stopped me. After a moment he turned the key and the engine gently hummed. I gripped the wheel so hard my fingers burned.

"Great job. Now close your eyes and envision yourself driving. Slow and steady. Just barely moving."

I did as he asked, but after a minute I felt stupid, so I opened my eyes. He kept talking, telling me to remember my best finish and the day I got my driver's license and where I went and who I went with. When I looked at the clock, I realized almost forty minutes had passed. I let go of the wheel and pushed out a breath I felt like I'd been holding since we got in the car.

"I think I'm ready," I finally said.

"Darlin', I know you are." Colt leaned over and kissed my cheek. "Nice and slow. We'll just drive around the parking lot once. Let you get your feet wet."

I wiped my palms on my pants and turned to Colt. "Wish me luck."

"Luck has nothing to do with this. You're ready."

I pressed the brake and put the car in drive. We crept forward as a car on the main road backfired and I screamed. "*I can't! I can't!* Please don't make me." I tried to put the car in park, but we were still moving, so the gears caught and the engine stuttered. Finally, we stopped and sat with my head on the steering wheel, tears running down my face.

I thought Colt would try to comfort me or at least say something, but he sat in silence until my breathing evened and slowed. "That was a good start," he said after a while.

"Please just take me home." I couldn't look at him. "This was a bad idea."

"You got it," he said, opening his door. We traded places, and after we were both buckled in, he took my chin in his hands and made me look at him.

"I'm proud of you, Pierson. Even if you don't realize it yet, you want this. And everyone knows whatever Piper Pierson wants, she works her ass off until she gets it."

I touched his cheek. "You're sweet to say that. Now let's get out of here."

We drove most of the way back to his house not talking—him singing to Supertramp and ABBA and me lost in my thoughts. He was right. I did want to drive again, maybe even race. But if the sound of a car backfiring wrecked me, there was no way I'd try it again.

When we pulled into Colt's driveway, we got out and I started toward his house. "Hang on a minute," he said. "Let's sit by the water. There's something I need to tell you."

He took my hand and we walked through the dewy grass. "If you're breaking up with me because I'm such a wuss bag, I am going to throw myself in the lake."

We got to the wooden loveseat with a striped cushion and sat. It'd rained earlier in the day and everything was damp. He shifted so he was almost facing me, and I did the same. "I hope you know I've only been pushing you to drive again because I can see how much you miss it."

"Hardly," I scoffed. "I'm rather fond of people watching on the bus and riding my bike straight uphill from my parents' house to yours."

"No you're not," he said. "I need you to know that if you can't get past this thing, it's okay. I love you no matter what."

"Is it, though?" I asked sharply. "How much longer are you going to put up with a girlfriend who is such a mess she can't even do something that teenagers do every day."

"Goddamn, Piper. Give me some credit." He got up, found a stone and skipped it across the water. It hopped a good fifty feet. He came back and sat. "When are you going to understand that I am in this for the long haul? You're it. I am off the market. Forever. You are my person." He reached in his pocket. I couldn't speak. We were so young, but he was right. There was no one else for us.

"What are you saying?"

He removed his hand from his pocket, and I saw he was clutching a tissue. "Here," he said, handing it to me. "Blow."

I took it from him and laughed. "Thanks." My nose honked loudly. We were too young. And he knew it. I'd been stupid to let myself think that for even a second. "Can we go in now? My butt is wet."

"Hold up. I'm not done. You are my person, and that won't change if you never drive a car again. But I need you to sit here, soggy bum and all, and really listen to me. I need you to *hear* what I'm saying."

"I'm listening," I said.

"If God himself came down from the heavens today and told me I could have another eighty-five years on this planet, but I couldn't ever race again and I couldn't love you, or I could die tomorrow with a heart full of love for you and cars and my family and your parents, I'd voluntarily take my own life."

"Colt! Don't you even think such a horrible thing."

"Horrible?" He picked up both my hands and kissed each finger one by one. "Living without loving you and loving what I do would be horrible. It'd be worse than death. I've lived more in twenty-five years than some guy who spent his life in a factory and never found his Piper, even if he died at a hundred and three. Don't you get that? My life is so good. Here. Now. With you. That's all I want. And if God sees fit to call me home tomorrow or the next day? Well, then I'll get to the pearly gates and get down on my knees and thank him for giving me such a blessed life."

I drank in his words, feeling a peace I hadn't felt since before Tennessee happened.

"Do you remember the day I interviewed you in Braselton, what you said to me when I asked you how important it was to you to win the Busch championship?"

"Sure do. I told you racing is a gift that could last thirty more years or could end tomorrow. Life is like that too, you know."

"That's exactly what you said. And I remember thinking that there was no one else like you. That you were an old soul trapped in a young man's body." I leaned in to him and kissed him. "Thank you, Colt."

"For what?"

"You know for what." I stood and offered him my hand. "Maybe we can go back to the school and try again next weekend."

"I'd love to, darlin', but I leave for Pocono in a few days."

•   •   •

Colt would be racing in Pocono the following weekend. I'd hoped that Tack would also send me to write another installment on the chase for the championship. But he said he needed me at home so I could wrap up a couple smaller projects and start a new big one.

The day before Colt left for the race, he called me at work.

"What's happenin', hot stuff?" Colt almost always greeted me like that. He sounded unusually happy given that he'd had only one top-ten finish and felt like he'd let down my father.

"I'm kinda frazzled. What's up?"

"Why? What's going on?"

I took the pencil I'd been chewing on and tied my hair up with it. "Tack just threw a little assignment at me and I'm freaking out."

"What is it?"

"He wants me to predict who will win the rookie title."

I could hear Colt zipping a suitcase. I hated the time we spent apart.

"I hate to brag on myself, but you know I have this in the bag."

"Oh no, my friend. Tack wants a two-thousand-word piece on *next* year's winner."

"Next year? That's crazy. We don't even know for sure who will move up to Winston Cup. What's he thinking?"

"Apparently he's impressed with the articles I've been writing about the big dogs. And he wants to see just how much magic I can spin."

"It makes you sound like a trick pony. You are awfully good at it," Colt said. "I've seen your spreadsheets. And I think you're right about who's going to win the Cup title."

"What I do is really just luck. People are going to think I'm a crackpot if I write about my methodologies."

"What are you worried about? You know more about stock car racing than most crew chiefs. Your research is impeccable and it's not like you base your picks on how pretty the cars are."

"Actually, I kind of do." After I took into consideration experience, records, number of wins, and a million other factors, I added a few points to the cute drivers, more if they had a cool name. Like Colt. "I guess it's just as well you're going solo this weekend. Tack wants a draft on his desk by Monday."

"Why? Next season starts in like six months."

"I have no idea. I just do as I'm told."

"Well, I have something to tell you that I think will cheer you up."

"Good. I could use some happy news right now. Spill it."

"Can I come over tonight? I want to say it in person."

Colt never asked if he could come over. Both Liza and I were used to him showing up unannounced when he wasn't at the shop or racing. "Sure. What time? Do you want dinner? It's Taco Tuesday."

"No thanks. I have to take care of something first. It'll be late. Just leave the door unlocked for me."

I'd tried to give Colt a key to my apartment many times over the last year, but he always refused. At first I thought he didn't want me to think we were more serious than we were. But then when we both realized that we did have a future together, I began to wonder. I asked him about it, and he'd said something about not wanting to lose it. It was a key, not the Hope Diamond. But still, he never took it from me when I offered.

• • •

I was asleep by the time he arrived that night. I'd gone to bed in a short, silk nightie, but Liza liked the apartment to feel like a meat locker when she slept, so by the time Colt slipped into my room, I had on fuzzy socks and a sweatshirt.

"I have something to tell you," he said, sitting on the edge of my bed.

I sat up and squinted. It was dark in my room, but the hall light was on, and I could see him in silhouette, grinning.

"Now?" He knew how much I loved to sleep and how I hated to be up in the middle of the night. "This better be good."

He held my hand. His was warm. "Oh, it's good. So very good." He switched on the light. "Less than a week."

I blinked with the light. "Till what?" I was grumpy and wasn't following his guessing game.

"I can't tell you now."

I didn't like where this was going. No great declaration of love ever began with those words. "You know patience isn't my strong suit."

He touched my nose with his finger. "I'm painfully aware of that. But that's too bad. You're just going to have to hold your horses until I get back from Pocono."

I flopped back on my pillow. "I mean this with love, but then why are you here?"

He pulled at a loose thread on my pillowcase. "I have big news, and although I can't tell you what it is right now, I wanted you to know it's coming."

Anything newsworthy relating to Pierson Racing would be vetted through our PR team. And I would know about it. "But you woke me up and now you're not going to tell me what it is? That's so mean."

He waggled his eyebrows. "It'll make the surprise that much

sweeter." I threw my hand over my eyes to block out the light.

"You are killing me here. Will you at least tell me when I'll find out?"

He kissed me quickly. "You know how much I love to celebrate. So, I'm going to throw myself a party and announce it then."

Announcement? What the hell was he going to say?

"I take it this is good news?" He looked much too cheerful to be about to tell the world he was retiring or defecting camps to open-wheel racing.

"You know it is."

"Does my father know?"

"Oh yeah. And let me tell you, swinging this idea by him was the scariest thing I've ever done."

"So, I take it that whatever it was, my father approved or you wouldn't be here telling me about it. Or kind of telling me about it."

"He's on board."

Colt was about as stubborn as me, and I knew that no amount of begging would budge him. So I switched tactics.

"Okay, then can you at least tell me what your announcement has to do with? A new sponsor? Another driver joining the team?" Those were things my dad would decide, not Colt. But I had no idea what he was talking about.

"You are clever. But I'm still not going to tell you."

I stifled a yawn. "In that case, I give up. Would you mind taking off your clothes and snuggling with me?"

"I wouldn't mind at all, Piper Patricia Pierson."

I laughed. "You know my middle name is Poppi." We kissed for a minute, then I asked, sleep already setting in, "When is this shindig?"

"As soon as I get back from Pocono we'll have a big ol' bash, and then the whole world will know."

"And more importantly, I'll know." And then I was asleep.

• • •

I spent the weekend of Pocono in my pajamas and watched
the race alone in my apartment. Liza was visiting Teddy, her
boyfriend, in Winston-Salem, and it was rainy and gross. After
a delayed start and an hour of the cars sitting on pit road with
canvas covers on them, the race began. Colt didn't drive well. The
few times the commentators cut to his in-car communication
with Birdie, his crew chief, Colt sounded tense. Normally he
would tell a couple jokes and predict that today was the day he'd
win his first Winston Cup race. But that Sunday he kept telling
Birdie that he couldn't feel her. All of Colt's cars were named
after girls from rock and roll songs. The one he drove in Pocono
was "Roxanne" from the Police.

Throughout the year, Colt had put Layla, Angie and Susie
Q in the wall, blew up Allison and Cecelia's engines, but he had
never finished DFL. He couldn't even say the words out loud—
dead fucking last. Somehow there was always another driver
who'd crash first, or Colt's crew would manage to get a bruised
and mangled car back out to limp around the track a few more
times. But Pocono did in poor Roxanne. He cut a right front tire,
spun, and a veteran driver took him out. The yellow flag came
out; Roxanne was loaded on a flatbed, and Colt took a mandatory
but unnecessary trip to the infield care center.

We talked while he was getting ready to leave the race. I could
tell by his fake perky tone that he wasn't alone. As disappointed
as he'd get when he didn't drive well, he never complained in
front of other people. He said it was unprofessional and made
him sound ungrateful.

"On the bright side, my dad told me you were able to catch
an earlier flight out this afternoon," I said, determined to cheer
him up. "What time will you be home tonight?" I was already
thinking about making him dinner and serving it to him naked.

"Well," he said, sounding a bit more upbeat, "since I'm getting home early, a few of us are going to Players to get dinner and make sure everything is set for tomorrow night."

I just wanted this flipping party to happen already. I couldn't take the suspense. I had an idea what his big announcement might be, but I wouldn't let myself even think about it.

"Sounds like fun. Do you want me to meet you and we can have dinner together? I can take care of anything that still needs to be done."

"Nice try, but we got this." I was disappointed that he wasn't coming straight home to me. But I'd been in this sport my whole life, and I understood how drivers operated. After a bad day, especially a *did not finish*, the men wanted to drink beer, play pool and not talk about the race or, God forbid, their feelings. Colt may have said he had more party planning to do, but I guessed he was mad at himself and wanted to mope for a few hours without having his girlfriend around.

"Have fun. I'll leave the door unlocked, and I'll see you when I see you."

"Pierson, has anyone ever told you you're the coolest girl on earth?"

"Of course, because I am."

I started to hang up when I heard his voice. "One more thing," he said.

"What's that?"

"I love you."

I smiled hard. "What a coincidence. I love you right back."

"No," he told me, sounding a bit forceful. "I love you like I'd marry you tomorrow love you."

It felt like my heart quit beating for a moment. "That's not such a bad idea," I told him. "Bye, Colt."

"Wait," he shouted through the phone. "One more one more thing. I can't wait for this party. Make sure you wear something that photographs well."

"Darn it. And here I was, going to show up in sweats. Hey, since you brought it up, can I ask you something? About the party?"

"Sure, but for the millionth time, I'm not giving away its theme."

"Oh, I know that. You're as pigheaded as me. Why are you having it on a Monday?"

"Because I'm away almost every weekend these days and I just can't wait any longer."

"Good answer," I said. "Tell the pilot to do a good job, and please be careful driving home."

"Darlin', I'm a race car driver. I got this. I love you, Piper."

"I love you, Colt."

I caught my reflection in an antique mirror hanging above the fireplace. I had the most ridiculous smile on my face.

•   •   •

I thought Colt might call after dinner and let me know he was on his way over. I waited till ten. Players only closed after everyone had left, so it was possible that Colt and his buddies were still there—eating wings and talking about the drivers who needed to retire or move back down to Busch. I wasn't one to call my boyfriend and check up on him, but I had a nervous feeling. I called his house, not really expecting him to answer.

"Hello?" he said.

"Hi." Excitement rushed through my veins.

"Hello?" he said again.

"Hey, you. It's me."

"I still can't hear you." He sounded like he was laughing.

"Colt. It's me. Are you okay?"

"Gotcha!" said his recorded voice. "You probably figured out that I'm not here. Leave a message. Ciao."

"Dammit, Colt," I said after the beep. "Where are you? I thought you'd be here by now. Give up plotting for tomorrow night and come over. I haven't seen you for four days and there are all kinds of naughty things I thought we could try. Call me. I miss you."

I told myself not to worry. Drivers could talk for hours about the shimmy they felt in the steering wheel or the slick spot in turn three or how much prettier the Hooters girls were last year over this year. They could spend hours discussing how a slow pit stop or a moment's hesitation may have affected the outcome of a race. I called it "turning left lingo."

I called my parents' house, and when they didn't answer, I remembered that they'd taken a later flight than Colt and were probably in the air.

At eleven o'clock, I thought about calling Players and asking the manager if Colt was still there. But I didn't want to embarrass Colt in front of the other drivers who were probably still at his table talking shop. So, I poured myself a glass of wine, put on one of his sweatshirts, turned on the TV and found a rerun of *The Love Boat*. I was just about asleep on the couch when the phone rang.

I grabbed for it. "Colt?" I asked. "Are you okay?"

"Hey, Pierson, I'm fine. I'm still at Players. Everyone showed up and you know how it is."

I sighed. "That I do. Are you still coming over?"

"Well, let's see. I could go home to an empty bed in an empty house or come see you. I'll be there in thirty minutes."

"I'll wait up," I told him. "And maybe I can seduce you into telling me what this party is all about." I was sure I already knew. He was going to ask me to move in with him. I'd feel guilty leaving Liza, but between her job and her boyfriend, she was hardly ever home.

"You can try," he said.

"Oh, I have ways of making you talk."

The wine I'd had was hitting me hard, and I barely made it back to my room before I fell asleep.

• • •

The next morning, I woke expecting to find Colt's warm body wrapped around mine. When I realized I was alone, I sat up and sniffed the air. A few times in the last year, he'd sneaked over in the middle of the night and I'd woken to the scent of coffee and bacon. But the room smelled of the dirty laundry on my floor.

I was a little pissed at him for not coming over or even calling. But he was the most responsible person I knew. He'd probably had too much to drink and got Scott or someone to take him home. His place was closer to Player's than mine. I didn't blame him for not asking for a ride to my apartment. We were too far away from Charlotte, the race shop and his house. If I was wrong, and he wasn't going to ask me to live with him, I needed to talk to Liza about moving even closer to Moorestown when our lease was up.

I turned on the TV and saw the crawl on *Good Morning America* flash something about NASCAR. Interested to know what big doings made national headlines and if I'd get to report on it, I waited for the news to repeat itself.

After a few minutes, the headline came around again. *NASCAR's young star, Colt Porter, was killed in a highway accident early this morning.* I saw the words but did not believe them.

"How could they make such an awful mistake?" I muttered. Half unconsciously, I dialed Colt's home number and got his answering machine. He often went to the shop early, although not usually the day after a race. But it wouldn't have surprised me if he had been at Pierson Racing since dawn, wondering what he could have done differently to avoid that old guy putting him in the wall. I hung up and dialed his extension at our shop. When his voicemail picked up I started to panic. I called Scott and got no answer. I called my parents, but they weren't there.

I fumbled through my address book until I found Liza's boyfriend's number. "Liza, is it true?" I asked when she got on the line. "Have you heard anything? I don't know what to do."

"Sweetheart," she said in a calming tone that was not hers. "What's wrong? What happened?"

"It's on the news. Is it true?"

"Teddy," I heard her say to the background. "Turn on the TV." The line between us was silent for a few moments. Then I heard her scream. "It's a mistake, Pipes. It's a mistake. It's a mistake." But I was sobbing so hard I could barely hear her. "I'll be home as soon as I can." And then the line went dead.

I called Tack's line at the paper, even though it was only a few minutes after seven.

"Tack Richards speaking."

It was then that I knew. I couldn't make myself talk.

"Hello?" he asked. "This is Tack. May I help you?"

"Tack."

I heard him breathing, pictured him rubbing his forehead, thinking of what to say. He spoke so softly I could barely hear him.

"Piper," he said. "Where are you?" I tried to answer him, but I couldn't. "Are you at your parents'? Is anyone with you?"

"Tack," I said again. "Tell me if it's true."

"Let me come get you. Where are you?"

I couldn't breathe. I wanted to rip off my skin. "Just tell me," I whispered. "Is it true?"

"Yes." I heard words and it took me a few seconds to realize he was talking again. "Piper, I am so sorry. How did you hear about it?"

"The news. It was on the news. I saw it on the crawl on the news. It was on the news."

"Dammit! No one was supposed to know until his parents were notified."

I dropped the phone. Tack was still talking.

19

After Colt's funeral, my parents had a reception at their house. I'd never seen so many people crowd into one area and then not talk. It was like none of us knew what to say. Liza stayed with me the whole time, holding my hand and bringing me food. We sat in a corner of the living room with Scott and Sasha. After an hour or two, I gave up trying to think of something to say to them. We were in an awful and awkward place.

Sasha had lost her brother and Scott his best friend. The love of my life—gone. Were we supposed to comfort each other? Take turns giving and getting sympathy? I opened the slider to the back deck, went down the steps, across the backyard and sat on the old stone wall that was there when my mom and dad bought the place. Tack spotted me and followed.

"Hi," he said. I looked at him but didn't speak. "I know there's nothing I can say that will make this suck any less. So, let me just tell you two things, and then I'll leave you alone again. If that's what you want."

"Please don't let one of them be that Colt's in a better place or somehow I'll get through this."

He squinted hard as if he were in pain. "Oooh—never. That's just stupid. The best place for Colt to be would be here with his parents. And you. And the team. Have people really been saying that?"

"We are in the Deep South." It was almost too much energy to talk. "There are Holy Rollers among us."

"That seems awfully insensitive." I thought he'd say more, but we were both quiet for a long moment. The ice in the soda I'd brought outside was melting, and it clinked as it settled.

"So, what did you want to say?" I didn't care; I just wanted him to speak his piece and leave me alone.

"No one expects you to come back to work right away. Take as much time as you need—for yourself and your parents. I imagine this is very difficult for them, too."

I'd never seen my father cry like this. "Thanks. I appreciate it."

"But I do want to give you one small bit of advice."

Tack's eyes were rimmed in red like he'd been crying. I wondered how many people across the country were weeping for Colt Porter. "I've been where you are and—"

"Really, Tack?" I couldn't stop myself. "Your boyfriend was killed in a car wreck that makes no sense?"

He kept his gaze level and his tone soft. "My best friend was hit by a car when we were fourteen. He was running into the street after a baseball that *I* hit." I was about to argue that it wasn't the same, but he kept talking. "Grief is grief. It doesn't matter who you lose. It's still a loss. Take all the time you need, but not too much. The longer you stay away, the harder it'll be to come back. The sooner you get back to your old life, the sooner you'll start to heal."

I slapped him across the face and then stared at my hand as if it had hit him on its own.

"There is no coming back from this, Tack. Colt wasn't the only one mortally wounded."

Tack didn't flinch. He grabbed me and held me hard against his chest and let me cry until I no longer could make sound or tears.

Tack kissed the top of my head and let me go. "I'm here if you need me," he said and stepped away from the stone wall where we'd been sitting.

"Wait," I said to his back. He turned and looked at me. "Was this supposed to happen?"

"Colt's accident? Of course not. It was bad luck."

"Are you sure it wasn't fate? His destiny."

He came back to me and we walked toward the woods lining the backyard. "What do you mean destiny? Like Colt was a serial killer in his last life and this was his penance?"

I stopped and picked a small, purple flower from the grass. My mother said it was a weed and wanted to kill the patch. I told her they were too pretty to be ruined. "I think that's karma—fate catching up to someone for a bad thing they did."

The wind died down and I tucked the flower in my hair. At a race up north, Colt had woven me a crown of flowers while he was waiting for practice to begin. He had a thousand talents he revealed to me over time and a thousand more I'd never know about.

"Colt had this whole theory that he had the best life ever, so if it ended now or in a week or a year, it was okay."

"That's awfully Zen." The wind shifted and the flower slipped. Tack tucked it behind my ear. "And a bit morbid."

Above us, clouds blocked the sun. "That's the thing. It really wasn't. He was trying to get me to understand how beautiful my life is. And how I'm wasting it by not doing what I love."

"Which is?"

"Come on, Tack. You've seen me at races. The way—"

"You run your hand across the hoods of your team's car as if it were a purebred show dog."

"Or a baby."

"And how you stand in the pits driving every inch of the track as if you were in the driver's seat." I smiled sadly. "So, Colt tried to convince you to drive again? That living the way you wanted was worth the risks?"

"He said I wouldn't feel complete until I got behind the wheel again." I felt like my legs would collapse. We'd lapped the backyard and I didn't know if I could keep going. "How am I ever supposed to move on now?"

He put his arm around me for a few steps. "Maybe he was right. The worst thing you could imagine happened . . . and you're still here."

I stepped away and stopped. "Is that supposed to make me feel better? I don't even know what happened. How does a race car driver lose control of a street car going forty miles an hour?" He didn't answer. "I mean it! How did this happen?" I had to ask the question I hadn't let myself think about. "Was he drunk? Like that paper said he was?" The day after Colt died, a rag of a newspaper printed a front-page article about him being at Player's and implied if he was at a bar, he must have been intoxicated.

"Fucking tabloids," Tack said. We walked back to the stone wall and sat. "I used my contacts at CPD to get a copy of the preliminary police report." He picked at a loose piece of rock. "Are you sure you want to hear this?"

"Yes. Whatever it is, it's better than not knowing."

"The report said the roads were wet and he was speeding. Skid marks indicated maybe a deer or a dog ran out into the road and he hit a tree trying to avoid it. But I promise you he wasn't drunk. The report also said his BAC was point-zero-two. He probably had one beer, but there's no way he was drunk."

"So that's it? And now he's just gone?"

"Let me get your parents," Tack said.

I picked at my fingers. "It's okay. I think I'd like to be alone for a little while."

• • •

A week later I showed up in Tack's office wearing dirty jeans, my unwashed hair in a ponytail.

"Piper," Tack said when I knocked on his open door. "What are you doing here?"

"I can't stop thinking about what we talked about at my parents' house."

He hugged me hard and sat me down on his couch. Then he closed his door and poured two shots of whiskey. He placed both on the coffee table in front of us.

"Oh, sweetheart." His tone was soft and sincere. "Come here." He reached for me, but I pulled away. I couldn't stand to be touched. "I know it must feel like all your fears have come true and the world isn't a safe place for anyone. But feeling that way won't last forever."

"How do you know?"

"Because I felt like that for a long time after Ben died."

"Ben? Your friend who—"

"Yes." He dropped his eyes. "I didn't want to come out of my house, never mind play baseball again. But it wasn't until I went out for the varsity team two years later that I stopped crying every day."

"I'll never get that far."

"Yes, you will. Because just like Ben wouldn't have wanted me to quit playing ball, Colt wouldn't want you to cry over him for the rest of your life. He'd want you to drive again."

I put my hand up to stop him, but he kept talking. "You don't have to drive in the Daytona 500, but he'd want you to make it to the drugstore." He leaned forward and picked up the shots. "Now, let's not let these go to waste." We touched our glasses together. The liquor burned. "I know I said you could have all the time you need, but we're a little short staffed around here. Any guesses when you'll come back?" I glared at him and he raised his hands in defense.

He refilled the shot glasses, but we didn't drink. "I'm kidding. I'm kidding . . . sort of. Amy's out again and, well, no one is as good as you."

"What's wrong with Amy? She seems like she's sick a lot."

He waved away my question. "Take all the time you need. But never forget that you're desperately missed around these parts."

•   •   •

Since Colt's funeral, I hadn't gone back to my apartment. Instead, I stayed with my parents. A few days after I went to see Tack, I came quietly up the stairs and listened to my mom and dad talking to Meri and Doug Porter.

"We have to do this," my dad said. He'd been weeping openly and constantly since the state police showed up on his doorstep, as if he were Colt's father and they were coming to do the family notification.

I peered around the corner as Doug went to my dad and put his arm around him.

"Listen, Planter. You all have become family to us. And we're grateful to you for loving our boy like he was your own. But this is too much for Meri." He was talking about his wife as if she weren't sitting two feet away from him. "She lost her only son. She can't think about replacing him now."

"I understand," my dad said. "But I've been through tough times before. And I can tell you the best thing we can do is stick together and make decisions like a family."

"What's going on?" I asked, stepping around the corner.

"Oh, Noodle." My dad held out his hand but didn't get up. "You don't need to be a part of this talk right now."

"Daddy. You just told Doug that we need to be a family right now. Aren't I a part of that? Now please tell me what you were talking about."

My father got up and led me to the couch. I sat next to him and he put his arm around me. "You are the heart of this family. I just didn't want to upset you anymore. But if we're going to keep Pierson Racing going, we need to start looking for a new driver."

Racing was the one thing that I knew would keep us going. But if my dad didn't have a team to lead and the Porters weren't a part of anything anymore, I didn't know if we'd make it. My breath caught in my throat when I tried to talk. Finally, I said, "I guess we do, don't we?"

Meri got to her feet. "I'm sorry, Planter. But I can't . . . I just can't." She ran out of the room and Doug followed her.

We watched them leave. "Do you have to do it now?" I asked. "The season is over in a few months."

"Five months," my father corrected.

"Still," I said. "Can't we find relief drivers or take a few weeks off?"

"I wish it were that simple, Noodle," my dad said, then got up to find the Porters.

●　●　●

The next morning when I got up, my parents were dressed in black and my father was talking to a journalist I recognized from a local morning show.

"What's happening?" I asked. I was in old sweats and hadn't brushed my hair.

My mom pulled me aside and spoke quietly. "We're having a press conference."

"Already?" I knew sooner or later we'd have to make an official statement about Colt and our team. But I'd thought we'd have more time.

"You know your dad. No point putting off what cannot be changed."

An hour later, I had showered and borrowed a dress from my mom. I stood in the same spot I had a year before when we'd announced to the world that Colt Porter was our new driver.

"Thank you for coming on such short notice," my dad began. He had a cloth handkerchief in his breast pocket. He took it out and clutched it. "I am going to make a statement and will not take any questions."

The front row of reporters looked at each other and started to talk. But my dad raised his hand and the crowd silenced. "Pierson Racing's future is uncertain. Without Colt Porter, we don't know what will happen." His voice broke and he brought the handkerchief to his eyes. "We must go on. Racing is all any of us know how to do. But, without Colt . . ." He grabbed my mother's hand and leaned on her so hard she stumbled but caught herself. "I just don't know."

My father stood there for a long time, not speaking, and the press started to look around, probably wondering if he was done talking. Finally, my mother whispered in his ear and he continued.

"We've had preliminary discussions with Jewel Petroleum and are immensely grateful to them for the support they showed us the first half of this year." Everyone knew sponsors rarely stayed with teams when there was a driver change. "At this point, nothing's been decided."

Standing between my parents, I noticed the reporters were also dressed in black, as if they'd known this would be a solemn event. I couldn't stand to hear my dad talk about losing everything that meant something to him. I recited state capitals in my head, something I used to do when I was little to pass the time on the school bus. I'd gotten to Cheyenne, the capital of Wyoming, when my dad put his hand on my shoulder.

"Come on, Noodle. It's time to go." As we walked to the race shop, the press silently packed their belongings and left, without a word spoken or a photograph taken.

• • •

Days later, my dad came roaring into the house, using curse words I'd never heard him utter. My mom was in the living room reading, and I was on the phone with Sasha Porter.

"Will you goddamn look at this?" I'd never seen my father that angry. He slapped a letter on the island. I recognized the logo and immediately knew who it was from.

"They want me to dissolve Pierson Racing. They say without a permanent driver we'll go down and they don't want to see a legend end his career like that."

"Sash," I said into the phone, "my dad just got home. Let me call you later. Love you, sister." Sasha and I had been friends since we met, but since Colt died we'd become family. I hung up and turned to my parents.

"What are you going to do, Daddy?"

"I'm going to goddamn prove them wrong. That's what."

He left the letter on the counter and opened the kitchen door. "Follow me." My mother and I exchanged glances and hurried after him. Once we got to the race shop, we went to the garage. Lined up were five identical cars. When Colt drove them, they were painted blue with a white *20* painted on the sides and roof and Jewel Petroleum on the hood. Now they were all black and had *In Memory of Colt Porter* written on the hood.

"What is this, Planter?" my mom asked.

"This is my answer to their letter," my dad answered.

"But you just got it today. I don't understand."

"Don't you see, Poppi? No driver equals no sanctioning body. I always knew this would happen."

"Then why haven't you chosen a driver?" my mother asked.

My father slammed his fist on the hood of the first car. "Because I won't be bullied into doing something before I'm goddamn ready!" I'd never heard him raise his voice at my mother. She took a step back, shaken. He wrapped his arms around her. "I'm sorry, Poppi. I'm so sorry."

"What do you think they'll do when they see these?" I asked after they broke apart.

"Oh, they already have. Remember the reporter who I was talking to before the press conference? I might have left him alone in here while I used the restroom. And if he leaked those pictures to the press . . . well, there was nothing I could do."

"Planter, why?" my mother asked.

As if the room was bugged, the phone rang.

"Pierson," he barked into the receiver. He listened for a moment, then said, "I'm sorry you feel that way. But we're not disrespecting anyone. Quite the opposite. That car is meant to honor one of our own. Our fallen son." He listened for a moment, then spoke again. "Show me where in the rules it says that." He was quiet for several more seconds. "No sir. That won't be a problem." He hung up the phone and turned back to us.

"Planter," my mom said gently. "What was that about?"

"Apparently, there's some archaic rule that prevents us from entering next week's race without a designated driver. The Colt Porter memorial car won't be allowed at Watkins Glen unless we get ourselves a driver right quick."

"Those fuckers," my mother said. It was the first time I'd ever heard her use that word. "What are you going to do?"

"I'm going to get us a goddamn driver."

"What can we do to help?" she asked.

My dad smiled for the first time in weeks. "Let's do this. Grab a line and we'll call everyone we can think of."

By the time we left the race shop, we had a designated driver and fourteen other men who all faxed letters stating they'd drive if need be—including me.

I hadn't sat in a race car since I was seventeen years old, and I didn't have a Winston Cup license, but I was fully prepared to drive if my dad needed me to. As the three of us walked back to the house, I realized I was where I was supposed to be—with my parents working in the family business. Even if it was just for one night.

•   •   •

The following week we flew to Watkins Glen. Buck Jenkins, our temporary driver, spent the two-hour flight with his hat clutched in his hands. "Planter," he said as soon as we boarded and got buckled in. He and my dad had known each other for a long time and were good friends. "Whether I drive one race for you or all the rest, it is an honor to sit in Colt Porter's car."

"The honor is mine," my dad said. "And I can't thank you enough for volunteering your time. As you may know, Jewel Petroleum decided to take their sponsorship in a different direction." They'd sent the official letter shortly after my father spoke to the press outside the race shop.

Buck reached for my dad's hand. "Even if you had three sponsors, I wouldn't take your money. This is what friends do."

Although we finished setting up and testing at the track in time for dinner that night, no one felt like going out. Gone were the days of big team dinners with the pit crew, my parents and the Porters. How could I make small talk over appetizers about who might be on the pole when Colt was dead? I might never have anything to talk about again. My parents and I ordered pizza and stayed in the motorhome pretending to watch TV until one by one we excused ourselves for bed.

I was still in my pajamas the next day when Meri knocked once and let herself in. "Piper. Goodness. I'm sorry," she said, taking in my Hello Kitty boxers and sweatshirt. She had a large, white bag in her hands that she put on the counter.

The roar of engines outside told me practice had started, so it was after ten. "Meri, I'm sorry. I should have been dressed by now. I just—" But I ran out of words.

Meri sat next to me and put her arm around my shoulders. Suddenly, I couldn't remember if I'd told her how sad I was for her.

"Oh, honey. I'd stay in my pajamas too, if I could. But here we are." She looked around the space as if she didn't know how she'd gotten to Upstate New York.

"I didn't want to come," I blurted.

"So why did you?"

"Because I didn't know what else to do. I don't want to be alone, but I can't stand to be at a racetrack without Colt."

"Well, that makes two of us." She got up and opened the paper bag she'd brought in with her. "How about we hide in here and eat donuts for a little while?"

"Can I stay in here forever?" My chest tightened and I put my hand over my heart. "I honestly don't know if I will be able to watch the race tomorrow. It's like I don't want to be here or in the pits, but I can't imagine not being where you and Doug and my parents are. I just feel so—"

"Lost?" she asked.

"Yes. Nothing makes sense without Colt."

She pulled two jelly donuts from the bag and handed one to me. "How about I come back tomorrow morning and we'll eat some more donuts. And if we decide to watch the race, then we'll do it together."

The next afternoon, Meri and I ate a few donuts in the motorhome, then ventured out to the pits. We had a couple minutes before the race started, so my dad wasn't on the spotters' tower yet. He and Doug sat side by side in director's chairs—both with watery eyes.

"Why are we torturing ourselves?" I asked.

Sasha, who didn't go to many races, heard me. "Because we don't know what else to do."

"If it's all the same, I'm going back to the motorhome to watch the race on TV. Does anyone want to come with me?"

"We might stop in if it gets too hot out here," my mom said. "Kiss your daddy for good luck before you leave."

I did as she said, but my good luck ran out after my year with Colt.

Alone in the motorhome, I ate a day-old donut and turned on the TV in time to hear the national anthem in stereo. Buck Jenkins had qualified well and was in the third row on the outside. Most drivers preferred starting on the inside simply because it was a shorter distance around the track, but in my brief career, I found if I let everyone immediately dive down toward the apron and I stayed high and wide near the retaining wall, I had a clearer path to the front of the pack.

About twenty minutes into the race, the ambient crowd noise both outside and on the TV went silent. Curious to see what happened, I left the kitchen where I'd been washing dishes and sat on the couch. The camera broke from the race to the commentating booth where both announcers were dressed in black suits. After a few more seconds, Benny Parsons thanked the crowd for honoring the moment of silence he'd implemented on lap twenty.

Watkins Glen was a road course, and it took the cars more than a minute to get once around. After it was over, Benny wiped his eyes and looked at his partner. "Watching that black memorial car of Planter Pierson's lumber around the track like a hearse was the saddest thing I've ever seen," he said.

20

Once a week since Colt died, I would meet Scott and Sasha for dinner. Liza and Teddy came when they were in town. Colt had cemented our group, and without effort, we'd fall apart without him. We'd meet at someone's house or Sandwich Construction and talk until we finally laughed. Then we'd laugh until we cried. Most of the time it took all the willpower I had not to pick up the phone and cancel.

If my father was still going to the race shop every day and my mother hadn't dropped her classes, then I could make myself do this one thing. But one Tuesday with Sasha and Scott made me miss Colt so bad that I had to get out of the house, talk to someone, go somewhere, do something.

I called Liza's office, but the receptionist said she was off-site at a meeting. Then I walked down to the race shop, but Scott's car wasn't in the parking lot, and I remembered the crew was at a training session in Charlotte. So, I called the paper.

"Piper Pierson. What a great surprise to hear your voice."

"Hey, Tack. I—"

"Are you okay? You don't sound good."

"Funny you should ask. I'm not having a great day and I was wondering if I could come hang out with you for a while. Everyone seems to be out, and I don't really want to be alone."

"Of course. Give me a few minutes. I'll come get you."

An hour later Tack and I were in his office, shoes off, feet on his couch, listening to the new Robert Cray album, *Midnight Stroll*. I sang aloud and badly to "Bouncin' Back." When I was done, Tack grinned.

"What?" I asked.

"Nothing. It's just nice to see a glimpse of the old Piper. So, what's going on? You sounded sad this morning."

"Do you think it's weird? How time keeps on moving and we're still doing all the things we used to. But Colt's not here."

"I felt the same way after Ben died. I thought they'd cancel school or let me stay home or something. But I got up the next day and there was my mother making my lunch. It just didn't make any sense."

I leaned my head back against the couch. "I'm so glad you get it. I half thought my father would just as soon sell Pierson Racing as go on without Colt—"

"But racing is all he knows how to do," Tack finished for me.

"Exactly. It's all any of us know. We keep on keeping on because without packing transporters and motorhomes and boarding planes or buses, we'd be lost."

My father had sat with our team before Watkins Glen and given each of them the opportunity to quit without any shame. Every one of our guys stayed, with Scott putting it best. "Sir," he had said, standing up and removing his baseball hat. "I wouldn't know what to do without racing. It's hard enough without Colt here. But if you took away changing tires and planning strategy and getting on planes or buses every week, I might as well lie down and die."

My suspicion was that that was how everyone, including my dad, had felt. Since then, it was as if muscle memory had taken over and our bodies went through the motions of going to races and driving cars even though our hearts were not beating, and our minds were blank with grief.

I opened a can of Mountain Dew Tack had handed me from his fridge when we got to his office. Then I said, "Most days I don't even feel alive, Tack. If I could will myself to stop breathing, to give up, I would. But my parents need me. My dad has fought so hard to keep our team together and for the right to keep racing. All these amazing people have come out of the woodwork. Like Buck Jenkins. He came out of *retirement* for my father."

"Is Buck staying? Driving for you permanently?"

I shook my head. "After Watkins Glen, my dad tried to hire him full time. But Buck said he was retired, except a dirt-track race every now and again. He'd only gotten back into a Winston Cup car to help out an old friend. So, we're back where we started."

Tack held his breath for a moment, then let it go. "This might be out of line, but have you ever thought of throwing your hat in the ring? Or your helmet?"

My stomach turned—but not in a bad way.

·   ·   ·

A week later Tack called and asked if he could stop by my parents' house. Ten o'clock came and went and he hadn't arrived. I called the newspaper, but his secretary said he hadn't been in yet that morning. I went upstairs and got a cup of coffee and wondered if Tack had an agenda. I couldn't stop thinking about the last thing he'd asked me. Before I could do anything about it, I needed to ask him about something else.

The coffee in the pot was cold, so I poured myself a cup and put it in the microwave. The whirring of the machine was like white noise, and for a moment it drowned out everything else. I didn't hear the bell ring or the door open.

"Piper?" Tack called. "Are you here?"

He startled me so badly I spilled my drink taking it out of the microwave, but it wasn't hot enough to hurt. "Hey there. I was starting to think you weren't going to show." I wiped my hand on my pants. "Want some cold, stale coffee?"

He smiled. "No, thanks." He was carrying a folder, and I wondered what was in it. "You look better today. How are you feeling?"

Tack was the only person who could ask that without me biting off his head.

"I feel like I showered this morning. So, there's that." I picked up a spoon from the counter and stirred my coffee even though there was nothing in it. "Come with me. I need to ask you something. Actually, I guess I wanted to ask you last week, but I chickened out."

"Uh oh," he said. "That sounds ominous."

I flicked on the stairwell light, and we went down the steps. "It's nothing that bad." This was the most normal conversation I'd had since Colt died, and I couldn't decide if I felt respite or despair.

We settled on either end of a dark leather couch facing a sliding glass door. Bright sunlight poured in through the panes and I had to shift in my seat to avoid squinting. I put my coffee on the table.

"I'm sorry, Tack. You came here for a reason. Did you want to talk about something specific?"

"Not at all. When you stopped in last week, it just made me miss seeing you every day. But you look like you have something on your mind. What's up?"

"I know I already asked you about Colt's accident, but I haven't told you everything. There are some things you don't know."

Clouds covered the sun, and the room darkened. "Now *that* sounds ominous."

I'd stretched out on the couch and playfully kicked him with my socked foot. "I'm serious, Tack. I need to know how my race-car-driving boyfriend died in a street car accident. Some weird shit has happened in the last year. I just need someone to help me make sense of everything."

He held up an imaginary glass as if he were toasting the occasion. "I am your guy. And I'm honored that you trust me with this."

I blew out my breath the way a horse would. "I don't even know where to start."

"How about at the beginning?"

"Ah, there you go again, using logic on me. Okay. Here goes nothing. After Colt and I had been hanging out for a few months, I was on the phone with him and he got a package delivered to his house. It was a dead fox in a box."

"A fox in a box? Sounds like a Dr. Seuss book."

I laughed for the first time in a long time. "Stop it, I'm serious. It was addressed to a taxidermy shop in Davidson, but it had his street name on it."

"Piper." He sat up on the couch and patted my hand. "Do you know what a taxidermist does? They stuff dead animals."

I pulled my hand away. "No shit. But I looked up the symbolism of a dead fox."

"I can't wait to hear this one."

His flip attitude was pissing me off. "You know what, Tack? Just forget it. If you're not going to take this seriously, I don't want to talk to you." I got up and dumped my coffee in the sink. "Have a good day."

He followed me into the kitchen. "I'm sorry, Piper." He stood behind me with his hand on my shoulder, but I wouldn't turn around. "Tell me about the fox."

I hesitated for a moment. I'd come too far to stop now. And I really needed someone to talk to. I knew Liza would listen, but she didn't have the same resources that Tack did.

"In medieval times, a fox stood for the devil." I wiped my hands on a dishtowel even though they weren't wet, then I faced him.

He swallowed hard. "Is that all?" he asked. Before I could react, he held up his hands as if defending himself. "I didn't mean it like that. Did anything else happen?"

I went back to the couch. "Yes. Last winter we were on our way out to dinner and stopped by his house to get dressed. When we got there, a pipe had burst and there was about an inch of water in his kitchen."

"Pipes burst all the time."

"In North Carolina when it's fifty degrees outside?"

"Well—" he said, but he didn't finish.

"A friend of my dad's is a plumber, so I called Hank. He came over and said one of the pipes in the basement was corroded. He also said he'd seen that kind of thing happen, but never around here. Apparently too much of some chemical or something in the water can do it."

"That makes sense. How does it tie in to the other things?"

"Hank said we don't have that chemical or whatever he was talking about in the water around here. Said if he didn't know better, he would have thought someone dumped it on Colt's land and it seeped into the ground and wrecked the pipes."

"That's a little weird. I'll give you that."

I wanted him to be more shocked. "A little weird? That's all I get? First a dead fox shows up on Colt's doorstep."

"A fox that was meant for a taxidermist."

I ignored him and kept talking. "Then his pipes burst for no reason, and then he dies in a car accident? Come on, Tack. He was a fucking race car driver. There's no way he would have lost control of that car if he hadn't been hit or run off the road."

Tack put his hand on the couch between us, palm up. "Those things sound like terrible, awful coincidences."

"I'm not done," I snapped. I had to think about how to phrase this next part. Tack didn't need to know what happened between Colt and Candice at the Busch banquet. "Scott and I both thought Colt was a little . . . off at the awards banquet in December. Not drunk, but definitely altered."

Tack stared at the ceiling for a moment. "Piper, I saw Colt that night."

"No kidding. We all did." I didn't want Tack to try to talk me out of my theories.

He softened his tone. "That's not what I meant. I saw Colt drinking at the banquet. He was with a bunch of guys I assumed were his friends or teammates and he was doing shots. I only remember because he asked me to join them."

"Are you sure? About the drinks?"

"Yes," he said. "Have you talked to anyone about this? About losing Colt?"

"Yes," I said impatiently. "I'm talking to you."

"I meant someone like a therapist."

"I knew I shouldn't have said anything. So now you think I'm crazy, too."

"First of all, I know you're not crazy. Secondly—what do you mean, too?"

"I told my parents right after it happened that I didn't think Colt could have died in a street-car accident. He was too good a driver for that."

"And what did they say?" he asked quietly.

"They said expert swimmers drown in backyard pools and commercial pilots crash small planes and even the most talented drivers make mistakes." I put my head in my hands for a few moments. "Look, I just need someone to listen to me. Even if I am off my rocker."

"I'm listening, Piper."

"So am I? Off my rocker?"

"Let me see if I understand everything you're saying. Because someone sent Colt a dead fox and then his pipes mysteriously burst, you think someone did something to his car? Caused his crash?"

"I sound batshit crazy right now, don't I?"

"No," he said sincerely. "You sound like you lost someone you loved and you're trying to make sense of it."

"Thank you for saying that; because I feel pretty nuts. It's just that . . . it could have been someone . . . my dad had a stalker who sent him underwear and pictures. And some lunatic broke into another driver's house a few months ago. What if some obsessed pit lizard fan went all fatal attraction on Colt and decided that if she couldn't have him, no one could?"

I thought Tack would dismiss me. My parents had listened, but gave me perfectly logical explanations that all came down to sometimes bad shit happened to good people.

"Had Colt been bothered by anyone? Any girls hanging around his motorhome at races or jealous boyfriends not liking him signing autographs?" I thought of Candice and her ex. Maybe he found out about the banquet and went crazy. But then I remembered Scott telling me he'd been busted for beating up his new girlfriend and had been in jail for the past six months.

I could only think of one person who constantly talked about Colt. "What about Amy?" I asked. She told me all the time how she met Colt first. And whenever he came to see me at work, she about broke her neck falling all over him. "You know, she has been missing a lot of work. Maybe she's—" Tack's expression soured. "Maybe she's unstable. I don't suppose she's been treated for—" I dropped my voice even though we were alone. "—mental problems. That would explain why she's out sick all the time."

I hadn't ever considered that Amy could have done something to Colt. It was ludicrous. But, now that I was piecing it all together, it made sense.

"Maybe she knew she was losing it." I was talking fast now. "And checked herself in to a hospital. But it didn't work. And she's always hated me, you know. She's the one who accused me of sleeping with drivers to get good stories." I shook my finger at him spastically, as if I couldn't control it. "And remember the time in the staff meeting when she got all huffy and threw my piece at me because you put a star on it? Isn't that what crazy people do? Hurt the people we love to hurt us the most?"

"Piper!" Tack's voice was sharp. I stopped talking and panted. "Stop it. I get that you're upset. And I will help you any way I can. But Amy didn't do anything to Colt."

My parents would have slapped my backside if they heard me talking like this.

"It makes sense. It all makes sense now. I knew the accident couldn't have been Colt's fault. We need to find his car and have the police check it again. Maybe she cut his brakes or screwed with the steering. Did the police even look for signs of foul play?"

"Piper," Tack said more softly this time. "It wasn't Amy."

I was out of breath again. "How can you be so sure?"

"Because she has breast cancer."

"What?"

"She has cancer. That's why she's missed so much work. Chemo is kicking the crap out of her. She's too weak to hold a coffee cup, never mind sabotage Colt's car."

I covered my face with my hands. "What is happening to me?"

Tack put his hand on my back. "You're grieving." He pulled me to him and hugged me hard.

"I'm sorry, Tack. Please don't tell Amy what I said. I didn't mean it. I just . . . I just . . . I don't even know."

"I'll get some answers for you, Piper. I promise."

• • •

I kept thinking about what Tack had said about not waiting too long to come back to work. With every day that passed, I felt a little bit more removed from my old life. And I found it more and more difficult to be away from my parents. My father almost died once, and my boyfriend was gone in an instant. Every time my mom or dad left the house, I feared I'd never see them again. My mother had taken a few psychology courses and said it was normal to have anxiety after someone I loved died. She said each day that I got through would help me realize that nothing bad was going to happen.

But that's not how it went for me.

Every morning at seven sharp, my father would fill his mug with coffee and walk down the sloping hill to the race shop. My mom said her eyes had been hurting and the light in the shop was better, so she preferred to study there, in one of the conference rooms. And me, not wanting to be alone, followed them and always found things to keep me busy. One of the new publicity people would ask me to proofread a press release, or a shop guy would ask for my input on a car that shimmied ever so slightly in the wind tunnel. Most of our team had been around during my brief stint with karts and Dash cars, and they knew how good I'd been. Whether it was respect for whatever talent I may have had or them just being nice, the guys asked my opinion from time to time.

I hadn't returned to work at the newspaper and was starting to look forward to the routine my parents and I had of making coffee and breakfast and then heading to the race shop together.

"Noodle, I need to talk to you," my dad said one morning after a staff meeting that I'd sat in on just to give me something to do. I could tell by his grin that he was up to something. I brushed a few crumbs off my skirt and licked apricot preserve from my fingers. My dad always brought pastries and coffee to meetings.

"Don't you think it's time for you to go back to work?"

I was stunned. "You mean for the newspaper?" I sat in my chair, sticky fingers and all, staring at my father. "I'll call Tack right now."

"You can call Tack, but I was hoping you'd want to work here," he said, getting up.

I stopped in the doorway and turned around. "You know that's not going to happen. Do you want me to go back to my apartment, too?" I still paid rent on the apartment I once shared with Liza, hoping that one day I'd want to go back.

"Settle down, you little hothead. I know you're not going to drive again, but I thought maybe you'd want to do something else."

I exhaled, suddenly not so resolute. Spending so much time at the race shop and with my parents had reminded me what my old life was like.

"Can I think about it? I always thought I'd go back to *Weekly* one day."

"Of course. And if you want to go back and work for Tack, that's great. I just want you to be happy."

• • •

That night I met Liza at a dive bar called the Tipsy Cow, halfway between Winston-Salem and Moorestown.

"Wow," Liza said. "This is the first time you've ever sounded like you'd consider working for your dad."

"I know. But I guess everything is different now." I took an onion ring off her plate and stuffed it in my mouth. "What do you think I should do?"

Liza stopped eating. "I think you need time to sort it all out." She took a bite of her burger, and ketchup dripped on her hand. She licked it off. "How are you? You look better than the last time I saw you." She poured a little salt in her hand, then dragged a French fry through it.

"I'm hanging in. Just waiting for life to feel normal again."

She touched my shoulder. "I know, honey. I think we all are." We ate in silence for a few minutes. Finally, she said, "So, are you considering your dad's offer?"

I pushed my plate away and took a sip of beer. "I honestly don't know. My parents are probably sick of me being home all the time."

"Are you ready?" she asked. "To go back to work? Either for your dad or Tack?"

I drank my beer slowly. "To go back, yes. I think I am. To go on, no."

"Sometimes I pick up the phone to call you and see if you and Colt want to meet Teddy and me for dinner. And then I remember. And it just makes me want to cry."

•   •   •

"Daddy?" I asked, standing in the doorway of my father's office the next day. He was sorting letters—resumes, I assumed.

"Piper." He neatly stacked the papers, flipped them upside down, then got up. "Come sit with your old man." Lines creased his eyes when he smiled. "I was just—" He glanced at his desk. "Looking through candidates."

"Do you remember the first time we did this?"

"Sure do. You came to tell me you'd taken the job working for Tack. And I was trying my darndest not to let it slip that I'd hired Colt."

"Did you really not tell me because you thought I'd blab it to the world before the press conference?"

He grinned for the first time in a long time. "Nah. I had some foolish thought I couldn't shake."

"Oh yeah? Are you going to tell me now?"

"You already know. I thought maybe Mack's retirement becoming official might kick you in the pants a bit."

"You never gave up hope that I'd drive again, did you?"

"Still haven't."

I scoffed. "You think I'll ever go near a car now? After . . . everything?"

He got up and went back to the pile of papers. "I guess we'll just have to wait and see."

I started to leave his office and stopped in the doorway. "When you told me it was time to go back to work, what did you have in mind?"

"Anything you want, little one. Whether you go back to Tack or write press releases for me. Or run the damn engine shop. You can do anything you want."

I walked up the hill to the house thinking about Colt. He wouldn't want this for me. To see me so stuck. Not working. Slipping back to the girl I was after my father's accident. I opened the slider in the guest apartment and heard the phone ringing.

"This is Piper," I said, feeling for one second like I was back at *NASCAR Weekly*.

"Piper," Tack said, out of breath. "I've been calling you. Look, I need to see you. Today. Can I come over?"

"Sure. Are you okay? Because I don't think I can take it if you're sick or hurt. Oh God, did something happen to Amy? I need to tell her I'm sorry. Should I make her soup? Or bread? Can she eat?"

"Piper!" Tack's voice stopped me. "Everything is fine. Amy is feeling better. I just need to see you."

"Okay. I'm downstairs at my parents'. Just let yourself in."

Thirty minutes later Tack knocked on the slider and came in. I'd showered and made coffee.

I handed him a cup as he entered. He took the mug from me, kissed me on the cheek and we sat.

"I'm just going to dive right in," he said.

"Okay." I couldn't shake the feeling he was going to give me more bad news. I sipped my coffee and waited.

"You know I'm a journalist, right?"

"Well, you do run a newspaper, so I figured."

He waved his hands as if he were trying to erase his words. "I mean, I'm your editor now. But I started as a journalist. And I have connections. I know people."

Tack was from the north. He didn't carry himself with the same swagger and bravado that the boys I'd grown up with did. He was so humble that sometimes I thought people didn't give him enough credit for his successes. I only knew about them because I'd looked him up in the library and read the few commendations he had framed and hanging in his office.

"I know you do. You know lots of people." I hadn't meant to mock him, but it came out teasing.

He blew out a heavy breath. "I'm just going to say it. The fox was a mistake. And the people three houses down from Colt had a hazardous spill in their yard. That's why Colt's pipes corroded."

"What?" I didn't understand.

"And just to be safe, I checked up on Amy. She was admitted to the hospital the night of Colt's accident. Complications from the chemo. There's no way she could have hurt him."

"I still don't understand."

Tack took the mug from my hands and set it on the table. "You were so broken when we talked. I just wanted to help you. So I did a little digging."

"Oh my God, Tack."

"I knew it. You're mad. I'm sorry, Piper. I just wanted to give you some peace of mind."

"No no no. I'm not mad at all. Please start from the beginning and tell me everything."

"Okay. Well, after we talked, I couldn't stop thinking about everything you said, and I could totally understand why you might think all those things added up to someone stalking and hurting Colt. I wrote down everything you said and went on a scavenger hunt of sorts. I started with the taxidermy shop. Turns out they remembered the fox because it was some family pet that needed to be memorialized forever. And when the package got lost, the family freaked."

"Who has a pet fox?"

"I asked the same thing. But anyway, the owner of the shop is super anal and he took a picture of the box to prove to the family that they misaddressed the package. The family confirmed that it was the husband's handwriting. The owner said they were so embarrassed that they paid double for the work." He smiled triumphantly. "So you can cross that off your list. Crazy fans may send drivers their panties and naked pictures of themselves. But no one sent Colt a fox. Not on purpose, anyway. It was truly a mix-up with the address. And by the way, I looked up the fox's symbolism too. And what I found said it means regality and grace." He looked at me sideways.

I got up and took a box of Double Stuf Oreos from the cabinet by the fridge. I came back and offered him the package. He took two and put the rest on the table.

"What else do you have for me?"

"I went door-to-door, asking everyone if they'd had problems with their pipes. This one guy got all squirrely, started talking really fast. All I had to do was stand there until he blurted out that he spilled some chemical composition in his yard and it basically ate his pipes."

"For real?"

"So real. Fear not. I called the EPA when I got back to the office. Good news is the chemicals didn't harm any of the lake wildlife and that guy's homeowner's insurance will pay to repair the neighboring houses. Colt's included."

I wondered then if Meri and Doug would keep Colt's house. The last time I'd gone to dinner with Sasha, she talked about moving into it. Thought it'd make her feel closer to her brother.

"And I guess the neighbor never said anything because he didn't want to get in trouble?"

"Bingo."

I got up and paced the length of the room twice. "So." I stood with my arms crossed. "What you're saying is that my race-car-driving boyfriend just died?" Tears burned my eyes. "Colt, who could weave in and out of forty cars going two-hundred miles an hour, swerved to miss a deer or a dog and died? He just died?"

"It happens." Tack's voice was soft. "It's sad and awful. But it happens."

"So no one did anything to him? There was no crazy stalker fan? No jealous boyfriend who punctured his tires or ran him off the road?"

Tack stood and brought me back to the couch. "Remember that I've seen the police report. Captain Callahan from the CPD shared it with me once, so I asked to look at it again, just in case I missed something. It's just like I told you last time. The only thing of significance in the report was that the roads were wet and he was traveling faster than the speed limit. I don't think we'll ever really know what happened. He could have been changing the radio station. Or swerved to miss a rabbit. " He held my hands in his. "But what we do know is this was a terrible accident."

"A pure kind of thing," I said. I leaned forward and kissed Tack on the side of his mouth. "Thank you." I opened the slider and walked Tack to his car, then waited until he disappeared from view. The house was still empty, so I grabbed my mother's spare keys from the hook in the kitchen and went back outside. Her car was in the driveway and I opened the driver's side door and sat in the seat and talked to Colt.

21

The next morning my parents entered my room. "Shoofly," my mom said. "You're up. Can I get you some tea?"

My family were hardcore coffee drinkers. Only grandparents and dying people were offered tea. "No thanks. But I'll take some coffee, black."

My dad had come in behind my mom. "That's my girl."

The day before, after I sat in the car for an hour, I went inside and found my mom. The moment I opened my mouth to talk to her, I started to cry. She called the race shop and told my father to hightail it home. I curled up on the sofa in the living room and cried until I couldn't breathe. I cried until I had no more tears. And then I lay on the couch until it got dark. My mother covered me with a throw and my father stroked my hair. If they had questions, they didn't ask. They just stayed with me. They knew what I needed and that they couldn't give it to me.

At some point my dad carried me to my bed. My mom slept with me, on top of the covers, singing lullabies the way she used to when I was little and had a fever. Now, when my mother came back with my coffee, I sat up and pulled my hair into an elastic that'd been on my wrist.

"It's over," I said, my voice barely above a whisper. My parents exchanged a look. "All this time I kept hoping that somehow the accident wasn't Colt's fault." I laughed like a lunatic. "Isn't that sick? I actually hoped someone had caused Colt harm. Does that make me a bad person?"

"Oh, little one," my dad said. "It makes you someone who has spent all this time trying to make sense of something that just doesn't. And probably never will."

I took a sip of my drink, but it was too hot. "But that's the thing, Daddy. It does make sense. It proves my point. What I've thought all along." My mother looked away and covered her mouth. "It's okay, Mama. Life is random. But Colt made me realize some things I never would have figured out on my own."

My mother put her hand on my forehead. "Piper. Are you okay? You're not making any sense."

"I am. I finally get it. Colt was right. We only get one life and we have to live it."

My father hugged me hard. "I'm so happy to hear that. But what changed?"

I spent the next half hour reminding my parents about the questions I'd asked right after Colt died and the crazy theories I'd concocted. I also told them about the research Tack had done. "I guess that's why I fell apart yesterday," I said after I'd told them everything. "Tack helped me understand that Colt was right all along."

"Piper." My mother's voice was firm and too loud. "We love you. But enough is enough. You didn't mean for Daddy to get hurt in Tennessee. And I loved Colt as much as anyone. But the police said he was speeding. Who knows what happened, but something did, and whatever it was, it was probably just some awful mistake that he made. You can't punish yourself for the rest of your life because of that."

"Have you been listening to anything I've said? Colt was

right." I picked up my coffee and drank some. It was cool now. "On the night of Mack's party, Colt drove me to the high school and got me to sit in the driver's seat of his car. He—"

"Colt got you to drive?" my dad asked, grinning. "I knew if anyone could get you to come back to us, he could."

"Don't get ahead of yourself, Daddy. I said I *sat* in the car. I couldn't make myself drive. But, I heard, I mean really heard everything he said. I believed him when he said he'd rather die young than live to a hundred and never get to do what he loved." I pushed back the covers. "It's time for me to start living again."

The doorbell rang before my parents could respond. "Oh my," my mom said, looking toward the bedroom door. "I guess the kids are here."

"Kids?" I asked. "Are you giving a tour of the race shop to the Boys and Girls Club?"

"We didn't know what to do with you last night," my dad confessed. "So we called Liza, Sasha, Tack and Scott and asked them to come over this morning. In case we needed—"

"Backup?" The doorbell rang again. "Coming," I shouted.

I let my friends in and disappeared into my room to brush my hair and throw on sweats. When I came out, Liza hugged me hard. "Are you okay? Your mom said you were having a hard time last night."

I smiled for what felt like the first time in forever. "I'm okay now. But I'm glad y'all are here. There's something I need to tell you and something I need to ask."

My mother brought out a pitcher of lemonade and a stack of glasses on a platter I had won at a kart race a decade before. She set it on the coffee table, and we all took seats. I'd brushed my teeth when I got dressed, and my first sip of lemonade tasted sour and minty.

"I don't have it in me to explain again the breakdown I had last night and the revelation I came to this morning. So, I'm just going to jump right to my question." My parents exchanged glances. "Does anyone know why Colt was going to have that party? I know he was going to surprise me with something. And I think he was going to ask me to live with him. So I just have to know. Because"—I swiped at my eyes—"maybe he would have left Players sooner if he hadn't been worrying about when to surprise me with a key to his house."

"Oh, Pipes," Sasha said, getting up from her chair and sitting on the arm of mine. "There's nothing you could have done to change what happened that night."

I shook my head. "I get it. I do." I looked up at her. "But I need to know what that party was about. Colt loved his life and his success, but he wouldn't have thrown a party on a Monday because he increased his points lead for the rookie title. It had to have been something pretty big."

Sasha made room for my dad. He took her place and held my hand. "Colt was a good boy. He asked my permission and I gave him my blessing." My mother came over and he put his other arm around her. "We both did."

"Permission?" I asked. "As in to marry me?"

Scott spoke from across the room. "He loved you so much. He wanted to get married at his house, by the lake. With birdseed instead of rice." We'd driven by a wedding once, and I'd rolled down the window and yelled at the guests that rice kills birds when they eat it dry. "And a band that would play until sunrise. And anything you wanted."

I looked around the room. "You all knew this? Why didn't anyone tell me?"

My father spoke. "We talked about it—after—but decided against it. We were afraid it'd unnecessarily upset you."

Anger flashed, but Liza spoke before I could say anything. "I told them not to tell you. You always said the what-could-have-beens were the worst." It was true. "Every time we saw on the news a story about someone dying on their way to graduation or crashing because they were late for work, you always said if they'd woken up five minutes earlier or didn't take that last phone call, it could have been so different. You said knowing how close those people had come to having a completely happy life was the worst. We were just trying to protect you."

"I would have been engaged now." I rubbed my ring finger with my thumb. "Was it pretty? The ring?"

"The prettiest," Liza said. "Colt took Sasha and me with him ring shopping."

"Said he didn't want to screw it up," Sasha added.

Colt had kept a secret so he could surprise me in front of all our friends. But he never had the chance to propose. And I'd been keeping a secret from almost everyone. I was so glad I'd told Colt about Tennessee. Since then, I'd felt like I needed to tell the rest of my friends. It was the only way I'd unburden myself. Now Colt was gone, and I was sinking in lies. The lie of omission my parents had told to not hurt me. And the one they had been telling the world for half a decade. And finally the happy one of what Colt's party had really been for. If that night had never happened or if I'd been allowed to tell the truth to the press and my boss and most of my friends, my whole life would have been different. I'd be a driver now, not a journalist. And maybe I never would have met Colt again and he'd still be alive.

"Mama? Daddy?" I reached out and took their hands. "It's time."

They understood my meaning. This secret had been simmering for years. "Those are troubled waters," my father said. "Let them rest."

"*I* am the trouble, Daddy. I never told you, but Colt knew. I told him." How could I not? "Please."

"Let her do what she has to do, Planter," my mother told him. They let go of my hands and sat on the loveseat on the other side of the coffee table.

"What's happening?" Sasha asked. "You're scaring me, Pipes."

Tack had gone into the bathroom and returned with a box of tissues. It was as if he knew what was coming. He handed them to me, and I thanked him. I sucked in my breath. If I was going to say these words out loud, I needed to do it quickly, before I lost my nerve.

"Y'all know that I've been staying here, right?"

"We do," Tack said. "Your parents must be so happy to have you home."

I thought about all the nights we cooked dinner together or grilled in the backyard. I'd always enjoyed spending time with my mom and dad, but now more than ever I loved being with them. "I hope so." I glanced at my mom and she smiled. "More and more I've been going down to the shop with them just to have something to do. And I like it there. For the first time in a long time, I feel like I'm home."

"You *are* home," my dad said. "And I don't just mean you're physically in the house you grew up in. You're with *our* race team, doing what you love." Sweat rolled down my spine. "It's okay, little one. I understand now. Say what you have to say."

I made eye contact with Sasha, Scott and Tack one by one. I'd told Liza long ago.

"You know that my dad almost died in an accident six years ago, right?" I got up and paced the length of the couch a few times, then sat back down. I couldn't find a comfortable position, and I felt like my skin was alive. "I told Liza when we were in college. And she's been a supreme secret keeper. Then, just a few months ago, I told Colt. And I thought that would be the beginning of really setting myself free. And then one morning I woke up and he was gone." I rubbed my temples. "Just gone." I looked up at Tack. "Can I tell you all? The people I love the most? Can I tell you what really happened that day?"

"Piper," Scott said. "What day? You're not making any sense."

"It was me," I said. "I caused the wreck that almost killed my father."

Everyone looked to my dad. He sat silently next to my mother. This was my story to tell. Scott stood and spoke. "Don't be ridiculous. It was a terrible accident caused by mechanical failure. We were testing in Charlotte that weekend and I remember hearing it on MRN."

"That's what my parents told everyone. To protect me. But it was me. I was the rookie kid in the car who begged my dad to let me run a few laps with him." I looked at Tack. "You knew that I drove when I was younger. Didn't you ever wonder why I quit so suddenly?" He held up his palms. "I know you, Tack. And as you proved last night, you're an excellent researcher. You really never put it together?"

His blushed. "Since we're confessing all our secrets, I have to tell you that I did do a little digging. It wasn't lost on me that your brief but promising career ended right after your dad's wreck. I figured you lost your nerve. Racing can be scary as hell."

"Oh, it was scary, all right. But it was also all my fault."

"It was not your fault," my dad said sternly. "It was an accident. Could have happened to anyone."

"Thank you for saying that, Daddy. But it was driver error. Plain and simple. My mistake." I looked at my friends. "My dad was supposed to be in Tennessee testing by himself, but I asked if I could drive with him." Then I told my friends the same story I'd told Liza and Colt. When I was done, I stopped to catch my breath.

"I almost killed my father. And I swore I'd never get in another race car again."

"You know we don't blame you," my mother said.

"I know. But how was I supposed to go on after that? As if nothing had happened?"

Tack rubbed his chin, thinking, reminding me more of a college professor than a newspaper editor. "The same way you're going on now. One step at a time."

"That's the thing. I haven't moved on. I've just moved around. And then Colt died and I came home. Being at the race shop every day with my mom and dad, I started to feel like maybe I could go back. Maybe I could start over."

My dad's eyes got bright. "You can, Noodle. Buck is driving for us until we find a permanent driver. That can be you."

"Slow down, Daddy. I'm just thinking out loud here. This is so not where I ever thought my life would go. But now that I'm here . . . I don't know. I'm just trying to figure it all out."

I took a sip of lemonade, just to give myself a minute to think about what I wanted to say next.

"I'd been convinced that Colt was too good of a driver to have wrecked his street car four miles from my apartment. But now, thanks to Tack, I know that that's exactly what happened."

Tack got up and sat next to me. "I didn't tell you any of this yesterday to hurt you. I just wanted to help you. I knew you'd never be able to heal unless you knew the truth."

"Thank you, Tack. I know what you did took guts. And you did help me. More than you know." I got up and topped off everyone's lemonade, then I stood in the middle of the chairs. "So there you go. I almost killed my father. My boyfriend died in an accident. An awful accident that could have happened to anyone. And I had a breakdown and then a breakthrough. Any questions?"

• • •

For a week or ten days after I confessed all my sins, I continued to go to the race shop because if Colt were alive, that's what he would have been doing. In my warped sense of loyalty, I somehow felt closer to him by being there. And if I was honest with myself, I was starting to miss the busyness of working. So one morning I stopped Frank from the PR department in the hallway. "Good morning," I said, handing him a coffee with two Sweet'N Lows and skim milk. "Any chance you might have a press release that needs proofing?"

Surprise registered on his face for the briefest moment, then he opened a folder and handed me a sheet of paper. "I don't have anything to proof, but I do need a quick five hundred words by the end of the day. Are you for up it?"

I read the bullet points introducing a new brand of baseball hats for the team. Sponsors were sponsors, and everyone loved to see their name in print.

"Thank you so much, Frank. You won't be disappointed."

He winked at me. "I don't expect I will."

As I sat at an empty desk, working on someone else's computer, I felt giddy every time my fingers hit the keyboard.

• • •

The day after the first press release went to print, Frank found me in the break room losing a battle with the coffeemaker. "It works better if you plug it in," he said from behind me.

"Huh," I replied. "I guess it would. Thanks." I put the end of the cord into the outlet and it immediately started gurgling. "What's up? Was my piece okay?"

"That's why I'm here." I noticed he was holding a folder. "It was more than okay. And I was wondering if you'd like a few more assignments. No pressure. Whatever you're comfortable with would be great."

"Hand 'em over," I said. "I'll get started right away."

"Awesome. Your parents are looking for you, so go find them and then come see me so we can go over what I need."

I left the folder on a desk and found my mom and dad in one of the conference rooms. "Howdy, parents," I said.

"Piper," my mom said, looking up from the table where several pages were spread out in front of her. "You're looking especially chipper today. It's nice to see you smile."

"It's a good day."

For six years I'd felt like there was a boulder tied to my ankle in the blackness of the ocean. But since I'd told my friends about my dad's accident, I stopped waking up every morning feeling like I was breathing water instead of air.

"What's up?"

My dad got up and closed the door, then motioned for me to sit. "We heard you're doing a bit of writing for Frank."

I reached for the folder he'd given me a few minutes before, then remembered I'd left it in another room. "Yes. Is that all right? I'm sorry I didn't ask you first. I assumed it'd be okay."

"Of course. This is the happiest we've seen you—" He glanced at my mother. "Well, in a long time. Did you go through the papers Frank gave you?"

"Not yet. He told me you were looking for me." I got that same funny feeling in my stomach as I did whenever I knew my parents were hiding something from me. "Is everything okay?"

"There's a paper in the folder Frank gave you that we want to talk to you about," my dad said. "We're expanding the team and we want you to—"

I knew how he was going to finish that sentence, and my breath caught in my throat. I was finally ready. "Yes?" I asked hopefully.

"We want you to write the press release announcing that we're actively seeking two full-time drivers. Your . . . awakening"—he made air quotes—"inspired us. If you're moving forward, then we should too."

I made myself smile. "Daddy!" I jumped out of my seat. "That's fantastic. I guess if you're looking for one driver, you might as well be searching for two. Have you found anyone worthy?"

"Not yet," my mom said. "We have lots of leads. People have literally been lining up since . . . well, you know. We just want to make sure we get it right again."

The phone on the conference table beeped, and the receptionist told my mom that the women from the auxiliary club were there.

"Sorry, honey," my mom said. "I've got to run."

I stood up and hugged my parents. "It's okay, Mama. I need to get something from the house." I walked out of the room with my parents, and after they went to their meetings, I headed up the hill. I stood in the yard between the shop and the house for a long time, trying to figure out which way to go. I needed to be sure.

I let myself in the kitchen door and took a can of soda from the fridge. My heart was beating hard, and I probably didn't need the caffeine. But I opened it and sat at the farm table. I finished the soda, threw it in the trash and went to a back staircase. I opened the door to the attic, and a wall of heat hit me. I flicked the light switch and climbed the steps, then walked to the back by the window. It took me less time than I thought it would to find the box marked *Piper's FS*. I opened the box, pulled out my old fire suit and held it up to my body, as if that would tell me if it still fit. I brought it to my face and inhaled.

It smelled of tar and fuel. It smelled like home.

Acknowledgments

My dear friend and amazing editor, Suzanne Kingsbury, gets most of the credit for turning *Drive* into a novel. Written, revised and rewritten many times, I just couldn't get the book right. I put it aside, wrote two more novels and finally came back to it only to decide it could live a happy life trapped in my computer. But something about it kept nagging me, telling me I owed it one more chance. So I called Suzanne and asked her to help me. I'd been round and round trying to end the book and even find its meaning.

Suzanne, in her typical Suzanne fashion, read it in a couple of days, called me, and in about three minutes explained what it was missing and how I could fix it. She helped me find this book's soul. For that, your friendship and your ceaseless encouragement, I love you, Suzanne.

Many thanks to John Koehler, Joe Coccaro and Hannah Woodlan of Koehler Books for signing me and doing an amazing job with the title, cover art and editing. You all are fabulously talented and super fun to work with. From the day you signed me, I've felt like I was home.

I'm eternally grateful to my agent, Lisa Gallagher, who gave me my start as a novelist. Your insight, support and friendship mean the world to me.

Thank you also to the countless people on social media who helped name *Drive* and choose its cover art. The support from so many friends, fans and strangers makes me feel like I can fly.

Most importantly, thank you to my family. My fans might make me feel like I can fly, but my mother is the reason I do fly. Mom—you've spent my entire life telling me I can do anything I want to. And you've shown up . . . for everything. You have no idea what that's done for my confidence and my drive. You always said I could do anything I wanted, so I did. I love you forever and ever. And thank you to my stepdad, Nick, just for being your awesome self. I love you.

Endless thanks and love to my dad and my brother, Robbie, who taught me everything I know about NASCAR. I miss you both every day.

I like to think everyone has a best friend, but even if they do, no one has a best friend as wonderful as mine, Sasha Sanford. You know by now that I named a character after you. Because you are just that amazing. Love you tons, Sash. And Sasha, please thank C Block for their help choosing the cover. I love it when I can get a whole classroom on speakerphone giving me their opinions. It reminds me I have the most fun job ever!

Thank you to my husband, Kurt, and my kids, Ainsley and Cooper. Kurt read an early version of *Drive* and had the unenviable job of telling me he loved the book and hated the ending. Without his honesty, I wouldn't have written these acknowledgments because the novel never would have been published. Kurtie, thank you for pushing me to be better than I thought I could be. I love you madly.

And Coop and Ainsley, thank you for helping me name so many characters, find a title and choose the cover. Thinking up names with you two is always the most fun part of writing. And thank you for being so awesome all the times that we were home together, but I needed to work. You two are the loves of my life. And the best part of me. I love you always.